A Very British Affair

Jane Chappell

First published in Great Britain

8th May 2025 by

PLUCKROSE PRESS LTD

PLUCKROSE PRESS
PUBLISHERS

ISBN: 9781838009519

Dedication

To the 1st Battalion, Queen Victoria's Rifles and their families.

Before the Second World War, the 1st Battalion, Queen Victoria's Rifles was a Territorial Army unit based in Davies Street, London. As part-time soldiers, these men trained on evenings and weekends, and at annual summer camps. These camps were often in rural parts of England, such as Kent, Sussex and Hampshire.

When war broke out in 1939, these part-timers were mobilised for full-time service. They were deployed to places like Paddock Wood in Kent to prepare for imminent service overseas.

These men and their families inspired this novel.

We will remember them.

CONTENTS

1
Wish me luck as you wave me goodbye

Where to begin? Gracie sat on the wooden stool by her dressing table; she gazed through tired eyes and dim light at her reflection in the tarnished mirror. The pen in her hand was poised, and the paper was set out before her, but where, she continued to wonder, should she begin? The emptiness of the page was stark, just as the stillness of the night had been; she at last determined that this was, perhaps, as good a place as any...

Monday, 20th May 1940

Dearest Edward,

In the still of the night, as I lay by your side with my head on your chest, I listened to every precious beat of your heart. I dared not close my eyes, not for a moment, in fear I might miss a second of us being together. As your breath deepened and its pace slowed, time stood perfectly still, and I began to pray it would forget what it was to move on... It must have been then that I drifted into sleep – a sleep I promised myself I would not have. It was a sleep without dreams, for dreams have left me quite alone. I pray they will return, my love, with you.

A cruel, eager sun has now awoken me. Time has remembered all I hoped it would forget; morning is hastening, and it seems I am unable to stop it. You are still sleeping, albeit a restless affair... I have been gazing at you, desperately trying to capture every part of you in my mind, so I might have you with me always. I swear to you Edward, every night, when I climb into our bed, you will be with me. In my mind, I will see you and hear you and feel your arms around me. I will kiss your soft, perfect lips, and you will hold me tightly and whisper softly to me, "I love you, Gracie. Everything will be fine."

Our darling girl has not yet stirred from her slumber. I imagine her head is full of tall tales set in a land far, far away, where her daddy is a strong, brave, handsome hero. You have done such a job with her – such a job of easing her delicate, young mind and of soothing her soul. As you told her your stories last night, as you tucked her into bed, I stood outside her door and listened... When you explained where you must go and why, I heard her laugh and giggle and gasp in wonder. As I listened, I held my breath and tried in vain not to cry. You are the most wonderful man, the gentlest father, and I know you will be the most honourable soldier.

I feared last night that my heart would stop...that every breath I ever took would be taken from me if I allowed myself to sleep...if I allowed today to happen. Light is here now, though; the morning has come, as it will again tomorrow, and I am still here. My heart is far from silent. It is pounding stronger than ever before. Tomorrow then, when you are gone, it will be stronger still. I have a strength within me, Edward, a strength born out of my love for you that I am only just discovering.

I know you will be safe. I know you will return, and that Primrose and I will be right here waiting for you. As you explained to our precious girl last night: there are little girls in far-away lands who need your help; little girls who have lost their fathers, whose mothers are scared and are being forced from their homes... I know they need you more than we do, that for a short time you must be strong for someone else. You are a good man, Edward, and those poor broken people need you desperately. I understand that you must go, and so, too, does Primrose. You must not worry about us; we will be fine because you have told us both so, and we believe you.

I will not imagine you at war. I will not allow myself to picture you in any way other than as you are here. I will not torment myself with scenes from a futile imagination – it will do no one any good. I will not cry. I will smile when I think of you and keep Primrose mindful of her wonderful father. Draw strength from us, Edward. On dark days, if ever you are cold, if ever you fear the worst, we are with you.

Check your pocket, my love. We are always there.

Your own darling, Gracie x

****

With that, Gracie folded the letter, slipped it into the pocket of Edward's laid out trousers and woke him with a kiss. Edward smiled. His eyes smiled – they were closed but they smiled nevertheless with telltale, mischievous wrinkles. Gracie laughed beneath her breath and cupped Edward's handsome, unshaven face in her hands. She kissed him again, and this time he kissed back. With strong, playful hands Edward grabbed Gracie's tiny waist, pulled her close and then rolled her over until she lay down on her back beside him. Their heads turned to face one another, their hands held, fingers entwined. Edward's clear blue eyes, now open, fixed on Gracie's and they were both overwhelmed. So much raced through their minds; so much could have been said, but, instead, the lovers simply melted into another kiss. This time, the kiss (and all that followed) was not to wake; it was not to play or even simply to love – this time, it was the start of saying goodbye.

There was an unexpected abandonment to the parting lovers' passion; they were not bound by sensibilities or troubled by expectations. The rawness of their emotion

3

was so intense that they were swept away and lost within one another. In those precious moments, Gracie and Edward secured what they were to one another; they became one another. They would never again be alone, no matter the distance or time that grew between them. They held their breath as they held one another and dared not let go. The lovers forged their way towards a shattering, deeply urgent and desperately passionate goodbye. Eventually, silent, strong echoes pulsed between them until, at last, they dared to surrender and gasp for air.

In the calm that followed, they knew without hesitation that everything between them was as it should be; there was no question as to how either of them felt. Everything was settled and, despite their silence, nothing between them had been left unsaid.

Given time to recover, and in an effort to ease the pain of their parting, Edward brushed Gracie's auburn hair from her forehead and whispered with renewed mischief in his eyes, 'This war of ours will never be won while men like me are naked, and women like you are...well, wanton!'

'Dear me, Mr Chatley, I can't think what you mean. Now, mind yourself out of my way, so I can make your breakfast. You're going to need to replace all that you've spent this morning!'

With a wry smile and a thankful heart, Gracie smacked the naked bottom tempting her from beneath the sheets before heading out of the bedroom door. Edward took a moment to watch his beautiful wife disappear from view and then another to make sure he could recall every part of her: the wave in her hair, the curve of her hips, her pale green eyes, her delicate skin and the lightness of her step.

He allowed himself a breath, to be certain he would remember all they had just shared. It was then he was struck by a thought. He took another breath, but this one was sharp and unbearable: he was mourning his future with Gracie. What was inevitably about to be stolen could never be replaced; it would never be found or even remembered. How long would he be gone? Would he return? Would she...?

The sound of tiny, dancing footsteps stopped Edward in his tracks and proved a timely reminder that to worry, as he had always said, was pointless. However, to pause and be happy, as Gracie always insisted, was everything. The reminder could not have been more beautifully packaged: six years old; missing bottom teeth; a white cotton nightie; thick, dark, shiny hair in rags; cold, quick, bare feet and a boundless energy.

The bundle of joy standing before Edward was Primrose. As she spoke, she ran on the spot with a mixture of excitement and necessity as a cold floor was her stage. She had rehearsed her tumbling words earlier that morning, in her imagination, whilst searching for an all-important and precious prop in her bedroom. 'Daddy! You have to get up, Daddy,' she chattered. 'The little girl will be waiting for you. If you're late, Daddy, she might cry. And, Daddy, I want you to give her this...it's my very best, favouritest, shiniest ribbon, but I think the other little girl should have it because I have a Daddy and she doesn't, and that isn't fair. So, I thought the ribbon would make up for it. If she already has a ribbon, though, can you bring it home with you please because it is my best one... I'll put it in your pocket, Daddy. Promise you won't forget?'

It was all Edward could do to not pick up his precious, beautiful girl, hold her tightly to him and sob. His angel had no clue what was happening; she had no grasp on how cruel life was being to them both. To Primrose, life was simple. Everything could be made better if you wrapped it up in a pretty ribbon and tied a bow. Her bright-blue, excited eyes gazed openly at her father's as she waited eagerly for his response. Edward, lost for words, simply smiled and nodded, and so his precious girl danced over to his trousers and unwittingly placed the ribbon with the letter her mother had written. She then skipped over to her father, jumped up onto the bed, hid her cold toes beneath her nightie and repeated her pleas. 'Honestly, Daddy, it is time to get up. Listen – it's the kettle's whistle! Mummy's making tea, and I'm allowed some this morning!'

As the whistle rang in their ears, Edward managed to whisper, fighting back tears, 'One quick cuddle, poppet, then Daddy will get up, I promise.' He held tightly to his little girl and prayed that time would stand still. His mind flooded with memories of times he had shared with his darling Primrose: the day she had been born; her first birthday; the day she grazed her knee for the first time – and only he could comfort her. How could he leave her? How would she manage without him? How would she...

'Would you two get down here! I've saved these eggs for today, and I won't have them going hard waiting for you!'

Edward's relentless, heartbreaking questions were interrupted by the obvious answer – his own darling Gracie would take care of it all. 'You heard your mother – quick now, jump to it or else you'll get me in trouble!' Edward lifted his baby to the ground and watched as she ran off onto the landing. He watched as she ran off into her future – into a life without him.

Edward was due at the hop farm at eight o'clock that morning. His colleagues, the local lads from the battalion, had agreed they would walk there together. The men had decided their goodbyes should be said behind closed doors, so that their families (and especially any children) could be spared seeing them go in any sort of contrived event. It was agreed that pomp and ceremony should be reserved until they returned home. The men were wise to think that if a fuss was made in public, and just one child cried, they might all join in, and where would that leave the women? The men of the Queen Victoria's Rifles were determined that their goodbyes were to be in the comfort and warmth of their homes, not the cold reality of the streets.

****

Edward was ready, he had been ready for over an hour. He was sitting at the small kitchen table with Primrose on his knee. Across from him sat Gracie, her hand in his, her eyes fixed on his. The ticking of the clock from the back room was the only sound to be heard. Little Primrose sat quite still: a teddy's hand in her grasp, both arms wrapped around her father, and her head nuzzled into his neck. Thoughts of girls in faraway lands, ribbons and heroes faded until they were lost. Primrose could only think of losing her father, and a strong sinking feeling began to consume her.

As the clock ticked and the seconds turned to minutes, the feeling that had begun in Primrose's chest slowly grew and rose up until it gripped her tiny throat. She began to draw deeper and deeper breaths, as though she were trying to rescue herself by drinking in every part of her beloved father. The fragile little girl, still wrapped in her cotton nightie, held on so tightly to Edward that he dared not move for fear of making matters worse. He knew he was powerless. He was weaker than he had ever been, void of control, unable to do the one thing he yearned to: ease his daughter's suffering. He conceded. He was beaten.

Gracie knew instinctively what Primrose was feeling and what her darling Edward was thinking. Yesterday, Edward had been brave for Primrose, but today he wanted none of it to be true. Today he wanted to take his little girl to the river, to go fishing, to paddle in the water; today he wanted to do anything but leave. Edward's eyes began to well with tears. Although she had no idea how, Gracie managed to smile. Edward blinked and a tear rolled, yet he was compelled to smile back – his heart swelling with admiration for his beautiful wife. How he would miss her: those knowing eyes, her lightly freckled nose, her suggestive smile, her wicked humour. No one knew him like Gracie did, so who was he, he began to wonder, without her?

The sound of the clock ticking from the back room grew ever louder and more urgent. Edward, Gracie and Primrose all knew that their time together was almost over. They sat and waited for the knock on the door: the knock from one of the men from the battalion. When the knock finally came, the pounding of hearts rendered the clock silent.

Primrose dutifully jumped down from her father's lap, her teddy hanging lifeless by her side, and answered the call. The man standing before her wore an expression that could not be reconciled with his face. Primrose was puzzled... How could a smile be worn, and a cheery hello spoken by a face so plainly washed with tears? Primrose pondered the face. She had seen such sadness and tears in her own reflection when she had fallen or been scolded, but she had never seen such stains on a grown-up man's face – never ever.

As Primrose locked quizzically at the face before her, Edward stood in the kitchen and pulled Gracie towards him. The pair clung to one another and held their breath, both knowing that no matter how painful it was they must not cry. If one tear fell, they would never stop. Tears would not help their parting; tears would make Primrose worry, and they had promised one another they would never allow that to happen. Edward pulled together more strength than he had ever needed before and, remarkably, more courage than he would ever need at war to whisper the words, 'I love you, Gracie. Everything will be fine.' With that, Edward kissed his wife's cheek and walked away, leaving her in the warmth of the kitchen. He walked towards the front door, picked up Primrose and whispered as he swung her round, 'Go and give Mummy a cuddle for Daddy; I've got to get going...' As Primrose's toes found the floor, she ran off to do as her beloved father had asked, longing to please him one last time.

Edward gathered his bag from the foot of the stairs and slung it over his shoulder. He did not look back. As he stepped over the threshold and pulled the door, Primrose spilled out, 'I love you, Daddy.' By the time the door was shut, Edward's face matched that of his companion. The pair walked, heads lowered, silent, resigned, towards their duty. The bravado, the comradeship, the stiff upper lip would all have to wait. Now was not the time.

The cold reality of the streets unsurprisingly bore no comfort for Edward, and (despite the warmth of the kitchen), no matter how tightly Gracie and Primrose held one another, there was an unmistakable chill from which neither of them could escape.

2
Keep calm and carry on

The road on which the two men travelled was long and straight; it was the hub of the small town's existence. At the far end, a good distance from where they had started out, was the railway station. Paddock Wood Station had changed the once sleepy backwater from a quiet village into an established rural town. Commuters from Paddock Wood travelled to the City to work, and many came in turn to the town for their holidays: to pick the hops, cobnuts and apples from the well-stocked farms, orchards and gardens.

Edward was a stockbroker and his companion, Thomas, a clerk. They were used to walking along the road towards the station in the mornings, but this journey would not see them board the train to London as they normally would. This was an altogether different affair.

The streets were empty and eerie – sinister even. The still air was stale and unnerving, and the terraced houses seemed oddly transformed: regimental and imposing. For the first time, the men noticed their footsteps echoing as they walked down the abandoned streets – their formidable army boots weighing heavy and transforming their footsteps.

As the heavily burdened souls journeyed towards the hop farm, the gravity of their circumstances slowly dawning with every step, the birds continued to sing. Blackbirds, robins, song thrushes and skylarks insisted on a cheerful chorus, disturbingly at odds with reality. Although the woeful figures could never have imagined the dangers they were soon to face, they were nevertheless troubled by the grim certainty of their situation: they were going to war, and they may never return.

Edward and his companion, Thomas Bennett, were both in the Queen Victoria's Rifles. The battalion was made up of volunteers (not conscripts): fellows who had been in the Territorial Army before the declaration of war. As such, these trained, dedicated soldiers were primed to be put in the line of fire. Thomas was a younger man than Edward, squat too in comparison, and he had fair, reddish hair in contrast to Edward's near black, slicked crown. Despite Thomas' stature, he was not to be underestimated. His size was, in many scenarios, a distinct advantage. Thomas was the short lad in school who had decided the only way to get on was to be tougher than all his peers. Thomas' strength, coupled with his acumen, meant he was a fine fellow to have by your side, and Edward was glad to have him as a comrade in arms as well as a friend. Thomas lived at home with his parents, and recently (aged eighteen) he had found love for the first time...he'd met the girl of his dreams: the girl he was going to marry. Mary worked on the shop floor of the local department store and had caught Thomas' eye when he was buying a Christmas gift for his mother. The couple often laughed when recalling the story of their meeting, as Thomas later confessed to spending a few more shillings than he had intended. This was not to impress his mother, of course, but to impress Mary. The seventeen-year-old shop girl was a petite, fragile doll; blessed with huge brown eyes; neatly curled hair; delicate, gentle hands; and a voice that almost whispered. Young Mary's softly spoken timbre melted Thomas' heart, and her endearing shyness allowed him to protect her. Thomas had a part to play with Mary: she needed him, and, goodness, how he loved being her leading man. Mary's enchanting vulnerability was now however the cause of Thomas' tear-stained face. He had arranged to meet his darling girl after leaving his parents' house. They'd held hands, kissed and whispered their goodbyes whilst sitting on the bench by the memorial. Mary had been bereft, and poor Thomas was torn and shattered.

The men had one other companion to meet en route to their destination: Charlie Webb. Charlie lived at the far end of the road in one of the slightly smaller terraced houses (one with a back yard as opposed to a garden). His mid-terraced house was close to the department store where Mary worked. He had, what the other two men considered to be, the best job in the world: he made beer! In his youth he picked hops, and, over time, he worked his way through the ranks at the hop farm until reaching the enviable position of brewer. Charlie lived very happily with his wife, Flo, and their two boys. He was renowned for being a bit of a card. His boys were aged two and four, and they were a true handful. However, if anyone could handle their boisterous antics it was Flo: a Yorkshire lass who was gritty and resourceful. Everyone joked that all Hitler really needed was a good telling off from Flo to put him in his place. At four-foot nothing, proud owner of a bust to be reckoned with, a rolling pin never far from her grasp, and a fag never far from her lips, she was formidable yet very much loved by all who knew her. Charlie, in contrast, was a wiry chap – well over six-feet tall. He towered over everyone and was the archetypal gentle giant. Together, Charlie and Flo were a proper team. Their priorities were to ensure the boys were well presented and polite but, above all, they wanted their boys to know they were loved. Neither Charlie nor Flo felt loved as children. Brought up in large families during the Great War, both were left without fathers and, thanks to grief, no mothers to speak of. When Charlie and Flo found one another, one fateful summer whilst hop picking, their lives truly began. Everything till then had merely been an existence. In their life together, the couple vowed to enjoy themselves: to love and laugh whenever they possibly could. The declaration of war, and Charlie's inevitable departure, simply strengthened their resolve to live every day as if it were their last.

True to form, when Edward and Thomas met Charlie at his door, he called to his wife, 'Remember love, I'm doing this to stop you lot moaning about the spam... When I get back, I'm expecting double egg, gammon and chips, followed by sponge pudding and custard.'

Flo did not miss a beat. 'Get out of here, yer dozy, great lummox. And remember (the three o' yer): first sign o' trouble, don't be no heroes – just run like blazes in't opposite direction!' The couple then shared the briefest of kisses, and the boys peered from behind their mother's apron to shadowbox with their father before Flo declared, 'Come on, let's get this here door shut before we heat the whole bloomin' street!' With that, a knowing smile and a nod was shared between the pair, then boom – the door was shut. The three men laughed, and the journey resumed with a spirit that was held onto from that moment on.

Charlie clapped his hands and rubbed them together playfully. 'Here we are then lads – peace and quiet away from them in doors for a while! No nagging of an evening or screaming nippers to content with.' Charlie was clearly on good form, and it was set to continue. Sucking air deeply between his teeth, he rallied. 'Mind you, Tommy me lad, you've had it easy. It's about time we got you away from those apron strings of ya mother's. We'll bring you back home a real man – put hairs on your chest.'

Thomas' retort was swift, 'I've more hairs on my chest than you've got on yer 'ead, old timer! I reckon most of yours have fallen out by now or gone grey!' With that, Thomas jumped up to snatch Charlie's hat from his head and ran off down the road. Charlie and the usually conservative Edward glanced at each other briefly before making chase. They caught young Thomas on either side (under each armpit and knee) and ceremoniously dumped his backside into a conveniently located dustbin. Charlie then retrieved his hat, recovered his slightly thinning locks and clipped Thomas around the ear. The three unlikely musketeers then continued on their way.

Anyone who thought men did not gossip did not know men. Thomas started, 'Did you hear about old Milly Pluckrose's son? He's only gone and signed up for that Local Defence malarkey...what's Eden calling it? LD something or other, ain't it?'

Edward, priding himself on being abreast of current affairs, promptly asserted, 'Local Defence Volunteers. The LDV. It's Mr Eden's latest plan to defend our...'

'...Crackin'!' Charlie boomed, before taking centre stage as usual. 'Send all of us (what knows what we're doing) gawd knows where, to do gawd knows what, and leave the country in the capable hands of the old, the infirm, the preachers and the bleedin' useless. Love a duck, it's genius!'

Thomas was in no doubt that Charlie was spot on. 'He's got a point, Ed... That boy can hardly see his hand in front of his face; he'll end up doing one of our lot in! It's plain dangerous.'

Edward tried to calm the waters. 'They won't give lads like him guns!'

'Well, you say that,' Thomas warned, 'but they were asking for weapons and that from the public to help arm this lot. My dad's handed his pride and joy in already. What if Pluckrose gets given one'a them?'

'But to arm the likes of Pluckrose would be insanity,' insisted Edward.

'The thought of my boys and Flo being protected by some sort of hotchpotch motley crew – well, it terrifies me. I plan on kickin' Hitler's backside long before he so much as gets a toe wet in the Channel. In fact, see this here boot, lads? It's goin' right up the bastard's arse!' Charlie had done what he was good at. The men continued with restored verve and vigour.

To keep the banter flowing, Edward turned the subject matter to something everyone had been talking about: Churchill. 'You know, this will be Churchill's tenth day on the job...he's been itching to get his teeth into this lot, and I'd wager he's got some pretty impressive plans under that hat of his.'

'I reckon you're right,' Thomas added. 'I've got a feeling we're about to find ourselves right in the middle of his plan "A". Let's hope it's a good'un!'

'Pound to a penny says it's a blinder,' Charlie enthused. 'He's just the ticket is Churchill. Just what we need. This is no phony war lads. Let's face it, it's kickin' off good and proper.'

Edward mimicked the stoic tones of Churchill. 'Umm, a..and together, with our *blood, toil, tears and sweat*, we are just the chaps to nip it in the bud!' The men fell about, all mimicking the man who had sealed their fate. Edward felt genuinely buoyant as he spoke those fateful words. He believed that, together with his friends, he was about to embark on something magnificent. They were going to defeat Hitler and save the families they'd had to leave from a dark, uncertain future.

After a brisk walk, the men arrived at the hop farm to join many others. As time passed, swathes more joined them. The men worked hard all day: practicing drills, parading the grounds and checking their all-important kit. They gave their trusty motorbikes the once-over – tyre pressures, oil, fuel... There was an air of expectancy hanging over them, and, by the evening, the tension was palpable. They managed, however, to keep their spirits high by singing, joking and drinking tea. By the time the men climbed into their bunks, they were so weary that the early order of 'Lights out!' was warmly welcomed.

Back on Commercial Road, Gracie had long since tucked Primrose into bed, and now she too was about to retire. So much had happened in their little terraced house that day – it had all been quite exhausting. Friends had rallied and visited with messages of love and support, and Gracie had lent her support in turn to Flo and young Mary when they briefly came to call. There had been all the usual work to be done: meals to make, shopping to do and, of course, time was spent distracting Primrose. Once Primrose had gone to bed, Gracie took out 'the books' from the department store and set to work as she had done most evenings since war had been declared.

Gracie had worked in the office at the store before getting married and was only too glad to help tidy up the books when the boss, Mr Spindler, had asked. He predicted that most of the men would be leaving to fight, so he thought it would be wise to get 'ship shape' as soon as possible. With the more than competent Gracie taking care of the figures, he could free up one (or maybe even two) of the girls in the office to work on the shop floor. Mathematics proved to be a welcome distraction from the empty room in which Gracie was sitting, and time passed quickly. Once all was tidied away, Gracie climbed the stairs to her bedroom, promptly completed her nighttime routine and got into bed, alone. She closed her eyes and did as she had promised herself – she imagined Edward holding her close; she felt his arms around her, felt his soft kiss and heard him whisper, 'I love you, Gracie. Everything will be fine.' With that, the exhausted Gracie feel to sleep with ease. It was not something she had expected to do.

A few hours later, both Edward and Gracie woke with a start. Edward's entire battalion had been woken at midnight. They were ordered from their bunks, instructed to prepare at once and then taken away. It was to be the beginning of their journey to France.

Gracie, however, had not been called nor had Primrose woken her. All was quiet, but she found herself quite awake and sitting up in bed. 'Oh Edward...' she gasped as she held her heart and her breath. She needed to speak to him – to tell him that she was with him, and he would be safe. She had not had a bad dream; she had not dreamt at all and was implausibly lucid. She hurriedly left her bed, raced to the window and looked out – searching for her husband. In desperation, she opened her box of precious paper, sat at her dressing table and began to write in a bid to appease her racing heart.

My darling Edward,

I know you'll think I'm foolish, my love, but I have woken quite suddenly, and I need to tell you something. You have only just left...it is midnight and the first night you have been gone. You must know that I love you, my darling. You must know that you will be fine. I am with you. Check your pocket. I am there.

Gracie x

With those few words, Gracie was strangely settled. Before getting back into bed, she gazed from the window again and sent a kiss to her husband. She may not have known exactly where he was (although she sensed it was no longer at the hop farm), but she knew they were under the same sky, and that brought her comfort. Gracie knew the note she had written would probably never be sent, but she vowed to keep it, to show her love when he returned. She thought it would make him laugh... 'Funny girl!' he'd say.

As Edward boarded the bus, he felt in his pocket for the ribbon his darling Primrose had left for him. As his fingers felt for the shiny ribbon they found, instead, the letter from Gracie. As he read the words from his darling wife, he was uplifted. He was protected and strong. As he headed towards Dover, in the darkness of night, the welcome distraction meant he quite forgot to be fearful. He was simply resolved to do his duty. Edward was going to be the husband, father and soldier Gracie had spoken of. As he sat on the bus holding his letter and the ribbon, he looked out of the window and into the blackness. He pictured Gracie and smiled as he thought to himself, 'Everything'll be fine.'

3
Make do and mend

Flo burst in through Gracie's front door in a fluster, calling after the boys to hurry up. She was still wrapped up in her apron with an appropriate dusting of flour on her nose and forehead. 'Sorry we're late, Gracie love. Hiya Mary, how do?' Flo dragged on her cigarette to calm herself down. Gracie and Mary smiled and shared a little titter before getting Flo an ashtray and a teacup and saucer. As Flo came into the kitchen, Gracie pulled out a chair from the modest but beautifully dressed table whilst Mary cut a slice of trench cake. 'The boys were being right little sods, and me pastry went t'wall 'cause I got so hot and bothered wi' flammin' Arthur.' Flo sat down as the source of her distress, Arthur, together with his little brother, William, ran past and into the garden to annoy Primrose. 'Ooh cake! Mary, was that you?'

Mary winced. 'Oh, I hope I've done it right. It's that recipe you gave me.'

Flo took a bite and mumbled, 'That's grand that is, Mary... We'll make a wife of you yet!'

Mary blushed as Gracie added, 'By the time your Thomas gets home, you'll be all set to become Mrs Bennett.'

Flo agreed before cautioning, 'We're gonna have to get more inventive with the recipes, mind, girls; I'd wager the rationing's only gonna get worse.' Gracie sighed at the thought of more restrictions, and Mary put her head in her hands. 'Oh no...don't worry. I could be wrong. In fact, I've told my Charlie to do Hitler in quick, so he can have his bacon again.' Flo stubbed her cigarette as she continued, 'There's nothin'll rile my Charlie more than the promise of some streaky rashers! It'll all be over before we know it; my Charlie'll sort it with your Edward and our Mary's Thomas.'

Gracie laughed wryly. 'All in the pursuit of a bacon sarnie!'

This was to be the first of many pots of 4 o'clock tea shared around the table in Gracie's prim, little terrace during the war. For the inaugural meeting, Gracie had dressed the table with spring blooms of oxlip and bluebells that she popped into a milk bottle, and she had made use of her late grandmother's best china. Mary's homemade trench cake had been placed on one of Gracie's treasured Johnson Brothers plates; its pretty rose design provided a fitting backdrop to Mary's culinary efforts. The sweets Mary had brought found a temporary home in a tiny cut-glass bowl that had been languishing at the back of Gracie's dresser. Mary had saved her sweets over many weeks. She had kept them as a special treat for both the children and the women alike, in the hope of sweetening their strictly rationed lives. As the three women drank their tea, ate their cake and shared their sweets, they, in turn, shared their burdens...

Flo and Gracie had known one another for years (long before the children had come along). They had supported one another on many occasions and shared many worries and joys over many cups of tea. But this was different... Gracie and Flo were about to start a brand-new chapter together, and they were under no illusion that it was going to be easy, so they were glad Mary was there to join them and perhaps provide a little distraction.

Gracie and Flo had met Mary when she started courting young Thomas, a lad for whom they held much affection, and they were happy to take her under their wing by inviting her to join in their evenings whilst the men were training at the hop farm. Mary's inclusion brought with it only joy; it enhanced what had always been. Gracie enjoyed teaching Mary about politics and reading good books, whilst Flo revelled in sharing advice on handling men and cooking...often the two went hand in hand! For all the two wise owls gave, they took in equal measure. Mary reminded them of life before the children and responsibilities. She reminded them that in the middle of all their family chaos, in the centre of the swirling mass of worries and bills and jobs to be done, there were two people hopelessly in love. In the glow of Mary's rose-tinted youth, Gracie and Flo realised that, at the very core of their lives as married women, they were unbreakable. Mary unwittingly invigorated both Gracie and Flo, so (to the men's delight) the welcome home they received after training was usually a very warm one indeed.

The afternoon sun shone, and its hazy, dust-speckled light streamed through the kitchen window before falling on the tea-stained table to dance on the sweet wrappers. The sun's comforting warmth mirrored that which the girls had for one another; both were reassuringly strong, not unlike the stewed tea in the pot! Gracie topped up Mary's teacup before venturing. 'How have you been coping? Did you manage to say goodbye to Thomas properly?' Gracie knew that neither Thomas' parents nor Mary's mother were understanding. They had long since forgotten what it was to be in love. The parents of the love-struck pair were patronising at best and dismissive at worst.

As Mary unravelled another sweet, she told the story of the goodbye she had shared with her love: her brave, handsome Thomas. 'So, there we were, up the road, sitting on the bench, and I tried not to cry – like we'd said – but I couldn't help it. My heart clean broke in two and so did Thomas'. If I tell you something, promise not to tell, not a living soul?' She paused to receive the appropriate, reassuring nods. 'Thomas cried too. He cried and told me he loved me, that he couldn't bear to leave me, that he was scared... I never knew he could cry. I never knew.'

Gracie and Flo were entranced. It was a real-life, romantic tragedy. Flo prompted, 'What did yer do wi' 'im? Out on the street with him in tears like that?'

'They weren't tears like we cry. They were sort of slow and sparse...they kind of fell almost by accident after his eyes couldn't hold 'em no more... I've never seen tears like 'em. They came straight from his soul.'

Gracie was enthralled. 'If you ever had any doubts that the lad loved you, those tears must have wiped them clean away.'

Flo was incandescent. 'Out in't street, no proper privacy...it's not right, my girl. I can't believe that's how you were forced to say yer goodbyes.'

'She's right, of course. Your mother ought to be ashamed of herself,' asserted Gracie. 'You should have been given the parlour to yourselves, at the very least.'

'And what about his parents? All pious and snooty. They're 'appy enough to see their lad set off to war – they think he's man enough for that – but not man enough to be afforded some time with the lass he loves. It's folks like that what make me sick! You deserve better lass. Don't let nobody nor no one make you think different.'

Mary was consoled. The support of her friends and the validation of her love for Thomas was like a blanket around her shoulders. 'I count my blessings,' smiled Mary, 'to have friends like you. I don't know how Thomas and I would ever have coped these past few months without you...'

To lighten the mood, Flo steered the conversation to a topic she knew would make everyone smile: hop picking. 'Don't forget to book your holiday with Mr Spindler, Mary, the first two weeks in September. It's gonna be grand!' All three ladies became animated as they discussed the prospect of picking the heavily scented hops from the huge gardens. The promise of earning some much-needed pin money brought a smile to all their faces.

Gracie beamed. 'I'm going to get Primrose new shoes for school with the money. I don't know who's more excited, her or me!'

'It'll do the boys good to help out with the hoppin' this year. With any luck, they'll use up some of that energy they've got and have less left over for mischief!'

The women looked out into the garden at the children. The two boys, Arthur and William, were happily playing alongside Primrose. They were amusing themselves with sticks and stones, building tiny shelters and fashioning riffles from their finds. Primrose was playing nurse maid to the 'fallen' (a few snails, odd bits of chalk and some shards of flint) by collecting them up and putting them in her makeshift field hospital, over by the Anderson Shelter.

Flo smiled and nudged Gracie. 'Would you look at your Primrose! She's got an 'ead full o' stories, that one. Mind you keep it that way, Gracie. There ought to be none of your politics and papers and harping on about the war when she's around. There's no need to go upsetting the lass with truths and facts and honesty. Let her be young, Gracie...young and naive. Let all this war nonsense be nothing but a game to her.'

Gracie looked hard at her daughter, playing in the back garden. Sure enough, Primrose did have a head full of stories (she could see her acting them out), and it was true, she was only young. However, she was not so young that she did not understand her daddy had gone to war. Flo's boys were infants, but Primrose was a child, and there was a big difference between them, even if Flo could not see it. Primrose was going to need her mother's help, and Gracie knew she could not afford to ignore the facts. She gathered her thoughts and found her voice. 'Primrose will be fine. She's strong, like her father.'

There was a pause. The mention of Edward's name prompted the three women to wonder where their men might be. Flo broke the silence with a jest. 'And my boys are like their father: too much energy for their own good and always up to mischief! I suppose I should enjoy the rest while he's gone!' They all laughed, before Flo suddenly noticed the time. 'Eee, would you look at that...' She tapped her watch then called to the boys, 'Come on you two. Time to be getting home and out of yer Aunty Gracie's 'air. The pie'll be burnt t'crisp.'

The boys ignored their mother's request for action on the first time of calling. They continued to play with their sticks, undeterred. They were waiting for the shriller demand that would inevitably come but, hopefully, not for some time. The boys had learnt, even at their tender age, that grown-ups usually get distracted. Arthur and William were right to have continued with their games since the women's goodbyes took a good ten minutes to play out. When Flo and her boys eventually made their way home, they were greeted by the unwelcome smell of burnt oyster pie.

Much was shared between the women around Gracie's old, wooden table before they went their separate ways: reassurance, laughter, advice, and, of course, recipe tips. But more than that, they shared a sense of womanhood. It occurred to them that whilst tea, cake and sweets may be in short supply, their support for one another was there in abundance, and that would be sustenance enough to get them through the war.

Everything was turning out just as the boys would have wanted. Their three girls really were looking out for one another; they were keeping each other strong. They were becoming the women they would have to be to carry on without them...

****

Saturday, 25th May 1940

My darling husband,

You would be so very proud of us all. We girls met up today and discussed how to help each other through, to have a chat and to be comforted. It was wonderful and most welcome.

Flo did not mention Charlie very much, and I did not pry... I know she is missing him and will speak to me about him when she feels the need. I expect Charlie will be much the same with you...

Young Mary told us of her parting from Thomas. She felt much better for sharing her sadness. Without breaking a confidence, I am compelled to say I am worried about poor, young Thomas. Please be mindful of his tender years...he is not as strong as perhaps we have been led to believe. Protect him and guide him whenever you can my love. He is, after all, still only a boy.

Our beautiful Primrose is well. She has spent much of the day playing in the garden, lost in her imagination. Tomorrow is Sunday, and I am looking forward to a quiet day with her... After Church, I plan on taking her for a walk through the orchards. After lunch, I thought we might play noughts and crosses before she takes her bath ready for the week ahead at school. I will take the opportunity to talk to her about you. We will smile and laugh and remember all that makes you so special to her. Perhaps, I will encourage her to write you a letter...yes, I think I will do just that.

I imagine you here with me, my darling, quietly reading your paper, occasionally glancing up and sharing a line or two with me. You keep me in good company...

You'd laugh because, earlier this evening, I made you a perfectly fine cup of tea! Imagine that – a cup of tea for a man who is not here. What was I thinking? Not of the rations, that is for sure. So as not to be wasteful, you'll be glad to know that

I did, of course, drink it. I heard your voice in my head saying, "Funny girl", as I placed your cup to my lips and indulged.

I am still smiling. You are with me as I am with you. I shall go to bed now and see you there.

Good night and God bless, my love,

Forever yours, Gracie x

4
Keep mum... She's not so dumb

In Gracie's eyes, Reverend Smith had always been old. When she was young, and came to church with her mother and father, Reverend Smith was a jolly, little, grey-haired chap with grandchildren a few years younger than her. His grandchildren were now grown. The boys, of course, were at war, and it hardly seemed possible that the dear old man was still there preaching to his flock. He was still jolly, still little (albeit a little rounder) and still grey-haired, although, admittedly, there was less hair to be counted these days. Gracie marveled at the old man's resilience. He had supported his congregation through many troubles, including the Great War, where he had lost one of his sons, George. His wife, Agnes, had died quite recently, and everyone assumed the old man would retire or be retired, but no. He remained and became an even better pastor than before. The Reverend's depth of understanding had somehow grown after the loss of his beloved Agnes. Though he grieved, he continued to support and comfort all those around him with an unbending faith and admirable dedication. Reverend Smith had baptised Gracie, married her to Edward, baptised her precious baby Primrose, and buried both her parents. He and the church had always been there. He was Gracie's comforting constant in a fragile, uncertain world.

The church service at St. Andrew's that day was inspired and uplifting. The church looked beautiful with brightly coloured spring flowers adorning not only the alter but the gabled entrance too. It was a rare and much appreciated display – one that was admired by all the parishioners. Gracie felt sure that Reverend Smith, together with old

Mrs Pluckrose (the ever-devoted church organist come florist *and* cleaner), had made a particular effort to brighten the day.

It had been announced by Churchill, some time earlier, that this particular Sunday would be, "A day of National Prayer for the British Army." All the soldiers, including Gracie's darling Edward, were remembered in the prayers. The children were the focus of the sermon, which Gracie thought was wholly appropriate. It was lovely for Primrose to hear how everyone in the community was mindful of her upset; they knew her daddy had gone away to fight, and it was a sad time for her. There was a great sense of unity in church that morning because everyone knew similar services were being held across the country. The nation was united in prayer, and the parishioners at St. Andrew's in Paddock Wood were very much a part of that heartwarming unification.

Mrs Pluckrose, with glasses perched on the end of her nose and frail fingers poised, was in fine form as she accompanied the congregation on the wheezy old organ. They sang the hymn, *Jesus Christ The Apple Tree*, which was one of Primrose's favourites:

"I'm weary with my former toil,
Here I will sit and rest a while,
Under the shadow I will be,
Of Jesus Christ the apple tree…"

Whilst singing, Gracie remembered times she had spent with her beautiful mother underneath the old apple tree in their back garden when she was a child. How she still missed her parents... She remembered her mother reading to her...she thought she must have been about the same age as Primrose was now. Gracie smiled at the memory. She realised that, although she would inevitably get tired and weary as the war went on, her mother's spirit would help her get through whatever lay ahead. When the hymn had finished, the Reverend continued to preach in support of his parishioners. He read to the congregation, 1 John 3:17-18:

"If anyone has material possessions and sees his brother in need but has no pity on him, how can the love of God be in him? Dear children, let us not love with words or tongue but with actions and in truth."

Gracie was inspired. She decided the rest of the day should be filled with deeds, actions and truths. She was not sure yet what form they would take, but she would not let that minor detail spoil her enthusiasm for the day ahead. Her life had been blessed with a wonderful mother and honourable father, a beautiful daughter and a remarkable husband. Gracie was determined to fill her war-torn world with some much-needed goodness and love by way of thanks.

Towards the end of the service, just before the collection, Reverend Smith declared, 'Each man should give what he has decided in his heart to give, not reluctantly or under compulsion, for God loves a cheerful giver.' Gracie thought that was very kind of the Reverend because money was tight. It relieved her of any shame or guilt when she put all she could spare, which was very little, in the offertory box. Compulsion to put in more than she could afford would be just as bad as putting in too little if it was to Primrose's detriment – the child had to be nourished and kept warm after all. Gracie left church renewed and assured that her day had divine purpose. She strode with Primrose from the graveyard towards home, set to embrace her mission.

As Mother and daughter walked the short distance from St. Andrew's back to the house, they chatted excitedly about what fun they could have surprising people with lovely deeds. Primrose decided that they should do something special for Mrs Pluckrose because she had played her favourite hymn in church.

Gracie struck upon the idea of rooting out some old clothes (no longer needed by the rapidly growing Primrose) for the evacuees living in the big house by the church. Primrose was prompted by her mother's good idea to have another of her own. 'What about my baby clothes, Mummy? They are sitting in that little trunk, doing no good at all. Let's give those to the new babies Reverend Smith was talking about.'

At this point in the excited chatter, poor Gracie was suddenly dumbstruck. Her daughter had hit a nerve and was unwittingly testing her Christian principles. The clothes in the trunk were treasures held very dearly by Gracie. They were a reminder of those precious early days of Primrose's anxiously awaited life. They were a testament to what had been a long and fraught journey to motherhood. Most notably, they were a symbol of hope... Gracie hoped that perhaps one day they would be worn again by a desperately longed for baby: a brother or sister for Primrose. It had taken Gracie many years to fall for her daughter, with many sad losses along the way. Since Primrose's birth (six, nearly seven years ago) not once had there been the slightest hope of being blessed with another child. To part with those clothes would not be a simple act of kindness or charity; it would be a resignation of hope and an acceptance of a painful truth.

The babies Primrose referred to were being born at Moatlands, a grand family house a mile or so further on from the church. The impressive house, set in generous grounds, was being used as a temporary hospital for mothers from all over Kent and London, and sometimes beyond, to give birth safely. The previous hospital, in Woolwich, had been bombed, and so everyone had been evacuated to the family estate in Paddock Wood.

Until recently, Moatlands had been the home of 'Old John Podmore'. Although he had died, his legacy was very much alive, and his reputation for generosity and charity was a source of immense pride to his family. It was no surprise to anyone, then, when his family agreed to their home being used for such a worthy cause. 'Old John' would have approved.

Expectant mothers arrived at Moatlands week upon week – often with very little. So, the makeshift hospital was keenly accepting donations of clothes and blankets, and that was why they had been mentioned in church that morning. It was the request for donations, together with her mother's encouragement to do good, that had given little Primrose her innocent yet provocative idea.

'We'll see...' was all Gracie could find in her heart to say before quickly moving the conversation on. 'After doing our good deeds, why don't we have a picnic in the orchard?'

Little Primrose squealed with joy and jumped whilst pulling on her mother's arm. 'Yes! We could pack everything up in your big basket. Good deeds first, scrummy tummy second...'

'...Bath time third!' asserted Gracie.

'Oh, Mummy!' Primrose protested with an upward glance from beneath her long, dark lashes. Gracie thought how much Primrose looked like Edward and smiled as she pulled her close. Gracie put the key in the lock and let the pair into their little sanctuary: Number 77 Commercial Road.

Primrose was given an empty jam jar to fill with spring flowers from the garden. She filled it beautifully with pretty weeds as well as genuine blooms, and Gracie thought it looked all the better for its childish charm. The left-over piece of trench cake from the previous day was wrapped in greaseproof paper and adorned with a simple brown tag, attached with string, on which Primrose wrote: *Thank you, Mrs Pluckrose. You are kind. God must love you lots.* The pair had decided not to put their names on any of their gifts because they were not giving to be thanked. They were giving simply to be good, and Primrose thought that was great fun.

Whilst Primrose was writing her tag, Gracie gathered up the ill-fitting clothes belonging to her daughter and bundled them up with string. Her tag read: *You are doing such a great and noble deed for the children in your care and indeed the war effort. These clothes are not charity, rather a gift of thanks for all you are doing and hopefully a welcome sight for one of your temporary house guests.* Gracie felt pleased as she wrote the note. She knew the clothes were needed because one of the evacuees she had seen in church was poorly dressed in comparison to most others in their Sunday best. Gracie imagined how thrilled the little girl might be, and it filled her with joy. After the gifts were prepared, work began on the picnic. It was a predictably small and simple affair, but the joy was as much in the preparation as it was in the anticipation of eating. Primrose stood on a wooden stall by her mother's side and Gracie mischievously smudged jam on her daughter's button nose. Whilst attempting to butter the bread, Primrose's intense concentration made her pull funny faces, and Gracie hoped she would remember the moment she was sharing with her daughter forever.

Time flew by as the happy pair enjoyed laughing and chatting about what fun they were going to have delivering their gifts. Once everything was packed in the wicker basket, Primrose hurried upstairs to collect her coat whilst Gracie waited by the front door. When Primrose returned to her waiting mother, she was carrying the small trunk of precious baby clothes and she glibly exclaimed, 'We nearly forgot these!'

Gracie stole a breath and then sat on the bottom step with Primrose by her side – the small trunk rested between their two laps. Gracie explained as well as she could, as honestly as she could, and with words she hoped her daughter would understand, how precious the items in the little trunk were. They opened the box and looked through as they had done so many times before. Gracie held matinee jackets to her cheek, and Primrose made booties dance on the tips of her fingers. Tiny woollen hats and peaked bonnets were marvelled at because they were so small, and a pair of immaculate navy-blue buckled shoes was held in the palm of Gracie's hand, evoking memories of days gone by... 'It would simply break Mummy's heart to part with any of these precious things.'

Primrose sat for a moment in quiet contemplation, worthy of a much older soul, and then asked, 'But what about the babies?' She searched in her mother's eyes for an answer to her question.

Gracie sighed, resigned. 'If anyone has material possessions and sees his brother in need but has no pity on him, how can the love of God be in him?'

Primrose was very impressed. She did not really understand what her mother had said, but she was impressed, nevertheless. 'Does that mean the babies can have my old clothes, Mummy?'

Gracie fell upon a compromise. 'Let's share them.' she conceded. 'We'll keep some for our memories but give the smallest and warmest bits to the babies who really need them.' Gracie kissed her daughter's forehead and then began placing the tiny gifts in her basket.

'God will be ever so pleased!'

As Gracie continued to fill the basket, she felt all too keenly that God was telling her to let go of her dreams of having another child. She would never again be blessed with a tiny hand to grasp her finger; no hushed coos or gurgles would melt her heart as she rocked a babe in her arms ever again... She had been given a message, Heaven-sent and delivered by her very own angel. It was as though Primrose was telling her, 'I am all you have, Mummy, so love me with all your might.' So, there it was: time to leave her fruitless hopes behind and move forward with a thankful heart and Primrose. As Gracie stood in the hall, about to open the door, Primrose took her hand and squeezed it tightly. Primrose's infectious excitement buoyed Gracie. It felt like encouragement, thanks and a new beginning rolled into one. For the briefest of moments, she felt Edward was there, right by their side.

The first stop on their journey was to be at Mrs Pluckrose's house. The mischievous pair had decided they would leave the gifts in a sort of 'knock-down-ginger' fashion. The gifts would be put on the front doorstep, the door knocked, and then the bearer had to run away as fast as they could so as not to be seen! Gracie had left Primrose in position and then crept around the corner (just a few doors down) to hide from Mrs Pluckrose. She was still, however, just about visible to Primrose's keen, focused eye. Primrose gently placed the jam jar of flora on the front step together with the careful wrapped slice of cake. She then looked about to be sure no one could see her before knocking as hard as she could on the imposing, black door. Heart pounding, Primrose then ran away as fast as her spindly little legs could carry her, back towards her amused mother. The covert pair huddled together, peeking around the corner of the bricked end terrace, trying to confine their infectious giggles. After a short while, Mrs Pluckrose came to the door: hair tied up in a scarf with two curlers adorning the front. She was wearing her double-breasted apron, slippers and a confused expression. Eventually, after scanning a line of sight in keeping with her own, she glanced down and saw the package together with the flowers. Slowly, she bent her old bones down and collected them up. The curious old girl smiled a puzzled smile and then, to her further intrigue, spied Primrose's tag. The dear lady tried to focus, but her glasses were not perched on the end of her nose to aid her. Instinctively, she stretched the arm holding the package away from her body and pulled her head back until she could read the carefully written words. It was then that she beamed! With one more look to see who might have done such a kindly thing, she took her tiny old bones back into her home, smelling her flowers as she did. She felt, for a fleeting moment, not seventy but seventeen.

The big house near the church was en route to Moatlands, which was in turn on the way to the orchard. Gracie left Primrose just the other side of the church wall, peeping over so she could check on her mother's progress. Gracie opened the gate at the front of the garden, walked up the path and placed the clothes on the impressive step. With her heart pounding in her chest, she knocked on the large oak door before her as hard as she could. To her own surprise, she then ran faster than she could recall ever doing in her adult life. She scrambled over the small stone wall to join her now awe-struck daughter in the waiting game. The game did not last long as the lady of the house answered the door, looked about quite puzzled and then lowered her gaze to spy the package. Gracie revelled in watching the relative stranger bend down to gather up the mystery bundle. As the message was read from the innocuous brown tag, the recipient was clearly overcome. Unravelling what was before her she exclaimed, 'Oh my!' She then called out as she took leave of the step and returned to her home. 'Agatha, Agatha come quickly.' The door was then shut, and the couple hiding behind the wall popped up and continued their journey, brimming with pride.

It was unrealistic to knock the door at Moatlands and run away unseen – the driveway must have been a good two hundred yards long. Instead, Gracie and Primrose approached the building quietly, holding one another's hands. Primrose knew how hard this was for her mother, and Gracie knew her daughter was trying her best to be grown up and supportive. By the time they reached the grand entrance, Gracie was quite calm and composed. She lightly tapped the door, so as not to upset the fragile residents, and waited to be greeted. A young woman, dressed in a simple, white nurse's dress with a scarf holding back her hair, answered the door with a smile and a hello. Gracie took the few knitted pieces of clothing from her basket, together with a small shawl and said graciously, 'Primrose and I no longer have a need for these few things, and we understand from the Reverend that you do. Please would you be so kind as to give them to any ladies who might make good use of them.'

The young nurse smiled again. 'Of course, thank you. Who should I say has called?'

'Oh, no one really...that's not important, but thank you.' With that, the nurse took the clothes and the shawl, they shared their goodbyes, and Gracie took *her baby* to the orchard for a well-deserved picnic underneath an apple tree.

The orchard was a profusion of blossom and wildflowers. Carpeting the orchard's floor were bluebells, occasionally punctuated with delicate, wild orchids, and even the odd, hardy (if slightly withered) primrose. The setting could not have been more perfect for mother and daughter to enjoy the simple pleasure of being together. Gracie had packed one of Primrose's favourite books, *The Secret Garden*, and the pair sat under an apple tree just as Gracie had done, once upon a time, with her own dear mother. Primrose was filled with delight as Gracie read from the pages of the book before them. They enjoyed their bread and jam whilst the sun shone down on them through the dappled shade of the obliging tree. For an hour or so, as far as Primrose was concerned, there were just two people in the world: there was no war, she did not miss her father, and she was as happy as she could ever have been. For Gracie, however, the picnic was bittersweet. She found herself missing her mother, but, moreover, she desperately missed her darling husband. She imagined her mother could look down from heaven and see her with Primrose, which lent her some comfort. But what of Edward? He could not look down on them both and smile. Gracie determined to write to Edward again that evening to share her day with him, so he might see in his mind's eye the day she was spending with Primrose. It might encourage him to be strong. In any case, she assured herself, writing was the best and only thing she could usefully do.

When late afternoon came and the tired adventurers at last returned home, Gracie drew a bath for Primrose in front of the fire in the back room. Gracie washed Primrose's hair and scrubbed her little, lean body until she was happy that it shone. She then topped up the bath with some hot water from the jug before settling down to talk to Primrose about her father. 'Do you miss Daddy, my love?' she started. Primrose shrugged her bony shoulders and remained quiet. 'Mummy misses him. She misses him lots...' she encouraged, but still nothing came from Primrose. '...I write to him every day. It makes me feel better. You could write to him if you like.' This time there was a shrug, followed by a carefully considered nod. Gracie did not push the conversation any further. Instead, she took the towel that had been warming by the fire and wrapped her daughter up tightly in it until she was dry.

A little later, in Gracie's bedroom, Gracie settled Primrose down in front of her dressing table and gave her a piece of paper from her box and a small pencil. She told Primrose to write whatever she wanted to her daddy. As Gracie put Primrose's hair into rags before bed, she looked on as her daughter wrote:

Dear Daddy,

Plees hurry up and giv the litel girl the ribbin. Then you can com home. I love you. I fink I made a mistak when I sed you can go. Sorry.

I love you. Plees do not be cros wiv me,

Love Primrose.

Gracie read her daughter's words as they spilled onto the page in front of her. It was all she could do to finish tying her daughter's damp, dark hair without breaking down in tears. She fought the lump in her throat and regained her composure sufficiently to whisper some words of comfort to her little girl, lost in the mirror in front of her. 'That's lovely, darling. Now, you mustn't worry...Daddy is not going to be in the least bit cross. We'll send him the letter, and I'm sure he'll be home just as soon as he can. Now, come on. Let's tuck you into bed.' With that, Gracie escorted her daughter across the landing and settled her into bed. They shared a prayer for Edward's safe return before Gracie kissed her daughter's forehead, turned out the light and returned to her own, empty, room.

Sunday, 26th May 1940

My darling husband,

I am quite overwhelmed by Primrose...she has taught me lessons today, guided me through heartache, kept me spirited and held my hand when I needed you. All without realising, she has been my saviour.

I was fooled for a while into thinking she was my rock – that our little girl was supporting me. I thank God I was reminded, shortly before bed, that she is just a little girl...a little girl who loves and misses her Daddy, who is confused and saddened by this terrible, awful war. She needs me, and I am determined to be here and do my best for her – for us.

The lessons she taught me today were not planned by her. She merely delivered them. The guiding light that shone so brightly from within her was not lit by her tiny hand – it was lit from afar and held by Primrose, so I might see it... I understand now that her spirit is a blessing from God, and that when I held her hand, and was so comforted, it was because she held all the love in heaven and earth in her small and perfect palm. I see now that Primrose and I are being protected and guided. We are truly blessed, and so I am grateful to God beyond measure. Be certain my love, as God holds Primrose and me, he holds you too, for our souls are together as one and He knows that... He knows everything.

I started my journey today with Primrose in church, and I thought it would be wonderful to end the journey with you by sharing this:

"Be careful not to do your 'acts of righteousness' before men, to be seen by them. If you do, you will have no reward from your Father in heaven. So, when you give to the needy, do not announce it with trumpets, as the hypocrites do on the streets, to be honored by men. I tell you the truth, they have received their reward in full. When you give to the needy, do not let your left *hand know what your right hand is doing, so that your giving may be in secret. Then your Father, who sees what is done in secret, will reward you."*

Rest assured, your good deeds and sacrifices will be rewarded my love...they are not going unnoticed.

I shall leave you with some thoughts for your dreams: Primrose and I shared in many good and wonderful deeds on our journey together today – ones which must, of course, remain secret! I can however tell you about the picnic we had underneath an apple tree in the orchard and the laughter we shared, the book we enjoyed and the bath Primrose had in front of the fire...it has been as perfect as a day can be all the while you are at war.

I pray that wherever you are, wherever you lay your head tonight, you remember I am with you. I am by your side, holding your hand and kissing you goodnight.

Sweet dreams, my love. I am forever yours...

Gracie x

5
Won't you choo-choo me home?

As Gracie settled herself in bed, she imagined Primrose's face when the first letter from Edward arrived at the house. Perhaps, she mused, it would be soon – perhaps it might even arrive tomorrow. With that comforting thought, and a prayer that Edward would sleep safely and dream of home, she fell to sleep. Sadly, though, her wish that Edward might sleep soundly and enjoy sweet dreams was not to be. For on that fateful night, 26th May 1940, Edward was destined, like Gracie, not to dream at all.

On Commercial Road the following day, everything carried on as usual. By midday, Gracie was drained of all her patience as she had been minding Flo's two boys. When at last Flo arrived to collect them (revitalised after a morning off duty as 'mother'), Gracie heaved a sigh of relief and happily waved them all goodbye. A few doors along, Mary had been busy working in the shop, serving customers and tidying the displays. The women's lives were being consumed, as they so often were, with their mundane (usually thankless) chores. As the day went on, so too did the predictable repetition: Gracie welcomed Primrose home from school, Flo settled her boys at the table for their tea, and Mary teetered home from work – eager to put her sore and tired feet up on the pouffe.

No letter from Edward had arrived in the post, but that was no real surprise; Gracie had not been expecting one for a few more weeks at least, and she had prepared Primrose for a long wait. Although they were desperate to hear from him, to be given some clue as to where he might

45

be, they understood they would probably have to wait a little while longer...

Monday rolled by, much like any other day, and the women of Commercial Road carried on as usual because there was nothing other than that to do. In the evening, however, as Gracie read the newspaper, she was reminded that these were far from ordinary times. As she turned the pages before her, her faith and optimism from Sunday was considerably shaken. There were reports of more fierce fighting in France, and she wondered where her Edward was in all the chaos. As she continued to read about the troubles in Dunkirk, she was startled by an unexpected knock at her door, which she approached with caution before nervously inquiring as to who was calling.

'It's Mr Spindler, Gracie. Sorry to call so late...'

Gracie was happy to hear the familiar voice and, with curiosity, opened the door to her boss. 'How can I help you, sir?'

Mr Spindler was a distinguished, older gentleman; he was also an astute, successful businessman who could afford the finest cloth. Naturally then, as a master tailor (of some repute) he was always impeccably dressed. Although not poetically handsome, he was always well groomed and presented. His affable nature made his Roman nose and sizable jaw really rather attractive. He was a very popular fellow amongst men, and (to their envy) adored by women – especially those with a penchant for silk, satin and lace. Any advances from admirers were, however, always wasted on him. He vowed he was married to his art and his business; he had no time to take a wife or entertain women with fanciful ideas of matrimony! His family, Jewish migrants from Poland, had started the business on Commercial Road generations ago. Originally, it was a simple tailor's shop, but it had grown (almost beyond recognition) over the years into a fashionable department store. Mr Spindler drove the business ferociously to ensure its continued success. He knew he was a custodian of a retail legacy and was determined to make his mark on the business before leaving it to his heir: his nephew. As Mr Spindler spoke to Gracie, he used his ever exuberant, expressive hands to convey the importance and drama of his late-night message. He began by rubbing his hands together, shoulders hunched, and exclaimed, 'My dear – it's not me. It's the men – the soldiers... The Station Master contacted me this afternoon about a train load of soldiers stopping off tomorrow at the station. He's been told they'll need tea and sandwiches and whatever else we can lay our hands on...'

Gracie invited Mr Spindler into the hall, so he could explain in full. It seemed that the train station was on standby for the next few days to provide sustenance to soldiers being evacuated from Dunkirk. They were not really sure on numbers or exact times, but they were to be prepared. Mr Spindler was hopeful of enlisting Gracie's help, for he knew she would be reliable and, better yet, resourceful. Gracie was, of course, only too pleased to have been asked and assured Mr Spindler she would happily coordinate operations from the shop. When Mr Spindler took his leave, Gracie could not help but wonder who might be on the train the next day. Mr Spindler had told her the train was stopping along the line from Dover to London and that men would be disembarking along the way. Who, she wondered, would disembark at Paddock Wood?

Little sleep was taken by Gracie that night; she was consumed with thoughts of Edward – hopeful that, perhaps, she might see him the following day. She resolved to make a particular effort with her hair, just in case, and she mused about what to wear. She decided not to mention a word to Primrose, however. It would be irresponsible to raise her little girl's hopes on the strength of her whimsical notions. Gracie tried in vain to put thoughts of seeing Edward to the back of her mind because she knew it was folly to imagine seeing him again so soon. Regardless, try as she might, her stomach kept turning in nervous anticipation of the day ahead. Every hour of the night was seen in by her bleary eyes.

The sun shone brightly on the following Tuesday afternoon, and the station platform was a hive of activity. The staff from the bank were in charge of tea; the water was provided by the fire service; and Smedley's Cannery (conveniently located by the station) provided all the cans to hold the hot, strong brews. Gracie had spent the morning coordinating the making of sandwiches from the store's canteen. The local butcher, baker and grocer, together with some office and shop-floor staff, had been involved in the effort to prepare them. Now, they all stood together, jostling for positions on the crowded platform, eagerly awaiting the train. Everyone had been warned that the men needed to be given food and tea as quickly as possible because the train was scheduled to stop for just eight minutes.

When at last the train arrived, the anxious anticipation gave way to a clamour of clumsy, heartfelt chaos. Men were leaning out of the carriage windows waving and smiling, and the platform erupted with excited cheers. Gracie and her fellow volunteers promptly set to work handing out tea and food. The servicemen thanked them profusely, explaining it was their first food in days. Everyone on the platform was shocked to see the state some of the men were in. Some were half-naked – their modesty preserved with blood-soaked blankets – and many were badly injured and in need of medical attention. It was as though the war had arrived, for all to see, in Paddock Wood, and there was nothing phony about it. It was no longer something those on the platform had read about in the newspapers or heard about on the wireless. It was real. The war was living, raw and bleeding, right there in front of them. Almost as soon as the train had arrived, changing everyone who had witnessed it for evermore, it departed again. As had been explained, after eight minutes the train (with its nourished occupants) drew away from the station and continued onward towards London. There was a cheer to see the soldiers on their way, then a sigh, followed by a brief reflective silence. Not a soul disembarked.

Gracie went about the business of tidying away, together with all the other volunteers, and she spoke to Mr Spindler about the refinement of procedures for the next day. Mr Spindler listened carefully to her and concluded that all his staff would be made available the following day to help. The shop, he decided, could shut for a few hours given the exceptional circumstances. Mr Spindler then asked if Gracie could hold the fort for an hour or so whilst he visited the warehouse posthaste for socks. He had noticed that, in most cases, the men's socks were in a dreadful state. He supposed that clean, dry socks were a simple comfort he could happily afford the brave, young soldiers passing through his hands. Mr Spindler's willingness to shut the shop, together with his resolve to buy socks without the hope of a penny's return, illustrated that these truly were exceptional times!

As Gracie walked the short distance back to her home, she felt proud to have been involved in helping the men. It was the first time she had really felt a part of the war effort. She had helped directly, and it felt very good indeed. Despite her feelings of pride, however, she could not help reflecting on the shocking state some of the men had been in. She had promised Edward she would never picture him at war, but what she had just witnessed was very real and not in the least bit imaginary. These were real soldiers with real wounds, and although Edward was not in their number he could have been. Would he be there tomorrow or the day after? Worse still, what if he was one of the fallen left behind? She shuddered as she turned the key in the lock. Once inside, she leant against her closed front door and spoke firmly to herself: 'Pull yourself together. Everything will be fine.' With that said, and a deep breath taken, Gracie set about preparing Primrose's tea.

By the time Primrose arrived home, news of the train stopping at the station with the soldiers was the talk of the town, and Primrose knew all about it. Flo, of course, knew all about the trains and had wasted no time in volunteering to help with the serving of tea, eager to be in the thick of things the following day. Mary, who had been enlisted to help at the store that afternoon, visited Gracie's after work. Together with Flo (who had 'popped in') they discussed logistical refinements. Both girls were keen to know what had happened at the station earlier and expressed their hopes that perhaps their boys might be on one of the trains due to arrive over the coming days. By the time everyone had gone home, and the excited Primrose had been tucked up into bed (assured that her Daddy was *not* expected to be on one of the trains), Gracie was utterly exhausted. The lack of sleep from the previous night had caught up with her, and she was more than ready for her bed when at last she finished all her chores and climbed the stairs to her room.

On the Wednesday, the platform was positively heaving. It occurred to Gracie there might be more volunteers than soldiers. However, when the train arrived it was even busier than the one from the previous day, and it was an all-hands-on-deck affair for a frantic, but productive, eight minutes. Once the train had departed, the excitement had passed and the cleanup had been completed, the three women walked along Commercial Road together and shared their disappointment in not seeing anyone disembark from the train...

Thursday came and went in much the same way. However, as she read the paper that evening, Gracie was alarmed to see the reports were getting ever darker. The optimism of Sunday's day of prayer, together with the positive sight of hundreds of men (alive if not necessarily well) on the trains, were in stark contrast to the reports she saw before her. Her blood ran cold. Try as she might, it was hard not to allow herself to drift into the darkness. Reports that the Belgian army had capitulated were difficult to ignore and made the situation seem all the more hopeless. The paper was full of harrowing, pessimistic reports from Dunkirk. She sat alone in the kitchen and read a telegram from the King to Lord Gort that had been published:

'All your countrymen have been following with pride and admiration the courageous resistance of the British Expeditionary Force during the continuing fighting of the last fortnight. Faced by circumstances outside their control in a position of extreme

difficulty, they are displaying a gallantry which has never been surpassed in the annals of the British Army. The hearts of everyone of us at home are with you and your magnificent troops in this hour of peril.'

As Gracie read, she felt herself bracing for the worst. She caught herself as her stomach tightened and her teeth clenched. She was furious and chastised herself – 'You don't even know where he is. He might be miles away from Dunkirk.'

The very next day, inexplicably, everything seemed to have changed. The bleak news and solemn wireless broadcasts of the previous few days gave way to the news of miracles and heroes overcoming insurmountable odds. It was a stunning turn of events. Everyone at the train station was wrapped up in the optimism and talking of nothing else. The mood was jubilant. The station was awash with schoolchildren (who had been given the day off!) and well-wishers, all of whom were milling with the usual volunteers. Young boys had written messages of thanks and support for the soldiers, which were to be handed out together with the tea, sandwiches and socks. Gracie was wary of the dramatic revelations; it all seemed too good to be true.

Flo, though, was happily convinced by everything she heard and read. She rushed over to Gracie, with her boys and Mary in tow, waving a newspaper that declared in its headline: *Disaster Turned to Triumph*. 'They've only gone 'n turned it on its head...our prayers have been answered, pet!' Flo was flushed and excited and clearly hopeful that her Charlie was in the number of saved souls the paper was reporting on.

Mary too was optimistic, a little more cautious than Flo, but still clearly excited by the revelations. 'If our boys were there, then it's hopeful isn't it, Gracie? They're coming home safe, in their thousands, in their hundreds of thousands. Chances are, our boys are with 'em. They've got a good chance, Gracie – a great chance!'

The three women looked through the paper together, but Gracie was not consoled; she tried to instill her reserve in Flo, but it was no use... Flo was happy to believe that Charlie was returning home a hero, and (more disturbing than that) she had told her boys so. She invited her young sons to look at the paper. 'Look, boys – look at the photographs. Can you see Daddy, boys?' Gracie flinched with unease as she looked upon the excited boys with dread. What might tomorrow bring, she thought? What if the reality of war was not the headline Flo was so eager and willing to accept? What would she tell her boys then?

The train came and went that day, as it had done previously, and the trains continued for a few days after that. In all that time, only one soldier ever disembarked at the station in Paddock Wood: a young man of nineteen, in a dreadful state. He was found by his mother and two sisters and taken home to be nursed back to health. Gracie, Mary and Flo were shocked to see the state of the poor boy being carried by his family. He was half-naked, had no shoes or socks and was stained with the cold, dark blood of battle. Despite their shock, the three women were all a little jealous – they did not want to be, and they uttered not a single word of it. However, it was there all the same – the feeling they wanted something someone else had: a loved one, home and safe, in their arms.

Like so many others, Edward, Charlie and Thomas were not destined to be reunited with their loved ones on the station platform in Paddock Wood. Their fate was an altogether different one, sealed back on the Sunday whilst everyone prayed for their safe return in church. Long before the first train had departed on its journey to Paddock Wood from Dover, Edward, Charlie and Thomas had begun starkly different journeys.

Unbeknown to Gracie, she had been quite right when she had told herself that Edward could be miles from Dunkirk. But for now, the only thing she knew for certain was that Edward had not been on one of the trains. She had no clue where he was or what fate had befallen him, and the anguish that caused her was something she had not even remotely prepared for. She thought it was just about as painful a feeling as she could bear. She was wrong.

A desperate fight had taken place. Edward, together with Charlie and Thomas, had been there... They were not in Dunkirk. They were in Calais.

Their battle scene had not been in the headlines, and few were aware of the brave men taking part in this small, tattered pocket of the war, least of all Gracie, Mary and Flo. The Queen Victoria's Rifles had been sent, together with a handful of other regiments, to Calais in order to protect the port. It was hoped their presence might act as a distraction to aid the colossal evacuation of Dunkirk. The thinking behind the audacious operation was to engage some of the German Panzer Division, thereby giving the allied soldiers in Dunkirk a better chance of evacuation. In theory, there would be a diminished German task force in Dunkirk if the allied troops in Calais could capture their attention and lock them into battle.

When Edward and his fellow men arrived in Calais, they discovered that a "logistical error" had left them without their trusty motorbikes: their nimble Nortons and sprightly Matchless bikes, their steeds, were still in England. Worse still, they did not have their rifles. They were given inferior pistols and told to make do. Food, water and ammunition were all in desperately short supply, and the German troops in Calais outnumbered their own by a staggering three to one. This was a fight they could never have won – and those who sent them knew it.

The efforts of Edward and his comrades in Calais may well have helped the three hundred and thirty-eight thousand men in Dunkirk evacuate. The price they paid, however, was desperately high. Of the four thousand troops who stood alongside Edward, a mere thirty survivors were brought home to safety. Edward, Charlie and Thomas were not in their number.

It would be some time before the girls back at home received any news of their men, and so they carried on with their lives as usual. They carried on unaware of their new realities; they lived cruelly false lives, littered with unknown truths that they would come to reflect on with grim and painful hindsight.

****

Sunday, 2nd June 1940

My darling husband,

We have had quite a remarkable few days here. I'm sure that when you at last receive my letters this one will be held by you as a favourite...

I have been a real part of the war effort here in Paddock Wood. Many thousands of men were evacuated from Dunkirk and transported by train from Dover to London. The trains stopped here so that we could provide the men aboard with hot tea, food and even socks! We were given just eight minutes to see to all those aboard the heaving trains...if only the preparation and subsequent tidying could have been as swift! As a consequence of the successful evacuation, spirits here are high as I trust they are with you.

I must confess that I mused about you being on one of the trains. I know – 'Funny girl!' It is clear to see where our darling Primrose has inherited her wild imagination and optimism... It was fun though, for a while, to imagine seeing you...to picture your face looking out of a train window: a face with an expectant smile, full of excitement in anticipation of surprising me. It may cheer you to know that I paid particular attention to my hair on the days that the trains came, just in case. You should take the time to picture me dressed in my best, hair curled, and all made up, my darling Mr Chatley because that is how I will be upon your return. I will be blissfully happy and so too will Primrose. That is a promise you must keep close to your heart.

You'll be pleased to know that I now have an address to send your letters (courtesy of Flo who pushed relentlessly to secure one), so I will bundle them together and post them to you on Monday. I'll post them after school with Primrose. She'll enjoy that. I do hope they reach you swiftly and find you well.

I am missing you desperately, my love; I confess, it is more difficult than I had ever imagined. Being without you is heart-wrenching at times, especially in the evenings when everything is quiet. I imagine you too have times when quietness finds you lonely and desperately longing for comfort. I suppose we should console ourselves with the knowledge that, although we are apart for now, we will be reunited soon enough. We will be together again when it is meant to be...we must simply learn to be patient until then.

Much love to you, my darling. Check your pocket...I am there.

Your own dear, Gracie x

6
Stiff upper lip

There was a knock on Gracie's front door.

There was a telegram.

DEEPLY REGRET TO INFORM YOU YOUR HUSBAND 46537 P/O E CHATLEY HAS BEEN REPORTED MISSING LETTER TO FOLLOW.

Gracie gasped. Her life began to fade as she stumbled in the hallway, falling to the stairs, staring at the telegram. She silently crumbled as the sound of the rain outside beat relentlessly against the window. The pulled thread in the rug at the foot of the stairs stared up at her as she dissolved to a washed-out blur. Hurried footsteps out on the street gathered in pace and thundered as she irrevocably fractured. It was merciless. She had no impulse to breathe. The Gracie who had enjoyed passion, mischief, desire and fun was no longer; she had disappeared just as surely as Edward had. The knowledge that he was missing in some war-torn corner, that he was without his fellow men, broke Gracie. She was beyond numb. She was nothing – not even Primrose's mother. She ceased to be. Anything she might become would have to be born again. For now, she was a void, capable of nothing – not even grief. Grief was reserved for those with loved ones who were dead. Gracie had not been afforded such a privileged position. Her life had been extinguished.

As Gracie disappeared and a poor impersonator embodied her, Flo screamed in agony and fell to her knees out on the street...

DEEPLY REGRET TO INFORM YOU YOUR HUSBAND 46433 P/O C WEBB HAS BEEN REPORTED MISSING LETTER TO FOLLOW.

Mrs Pluckrose, who had been queuing, nestled under her umbrella at the butcher's opposite, ran over to Flo as quickly as her arthritic joints would allow. She tried to make sense of Flo's outburst but was unable to tear her from the pavement or distract her from her screams. Mrs Pluckrose was soon joined by others from the queue. Some knew Flo and were genuinely concerned, while others were merely curious to see if they could assist a stranger in need. Those who remained in the queue valued their rations dearly and moved happily along the shortened line, content with their view of the spectacle from across the street. Flo's two boys ran out after their distraught mother. They were clearly confused and scared by the scene that greeted them. Mrs Pluckrose tried to reassure them and had them swiftly taken to her house, where her son Bill would entertain them. Mrs Pluckrose asked her elderly neighbour, Mr Jones, to escort the boys to her house, and she asked a relative stranger to fetch some brandy. After a short time, Mrs Pluckrose managed to prise the apparent source of Flo's distress – a clenched telegram – from her weakening grasp. After reading the desperate news, Mrs Pluckrose resigned herself to accompany Flo on the wet pavement. The frail, elderly soul joined Flo with a profound empathy, and they both began to weep. As Mrs Pluckrose cradled Flo in her arms and gently rocked her, she repeated all the while, 'I know, my darling girl. I know...' For Mrs Pluckrose did know all too well. The telegram Flo had received was the beginning of what was usually the end, and everyone knew it. First the telegram stating they were missing would arrive, then, in most cases, the letter that told you they were dead – or even worse, still missing – would follow. For Mrs Pluckrose that was how her dear husband was categorized; he was still *missing*, now *presumed dead*. Mr Pluckrose had held his unfortunate status since the battle of the Somme. There had been no funeral for him, no flowers, no single day of unadulterated grief...just a lifetime of unanswered questions. No body. No grave. It was true, Mrs Pluckrose really did know. She knew all too well.

From nowhere there appeared a blanket to cover the shoulders of the two women on the street floor, and the brandy ordered for Flo was shared with Mrs Pluckrose. Those standing around the sodden pair used their umbrellas to shelter them, not only from the elements but from the prying eyes across the street. No one rushed Flo or Mrs Pluckrose to their feet. They rose in their own time, sharing an unexpected laugh between themselves as they did. They then thanked those who had shielded them before slowly walking to Mrs Pluckrose's house for another brandy and a cigarette or two. In Mrs Pluckrose's parlour, as tears were shed, brandy was poured and clouds of tobacco plumed, Flo found herself immersed in a sea of emotions – a rough, turbulent sea, with unexpected swells and crashes. Wave after wave of crushing emotion rolled over her as she surrendered to the immense, relentless force of it all. She did not fight; she hadn't the energy to struggle. She simply allowed herself to be drenched, to begin the cleansing process. It was to be a long journey at sea for her and the boys, but their journey, unlike Gracie's, had at least begun.

As Gracie sat motionless on her stair and Flo sipped brandy, young Mary received news of her own...

Thomas' father had taken receipt of a telegram the previous day, and he was on his way to visit Mary's house to share its contents. His visit was performed as an act of duty, carried out in respect for his son. It was not in any way intended to be respectful of Mary's feelings, and sadly, as intended, it was not. Mary greeted Mr Bennett at her mother's door. He was dressed in a long, black overcoat and a black trilby hat. He wore a stern expression, and his narrowed eyes were fixed, quite purposefully, away from Mary's contrasting wide, brown orbs. As Mr Bennett spoke, he slowly rocked to and fro on his agitated feet, and he tapped the gloved fingers he had tightly grasped behind his back. His errand was an uncomfortable one. He was uncomfortable in Mary's presence, and if his stiff, awkward body had not portrayed that clearly enough, then his cold and blunt delivery of his shocking news most certainly did. 'My wife said I should let you know that we have received news. She was insistent that I visit you this morning, for Thomas' sake. It's rather awkward, and I'd really prefer it if you didn't make any unnecessary fuss because it would only make matters worse...it would make it harder for the family. The crux of the matter is that we received a telegram yesterday, and it seems that, most regrettably, our boy – *our* Thomas – has been killed in action. It's terribly upsetting for us all. I'm sure you understand. The family are devastated.'

There was a pause. Mary was stunned, struggling to process the words hanging around her, unable to take a hold of their enormity. Her eyes glazed, and they became framed by deep furrows that burrowed into her fragile, porcelain forehead. As the furrows deepened and Mary's eyes filled with tears, she quite forgot what it was to breathe. Her heart beat so hard and so fast that she was overwhelmed by it.

Mr Bennett, too, held his breath. He was on tenterhooks – waiting for the kind of inappropriate outburst he had imagined on his walk over to the house (the type he had tried to prevent with the carefully chosen words of his speech). After a few seconds, Mr Bennett was reassured that his pre-emptive, scripted monologue had been successful, and so he endeavoured to execute a quick getaway. Mary, feeling faint thanks to her racing heart, heard nothing of Mr Bennett's clumsy, unrehearsed parting ramble: 'Right, well, there it is then...I must take my leave, I'm afraid. Mrs Bennett needs me, you understand? Right, well, good to see you've taken it so well...good show. I'll be off then. Good day to you, Miss.' With a tip of his hat, he turned on his heel and left Mary barely able to stand against her mother's doorframe – bereft. Alone.

Eventually, Mary gathered her thoughts sufficiently to grab her coat from the banister, slip on her shoes and run to Gracie's. It was the only thing she could think to do... She pounded on Gracie's door, yelling her name from the street. Inside the house, a woman began to stir. She did not know what to do, so she did not move from the confines of her step. At last, Mary looked through the letter box and called to Gracie, 'Let me in, please. Gracie, please. I don't know what to do....'

The woman resembling Gracie was thrust into her new world with a role to play and expectations placed upon her tiny, ill-prepared shoulders. She was expected to be a supporter and carer. She had been called upon to nurse the broken-hearted – those who were permitted to grieve. She rose to the challenge admirably. Edward would have been proud of her.

'It's all right, my love,' she found herself saying, 'I've got you, and everything will be all right. You'll see...give it time, my lovely girl. Give it time, and you'll be able to breathe without it hurting like this. I promise.' For an hour or so, Gracie cradled Mary just as Mrs Pluckrose had cradled Flo. After a while, the pair shared some hot, sweet tea with a nip of brandy in it. Mary found the strength to sit at the table and share with her dearest friend the horror of how Thomas' father had told her the heartbreaking news of her precious love's death. Instinctively, Gracie knew to listen intently, to gently tilt her head and nod slowly in all the right places. She knew when to pour more tea and when to hold Mary's hand, but what she did not know was how to share her news...how to let Mary know about Edward. The pair spent the best part of the day huddled around the teapot in Gracie's neat and tidy kitchen, but Edward's name was never mentioned, not by either one of them.

By mid-afternoon, before Primrose was expected home from school, Mary decided that a walk alone in the fresh air would do her some good. She thanked Gracie and promised to return the following day for a repeat prescription of tea and sympathy. Gracie performed the perfect goodbye, complete with reassurance and affection, before closing the door and returning to the stair where the telegram lay awaiting her. She resumed her position. The pulled thread in the rug at the foot of the stairs stared up at her, and she held the telegram in the palm of her hand. It was as though the visit from Mary had not happened; the performance had ended and, in an instant, been forgotten.

It was an hour or so later that Primrose burst excitedly through the door with news of her day, and Gracie, on cue, acted her part as mother admirably – drawing inspiration for the role from instincts buried somewhere deep inside her new self. Gracie prepared and served tea for her growing daughter, then promptly tidied away all the dishes and cutlery. She listened to Primrose read and sat with her whilst she practised forming her letters with her sharpened pencil. As the afternoon wore on, Gracie stayed in the room whilst her daughter played with her china doll. She sat silently in her chair. She did not sew, read or knit. She did not listen to the wireless or even look at Primrose. She simply sat and stared blankly at the bundle of letters, tied with string, waiting to be sent to Edward, sitting on the mantelpiece. Time passed slowly but eventually bedtime came, and so Gracie escorted Primrose up the stairs and helped her into her nightdress. She then filled the china washbowl with water from the jug to wash Primrose's face before helping her to brush her teeth. By the time Gracie left Primrose in her bed, set for a good night's sleep, all the necessary duties had been carried out. Edward's beautiful little girl had been fed and watered, she had played, been educated and cleaned. She had been set to her rest, ready to grow, and so Gracie thought her act was sound and complete. She could now return to the sanctuary of her step and resume her silence, holding the telegram tightly in her grasp.

Although Gracie thought her act convincing, she had omitted many things that evening. Things of such importance, of such significance, that it alerted Primrose to the stale, heavy air that hung ominously in the usually bright and breezy terraced house that was her home. As a sad but inevitable consequence of her mother's lack of attention to detail, poor Primrose was very uneasy in her bed that night. Gracie had shown Primrose not one ounce of love or affection since she had returned home from school, and so young Primrose knew something was very badly wrong. She was unable to sleep. The more the little girl thought, the more she realised how bad things must be. With every recollection of what her mother had not done that evening, Primrose fell deeper into despair. From beneath her winceyette sheet and patchwork quilt, she curled into a ball and gently rocked to comfort herself. Her mother had not asked about her day, she had not tapped her bottom as she followed her up the stairs, she had not looked for potatoes or carrots growing behind her ears when she had washed her face...she had not kissed her forehead, wished her a goodnight or promised that the bugs wouldn't bite. Crucially, she had not prayed with her for Daddy's safe return or said 'God bless' as she finally left the room. Primrose concluded that she must have done something very wrong, something very naughty indeed, and that her mother must be terribly cross with her. She lay awake for hours, desperately trying to remember what it was she must have done... Was it because she had scuffed her shoes on the way home from school? Had her teacher told her mother about the spelling she had got wrong that morning in the test? Was it because she had not wanted to play with Daisy at playtime? But how could that be? She had only *thought* bad things about Daisy...she had not said anything aloud. She had not said, 'I think you're smelly, Daisy Patterson, and I shan't play with you.' For hours and hours on end, the innocent six-year-old grappled with unanswerable questions; her situation was desperate. She felt as though she would never be loved by her mother again, that she must be an awful person, that perhaps God too was cross with her. Father Christmas was bound to know that she had been bad, and, worst of all, perhaps Mummy would write and tell Daddy what an awful girl she had been. The poor, exhausted child eventually cried herself to sleep with her head pressed into her pillow so as not to make a sound and risk angering her dearest mother any further.

The following day began quietly for Primrose, who woke quite alone and unnerved. Her mother usually woke her by throwing open the curtains and cheerfully singing, but today she had woken without prompting and felt certain things were still very wrong. After summoning the courage, she slipped out of her bed and tiptoed tentatively towards her mother's bedroom. Peeking through the keyhole, Primrose spied her mother, perfectly still and sleeping, wrapped up in her blankets. Primrose tiptoed back to her room and dared herself to peel back the corner of her curtain to reveal the street below. She discovered, to her alarm, that friends were up and dressed and on their way to school. Primrose did not waste a second. She immediately dressed herself as best she could, remembering to tuck her blouse neatly into her pinafore and ensuring her socks were pulled up straight. The buttons on the blouse were misaligned, but Primrose knew she had no time to correct them. She supposed that, as long as her socks were neat, no one would notice the buttons hidden from view beneath her navy-blue pinafore. Primrose then quickly brushed her hair and tried her best to tie it into a neat bow, which she was confident she had done. Luckily, there was no mirror to dampen her spirits with the reflected truth of her scruffy, tangled locks. She peeped from behind the curtains again to see just a few children running up the road. She guessed they must be running because they were late. In great fear of letting her mother down, and perhaps failing some sort of test, she ran swiftly but silently down the stairs, threw on her coat and shoes, and left the house. Her tummy grumbled all the way to school, her heart pounded, and her throat was mercilessly dry. As she ran to avoid reprimand (the school bell ringing in the distance), Churchill worked on his speech that would, later that day, ring out to the nation from the House of Commons.

"The Rifle Brigade, the 60th Rifles and The Queen Victoria's Rifles with a battalion of British tanks and about 1,000 Frenchmen, in all about 4,000 strong, defended Calais to the last. The British brigadier was given an hour to surrender. He spurned the offer, and four days of intense fighting passed before the silence reigned over Calais which marked the end of a memorable resistance.

Only 30 survivors were brought off by the Navy, and we do not know the fate of their comrades. Their sacrifice was not, however, in vain. At least two armoured divisions which would have been turned against the British Expeditionary Force had to be sent for to overcome them. They have added another page to the glories of the Light Division. The time gained enabled the Gravelines water-lines be flooded and to be held by the French troops. Thus it was that the port of Dunkirk was kept open."

The Prime Minister's finely spun words – his glorious tribute, his patriotism woven into memorable prose – were no consolation for the confused, scared, hungry and thirsty six-year-old, who had run with all her might to reach school before the bell stopped ringing. Primrose heard none of the fine words from the great orator; she heard only the bell ringing in her ears. Her poor, dear mother heard nothing at all. Back at home, Gracie slept, unaware of her daughter's anguish...unaware that her little girl was hopelessly lost without her. Just like Edward, Primrose had been lost in the chaos of war. No one had noticed her, and so she too had become an unaccounted casualty of battle.

★★★★★★★★★★★★★★★★★★★★★★★★★★★

A strange and clumsy existence replaced life on Commercial Road for the rest of that week. Primrose woke alone each morning and readied herself for school. By the Friday, she had become quite adept at preparing her breakfast, and her hairdressing skills were much improved. In stark contrast, Gracie, who was lost somewhere within herself, ate the tiniest morsels of food and did not bother to so much as run a comb through her dishevelled locks. It was the Saturday afternoon when Primrose at last confronted her mother, when she cried and apologised profusely for scuffing her shoes, for not learning her spellings and refusing to play with Daisy Patterson. To Gracie's credit, she asserted that Primrose had nothing to apologise for. Gracie tried to convince her that she was just a little 'off colour' and that soon she would be well again. The astute Primrose, however, was not in the least bit fooled. It was true enough that her mother had taken to her bed for many hours and had not eaten, but she had no fever. She had taken no medicine, she had not coughed, sneezed or even been sick, nor had she called for the doctor. Something was wrong with her mother, but sickness was most definitely not the cause of her troublesome state.

As each day passed, the weight of Gracie's burden bore down heavier on her fragile shoulders, and she grew weaker. Eventually, the weight became unbearable and impossible to lift or share. As Primrose and Gracie stumbled along, dearest Mary's condition worsened, and so she took to her bed – heartbroken and inconsolable. She was crushed by her grief, a grief few bothered to acknowledge. Her own mother mocked her, and not one soul called to sympathise, or lend an ear, or even offer a simple card of condolence. These were desperately dark days. Flo, crippled by her despair and eager to escape her reality, packed her bags, all set to stay with her sister in Yorkshire for a week or two. The boys would be cared for there, and so she would have the time to collect her thoughts and make plans for their uncertain future. She posted a hastily written note through Gracie's letterbox before she departed:

I got the most awful news, Gracie. I called to tell you, but you weren't home. Charlie's missing. I got a telegram the other day. I'm off to my sister's place for a rest and some help with the boys. Mrs Pluckrose has got a key to my place, and she's going to open the post for me and let me know if there's any news.

I heard about young Thomas. Poor Mary told me. I know she's spent time with you, and you were a comfort to her. She told me all about the brandy when I saw her... You mustn't feel bad, Gracie. It's just one of those things. I'm pleased for you that Edward is all right – I am, honest. If you hear from him and he says anything in his letters about what happened, you must let me know...

Take care. I'll be back in a week or two.

Flo x

Just as their men had been separated some weeks before, so too now had the women of Commercial Road. The division weakened their steadfast resolve to walk through the war together. They had been blown apart — each struck by cruel, indiscriminate shrapnel. Their invisible wounds would never truly heal; they would forever bear the painful, unspoken scars of war — destined to join the ranks of the unseen and unsung.

7
Rally round the flag

Despite the cold reality of life behind closed doors on Commercial Road, the sun shone brightly on Primrose's face as she walked towards church, alone. As the bells pealed, Primrose raised her little head to look at the impressive spire in the distance. As she did, she tried to shield her eyes from the sun's rays with her tiny, pale hands, but the rays found their way through her ineffectual fingers, so she squinted against the glare. The warmth from the sun against Primrose's skin made her smile. She had not smiled for some time, but the warmth felt like a much needed, reassuring hand cradling her face. It kept her company as she unwittingly made her way towards salvation.

Primrose walked slowly towards the church, enjoying the sun and her freedom, and the lighter, brighter air than she was accustomed to of late. The little girl arrived just as the service was about to begin, only to find a packed church, with not a free pew in sight. She stood at the back of the congregation, behind countless dresses and suits, unable to see the Reverend or her dear Mrs Pluckrose. As the service went on, Primrose grew all the more weary from standing in her Sunday best. The heat was stifling, and she could not understand what was being said. She decided that God would not mind if she sat down on the floor for a while. The cold stone floor offered her immediate relief, and she rested her tired head in her hands before shortly nodding off to sleep. She stirred when the organ struck up, but merely settled herself into a comfier position (curled up like a church mouse) as the congregation dutifully sang their hymn, which doubled as her lullaby.

Primrose slept soundly through the remainder of the service. She slept through the prayers and the collection and was only noticed by a few amused parishioners as they filed out of church. At last, Mrs Pluckrose (made aware of the sleepy mouse by her son, Bill) gently woke Primrose with a rub on her shoulder. 'Come on now my little sleepy head. Wakey, wakey! Time to get up now, poppet...'

For the briefest of moments, somewhere between sleep and consciousness, Primrose felt quite wonderful. She was being woken with love and affection, and everything was perfectly well with the world again. As she stirred, Mrs Pluckrose was joined by an enamored Reverend Smith who playfully enquired. 'What in the world have we here, Mrs Pluckrose? Well, look at you, little Miss Primrose – as pretty as a picture, all sleepy-eyed!' Primrose blinked and tried to focus. 'How would you like some milk? And perhaps I could find a biscuit to go with it, to help wake you up?'

Mrs Pluckrose scooped Primrose up with the help of Reverend Smith, and she sat the slightly embarrassed, slightly confused bundle onto her lap whilst the Reverend went to collect the refreshments. It was then that Mrs Pluckrose realised something was very wrong with the cherub resting on her knee. Primrose had filthy, unkempt fingernails, her hair was matted on the crown and her shoes were on the wrong feet. Most noticeably, although it had only just occurred to the old lady, she was without her mother... Mrs Pluckrose gently and rhythmically rocked Primrose on her knee as she began her questioning. 'So, how are things? How is Mummy? You know, now I come to think of it, I've not seen her this week... I've been so busy with one thing and another – you know how it can be! Is she all right. Primrose? Is Mummy well?' Primrose shrugged and kept her lips tightly shut, in fear that whatever she said would be wrong; saying nothing, she supposed, would be her safest option. 'Rightio then, well...how about you? Are you well?' Primrose shrugged again, lips tighter still. Mrs Pluckrose sensed that her questions were troubling Primrose, and so a cuddle was probably all the little girl needed for the moment. Eventually, a very proud Reverend emerged, carrying the source of his pride. 'Oh look, here comes the Reverend with the tea tray no less!' Mrs Pluckrose declared. 'Goodness me, what a treat. That's usually my job, Primrose.' As Reverend Smith approached, Mrs Pluckrose hinted to him, 'I was just asking how Mummy was, Reverend Smith, but poor Primrose seems to have lost her voice – so she can't tell me.'

'Not surprising, Mrs Pluckrose, not surprising at all. In my experience, I've found that young ladies with delicate voices (such as our Primrose here) need milk and sweet biscuits to help them get going after a little doze.' The Reverend passed Primrose her milk. 'We'll all have a drink and a biscuit, and by the time we're done we'll all be chatting and laughing. Then, after that, we'll pop around to see Mummy and get her chatting and laughing too. How does that sound, Primrose?'

Primrose, quite overjoyed at the prospect, spilt out, 'Oh yes, yes that does sound good because Mummy won't talk to me, and we haven't any biscuits. Perhaps they might cheer her up, and make her smile, and stop her from being quite so sad about things...and stop her from always sitting on the stairs.'

Mrs Pluckrose quickly ran with her lead, 'Why is Mummy sad, Primrose?'

'I'm not really sure, but she says it's not my fault. It's not my shoes or the spellings or because Daisy Patterson smells.'

The Reverend chuckled, and Mrs Pluckrose smiled through her sigh. They both knew they had a long day ahead of them at Number 77 Commercial Road; the church service had merely been a warm-up for the real work that was soon to begin. For now, though, the most important thing was feeding the very hungry Primrose as many sweet biscuits as she could possibly manage before their departure.

****

Primrose pushed open the latched door, and Gracie looked up from her resting place halfway up the stairs. She was troubled to see the Reverend and Mrs Pluckrose. However, she was not half as troubled as they were to see her. Still in her nightclothes, with hair dishevelled, sitting in the dim light created by the draped windows denying the sun passage into her home, Gracie had pale skin, dark eyes and sunken cheeks. It was plainly obvious to both the Reverend and Mrs Pluckrose that Gracie was in a great deal of trouble. They supposed, quite rightly, that the cause of her troubled state must have derived from receiving news concerning Edward. There was a palpable tension between all parties as they held their positions in the hall, but Mrs Pluckrose's quick thinking soon resolved the stand-off. 'Right then Reverend – tea you said, was it not? Tea and a biscuit or two? I'm sure Primrose can show you the way to the kettle, can't you, Primrose?' With that, Primrose happily took the Reverend by the hand and led him, with a skip, off toward the muddled, messy kitchen. 'Have you room on that step of yours for one more, Mrs Chatley? Only I've a feeling you and I are going to need to have a bit of a chat whilst that kettle boils.' Mrs Pluckrose was quietly amused as Gracie shrugged her shoulders and kept her lips shut tight; the mirror image of Primrose not half an hour earlier... For the second time that day, the Reverend mastered the art of making and delivering a fine cup of tea. He then left the recipients alone on the stairs to enjoy the fruits of his labour whilst he got down to the serious business of playing dolls with Primrose in the back room. The round, grey-haired, bespectacled gentleman was satisfied that he was best suited to playing dolls rather than sharing tea and sympathy with Gracie. Experience had taught him that God often sent angels to help him with his work, and today he realised that Mrs Pluckrose was his angel, and he her tea boy.

Most things, it seems, can be dealt with over a cup of tea; it is so often the heartiest of gestures. There is no finer cup than that drunk after childbirth, and whenever there is a shock, hot, sweet tea usually follows to soften the blow. On hot summer days, tea somehow cools you, and on the bleakest of winter afternoons, it warms you through... Tea it would seem is the answer to all our problems – so long as it is served with love, a listening ear and perhaps a tiny nip of brandy!

'Something is clearly very wrong here, Gracie, and I'm sorry I've not called sooner or noticed something was troubling you, but I'm here now, my love. I'm here. I'm listening, and I'm not leaving until whatever *this* is, is sorted out.' Mrs Pluckrose took a sip of her tea and then waited for Gracie to find her voice. She did not have to wait long.

75

Gracie stared into the middle distance, eyes wide and painfully dry; she fought for the strength to speak each unbearable, hitherto unspoken word in an attempt to finally share the weight from her shoulders. 'They've lost him... He's missing.'

'And all this time you've not said a word? Not told a soul? My darling, silly girl, what have you been going through here all alone?'

The two women sat and finished their tea. By the end of the cup, Gracie was reviving, blinking her eyes and focusing on the world around her. Mrs Pluckrose tried her best to make Gracie see that no matter what, she had Edward always in Primrose, and she owed it to him to be brave and carry on: small steps, bit by bit, day by day, and with the help of her friends she would manage. No matter what news might come, they would face it together. Mrs Pluckrose took hold of Gracie's hands, looked into her newly opened eyes and asserted, 'Don't give up on him, Gracie. You're all he's got right now. Have a little faith in him.'

'I haven't been able to think. I haven't been able to do anything.' Gracie was suddenly struck; she took a deep, desperate breath, and her voice trembled as she exhaled, 'Oh my poor Edward. I just gave up on him. Just like that...after all I promised. I do have faith in him, Mrs Pluckrose. You must believe me. I have faith in him, and I love him so desperately.'

Mrs Pluckrose was nothing but reassuring, 'No one would doubt that, Gracie. How could anyone doubt that? It seems to me that you have love and faith in abundance. All you need now is a little hope to keep you going.' Gracie smiled and Mrs Pluckrose took hold of her hands before continuing, 'In all honesty, Gracie, if faith, hope and love is what you have left to hold onto, you have a great deal in these hands of yours, my love. They're positively overflowing.'

Gracie paused and then quizzed her beloved friend. 'Isn't hope for fools? False hope I mean. I don't want to be a fool, Mrs Pluckrose. Nothing scares me more than that. To waste my life and Primrose's on false hope would be too cruel – too cruel for words, wouldn't it?'

'I'm a happy enough fool.' Mrs Pluckrose put an arm around Gracie, and she, in turn, rested her head on the strong, wise shoulders of her dear friend. 'Without hope, false or otherwise, I would have stayed sitting on the stairs, just like you, staring at the floor, listening to the world go by. Worst of all, my young Bill would have been left with no father *or* mother to speak of.' Mrs Pluckrose took a handkerchief from her sleeve and dabbed her nose. 'I've seen it happen, Gracie, time and time again: mothers who give up hope, and it's the children that suffer. Ask Flo, she'll tell you straight enough.' With a quick sniff, the handkerchief was hidden again beneath the chiffon, buttoned cuff. 'You need to think about your Primrose. Think about what Edward would want for her. You'll be no fool Gracie, not if you live up to what he would want.' Gracie was listening intently, clinging to Mrs Pluckrose's words like a lifeline. 'One way or another, you'll see Edward again. Have faith in that, Gracie. You must have faith in that...' Mrs Pluckrose squeezed Gracie's arm as she continued, tears welling in her weary, old eyes. 'I'll see my William again, you know, when the time is right. He'll see me coming, and I'll be no fool – not to him. He'll be waiting, arms outstretched, and he'll say, "I've been waiting, my love," and I'll say, "So have I..." and it will have been worth the wait. Worth every second to this old fool.' Mrs Pluckrose retrieved the handkerchief once more from her sleeve and attended to her rolling tears.

Gracie drank in Mrs Pluckrose's words as well as she drank her tea, and she felt all the better for them both. She was weak but resolved to make Edward proud of her, and to be the mother Primrose so desperately needed her to be. Before too long, Gracie was upstairs dressing and sorting out her hair whilst Mrs Pluckrose saw to the kitchen and Primrose's bedroom. The Reverend was ordered to throw back all the curtains and open the windows, and Primrose was directed to assist him with his task. By mid-afternoon, Mrs Pluckrose had cobbled together a meal, and all four souls sat around the kitchen table and shared in the delights. It fell to the Reverend to explain to Primrose that her daddy had 'got a bit lost' and that was why Mummy had been so sad. He assured her, however, that God was busy looking for him, and that he was sure he'd turn up soon enough.

That evening, once the Reverend and Mrs Pluckrose had returned to their quiet homes, Gracie and Primrose snuggled up in bed and shared some much-needed time together. Happily, whilst Primrose was being held close by her mother, having her forehead kissed and her hair stroked, she quite forgot about the sadness of the past few days. Gracie read from Primrose's favourite book, and the pair were consumed by the magical world of *The Secret Garden*. Primrose, quite exhausted by her salvation, soon drifted off to sleep, listening to her mother's soothing voice as she fell away to her dreams.

When Gracie was satisfied that Primrose was sound asleep, she snuck out from beneath the covers and revisited her dressing table, where her box of papers and her pen lay patiently awaiting her. She took a single sheet, lifted the pen and returned to her bed and to Primrose. Resting the paper on *The Secret Garden*, she began to write her letter; a letter that was destined to join the others on the mantelpiece, destined not to be sent. It had nowhere to go.

Sunday, 9th June 1940

My darling husband,

Little has changed. I still have no idea where you are. The only thing that is different is that no one else does either! Well good for you, Mr Chatley. If I'm not allowed to know where you are, why should anyone else? I have to laugh, my darling, or else I'd cry, and that would do no one any good – least of all Primrose...no good at all.

I got a telegram with the awful news bluntly punched out before me – so too did Flo. As you may know, young Mary received the worst possible news. Poor Thomas, poor young boy...it's just too awful. Too awful for words. I do hope it was quick, that he did not suffer unnecessarily and that he was not alone. I do so hope that, perhaps, you were by his side... It would bring Mary such comfort, I'm sure, to think he was with someone – that someone held his hand as he left our wretched world on his journey to the next.

I have been feeling a bit hopeless since receiving all the news. I was shocked initially, you see, when I read the telegram. I was shocked and struck down by a sudden darkness. Today though, happily, I saw the light. Today I was awoken by our dearest Mrs Pluckrose. I drank tea made by the Reverend, and I was quite revived. I suspect I'm a little different from before, perhaps a little older (I fear a little grayer). I am certainly a bit wiser, but most of all, I am still yours and Primrose's alone.

Flo has had to go away. She is visiting her sister. It was a dreadful shock for her too (the news of Charlie's disappearance), so she's taken the boys with her to Yorkshire for some much-needed support and rest. I miss her. I must write and tell her about you. Before she left, I couldn't find the words to explain that you were missing too. I'm ashamed to say I avoided her. How things have so suddenly changed between us: friends and neighbours for so long, now suddenly miles apart and not a word spoken in days. I must not allow the war to separate us too. Flo is too dear to me, and we need one another more than ever now.

I suppose we must expect change, must we not, my darling? As time continues to pass and we live each day, change will come upon us both. Primrose will have altered so very much by the time you see her again. She is growing every day. Although perhaps I do not notice it all that much, she is growing, nevertheless. The changes in her, viewed in time by your long-absent eyes, will no doubt be breathtaking. Primrose will have blossomed, my darling, by the time you see her again (I will make sure of that), but I fear I will have weathered – just as any strong and determined steadfast rock would. I will be defiant in this raging storm of war, and I will protect and shield Primrose from the angry tides...but the elements will take their toll on me. I know the longer I am without you, the more I will be battered and worn. I imagine you too will have changed by the time we hold one another again. My mind fills with images of you constantly. Sometimes you are strong and handsome and full of laughter and stories, but at other times you are quieter, reflective, frailer and grey. But always you are Edward. Always you are mine. And always I love you – just as you love me. No matter what. No matter how we have changed, we are always each other's.

I shall continue to write, and the letters will collect on the mantelpiece, awaiting your return. I will buy a ribbon to wrap them in, to keep them safe until you come home... But if you do not return soon and it transpires that we should sit together on high and read these letters as children by God's knee, I pray that you remember your letters to me, Edward. I so desperately yearn to read them – to find out what has happened, to understand at last what has become of you. I will wait to hear from you all my life, if I must, my darling. My faith, hope and love are strong enough to see me through to eternity.

I intend to live each day as it is presented to me, as Mrs Pluckrose explained. It will do me no good trying to predict tomorrow, for God has a plan for us, and I must learn to trust in Him. I am reborn today because in faith I have found some peace in my heart, and I have embraced hope that all is not lost. Together with the love I have for you, these three things (faith, hope and love) have created a sacred place for us to rest together until we can meet again.

Until tomorrow then, my love, and whatever it may bring.

Your happy fool in love, Gracie x

8
Get that light out

Gracie endeavored to live each day as it was presented to her. She wrote to Flo to tell her of Edward's missing status and begged forgiveness for selfishly hiding away and not being there for her. She tried her best to be supportive of Mary in her desperate grief, and a little over a week after Mrs Pluckrose had consoled her, she accompanied Mary to Thomas' memorial service.

The service was orchestrated by Thomas' family and Reverend Smith carried out their wishes to the letter. Like an accomplished conductor, he pulled everything together beautifully, but Gracie and Mary felt the service could have been for a complete stranger. It contained nothing that spoke of the Thomas they knew and loved – nothing of the young man they had lost. It made the ordeal of saying goodbye all the more painful. There was no recognition of Thomas' passions, no remembering of his achievements or endeavors as a young man; words were spoken about the baby, the toddler and the young boy, but nothing was spoken of the man Mary so dearly loved. There were Hymns – hollow, tuneless hymns – that Thomas' mother loved, but not ones Thomas would have chosen. Inexcusably, Mary was not mentioned in the prayers, the sermon or any of the readings – such was the family's dismissal of their son's blossoming courtship. In their instructions to Reverend Smith, they had expressly forbidden the mention of Mary.

Each time the organ struck up to play, Gracie helped the broken doll beside her to stand, but she was unable to sing or even whisper 'Amen'. For the most part, Mary sat, invisible, at the back of the church, and wept silent tears.

The end of the service came as a relief; Gracie and Mary's passage towards the exit was swift. Reverend Smith met the women at the door and promised Mary he would pray for her that night. Mary's deep distress was plainly obvious: painted vividly across her porcelain face. Though Reverend Smith was saddened to see her so bereft, he was somewhat reassured by Gracie's supporting presence. He made a point of thanking Gracie for her support, particularly in light of her own troubles, before returning to his duties in offering his condolences to Thomas' immediate family.

As Gracie and Mary walked arm in arm along Commercial Road, towards Gracie's house, Mary struck upon the idea of having her own memorial service. It would be a quiet affair, and only Flo and Gracie need join her. She would read poems and passages Thomas had loved and bring bright summer flowers rather than a sombre wreath. She would write something especially for the occasion and ask Flo and Gracie to do the same. Gracie was wholly supportive. 'We'll come back to mine after if you like. You can prepare everything, my love, and use the house as though it were yours. Do everything the way you want it to be done.'

'The way Thomas would have wanted it.' Mary trembled as she took a deep breath in and smiled.

'Exactly.' Gracie tried to veil her own grief. She was grieving for Thomas, but, moreover, she was grieving for Edward. She tried not to think dark thoughts, and told herself with every step, *'At least I have hope. I still have hope.'*

As the pair neared the house, they were pleased to see an excited Primrose running towards them. Mary was immediately uplifted. 'Well, aren't you a sight for sore eyes? Is it that time already, Primrose?'

'Home time!' Primrose was beaming as her pace quickened.

'And why is home time so special?' Mary teased.

'Because Mummy gives me a great big cuddle!' As Primrose spoke, she ran and leapt up to her mother, who caught her in a tickle! Primrose squealed with delight as she was tickled relentlessly, and Mary (caught up in the moment) could not stop her playful fingers from joining in. The laughter lifted their spirits, and, for a moment, Mary thought what fun Thomas would be having looking at the three of them from up above in heaven. As Gracie listened to Primrose's laughter swell, she thought of Edward... She wished he were there to see his beautiful baby girl laughing. By now however, Primrose had no such thoughts; she just imagined that, although she was now seven, she may very well wet herself if her mother and Mary didn't stop tickling her very soon!

Gracie invited Mary in for tea, but she graciously declined. She was keen to get home to rest and then write to Flo to tell her of the plans for their own little memorial. Mary explained that she would set to work over the next few days on preparing Thomas' farewell, and that she would keep Gracie posted on the developments.

Primrose, who thought she was missing out on something important, asked if she was invited, to which

Mary replied, 'Most definitely and Flo's boys too. Thomas would have wanted you there.'

'Will we be saying goodbye to your Thomas because he's had to move to Heaven?'

Mary smiled. 'That's right, Primrose, my love.' Her eyes glazed with tears.

'You mustn't be sad, Aunty Mary, because now Thomas is your very own angel.' Primrose smiled, thoroughly pleased with her deduction.

Mary smiled too. 'I suppose he is.'

'And you mustn't worry about him, Aunty Mary, because Mummy says he's with Jesus.'

Mary half laughed in wonder at the words tumbling from the babe's mouth. 'That's right.'

'And Jesus is very kind. He's looking for my Daddy because he's got a bit lost...or was it God, Mummy? Is God or Jesus looking for Daddy?'

Gracie stole a quick breath to steady herself before replying, 'I think they're both looking, darling.' She continued, almost in prayer, 'But I hope Mummy finds him first...'

'Or I might!' Primrose declared playfully. 'I always find Daddy when we play hide and seek – he's not very good at it.'

After Mary had hugged Gracie goodbye, more mindful (thanks to Primrose) of her friend's troubles, she headed home for a quiet, reflective evening. She prayed that night for Gracie, not for Thomas; she knew Thomas was being well looked after... Gracie needed her prayers more than anyone else that night.

As it transpired, Mary did well to dedicate her prayers to Gracie that evening – she was going to be in desperate need of them.

The effervescent Primrose had quite exhausted her mother; she'd talked incessantly about the impending memorial service (and what dress she might wear), so by the time the seven-year-old's bedtime came, it was welcomed with a sigh of relief and a hot, strong cup of tea. Gracie made herself the tea as a reward for making it through another tough day without her husband. The cup was not half empty, and the day not nearly done, when there came a knock at the door. With a heavy heart and an even heavier body, Gracie forced herself from the comfort of her chair to answer the door. It was Mrs Pluckrose.

Mrs Pluckrose was clearly uneasy as she started, 'I've got some news, Gracie, my love. Shall we go in and sit down?' Mrs Pluckrose had come with news: Flo had received a letter. A letter from the records office. Charlie was found.

Gracie hadn't the faintest clue how she should react; she was literally dumbstruck. Mrs Pluckrose explained how she had discovered the news: 'I picked up her post yesterday, like she'd asked, and the letter was there. I've spoken to Flo – I managed to get hold of her on the telephone today – and she asked me to come and tell you the news.' Gracie struggled to process the information. 'She's going to come home tomorrow. That's what she said. She's coming home tomorrow with the boys.' Gracie stared blankly. 'Gracie, my love, are you all right? Say something...'

Gracie was confused. 'I haven't got a letter. I didn't get one yesterday, and I haven't got one today.' She continued as though she were trying to work out a puzzle: 'If Charlie is alive and a prisoner of war, and poor Thomas is dead...what's Edward? Where's Edward?'

Mrs Pluckrose calmly but firmly responded, 'He's missing, Gracie. Nothing has changed. He's still missing.'

****

Flo's return with the boys brought with it much-needed distraction. There was plenty of catching up to do, plenty of gossip to share and of course plenty of tea to be drunk. Flo's homecoming, together with the planning of Thomas' farewell, helped fill Gracie's long evenings with a semblance of purpose and meaning. The fragile world Gracie was spinning for herself was all she had to hold on to, so she worked with all her might to spin as elaborate a web as she possibly could. She filled her days and nights with work, baking, meeting for tea, shopping, cleaning, playing with Primrose...anything she could think of to stop her from sitting quietly and thinking.

****

The day of Thomas' remembrance dawned. Mary stood with her friends by the statue at the Great War Memorial, at the end of Commercial Road. It was a beautiful morning: the church spire gleamed in the distance, and just a few wisps of soft, white cloud hung in the sky. She felt, as she looked at the idyllic scene, that Thomas must have painted it for her because everything was perfect. Mary started proceedings by reminding Gracie and Flo of the goodbye she had shared with Thomas on that very spot, before she placed her flowers (a hand-tied melody of red campion and foxgloves) by the statue and sat with the girls on the bench. Flo read a beautiful passage that began, "Do not let your hearts be troubled...", and Gracie shared a story about how Thomas had asked for her advice on courting Mary. He had wanted to know how best to deal with Mary's mother, otherwise known as 'The Old Dragon'. Gracie's advice, it was revealed, had been floral... She confessed she had given Thomas the flowers that so impressed Mary on their first date, and that they *had* been intended to sweeten up her mother, not sweep Mary off her feet! Mary laughed. She recalled how she had answered the door, seen the flowers and grabbed them. She giggled as she finally understood Thomas' panicked expression. She had thought, at the time, he was just nervous. Mary was glad she had got the flowers instead of her mother, but not half as glad as Thomas had been. Her mother would have been ungrateful for the blooms, but Mary showed her appreciation by giving Thomas his first kiss. They were all happy memories, and Mary enjoyed sharing them with her friends. Primrose showed Mary the picture she had drawn of Thomas in his uniform, and the boys ran around and played. Peace and solace were found that morning, and an unexpected calm washed over Mary as she prepared to read her final tribute: a poem she had written for the man she had kissed goodbye on that very spot... Once read, Mary left it nestled amongst the blooms for Thomas to gaze upon at his leisure.

I'll think of you
When a snowflake falls
And brushes gently my cheek

Then drifts into a blanket
Full of comfort at my feet.

And on some summer morning
When the beauty of the sun
Is a tender hidden promise
As yet not quite begun.

I'll think of you when singing
On some Tuesday afternoon,
When it's quiet, when it's rowdy,
When I'm walking - sometime soon...

Rest assured you are not forgotten,
Rest in peace, I pray you may...
Rest my mind in dreams of promise -
I will see you once again.

Upon their return to the house, the children were treated to sweets, that Mary conjured from her cardigan pocket, and the three women of Commercial Road toasted Thomas with a sweet sherry. They enjoyed perfect little sausage rolls, bloater paste sandwiches and honey cake...all of which had been prepared by Mary, and all of which were Thomas' favourites. Leaving the others momentarily in the beautifully laid-out parlour, Gracie popped to the kitchen to fill the kettle. For a brief moment, she let her guard down, and found herself not filling the kettle but rather filling with tears. Determined not to spoil Mary's special day, she threw back her head, quickly wiped her eyes, blinked and sniffed with great purpose before gulping, sighing and finally composing herself. She was relieved that not a single tear had fallen, and so she had not cried, just as she had promised Edward. How she wished, as she stood in the kitchen, that he was there...that he would place his hand on her shoulder as she filled the pot and say to her, 'I love you, Gracie. Everything will be fine...' As she stood there, with no distractions, quiet for those few seconds, they were the words she needed to hear to summon the strength to rejoin the others and carry on.

'Can I have another sweetie, Mummy? Aunty Mary says I have to ask you.'

'Fine...' Gracie spoke with light-hearted resignation as she was stirred from her troubles. 'Yes, of course.' Had Primrose been sent by Edward to revive her? It was comforting to believe that, somehow, she had. Primrose ran back to the parlour. As Gracie watched her little girl excitedly run off, she quietly laughed to herself and shook her head in amusement before saying aloud, 'I know you love me, Edward. I know everything will be fine...' With that, she patted her own shoulder and squeezed Edward's hand.

****

That night, Gracie snuck out from her bed (so as not to wake Primrose who was curled up by her side) and took a single sheet of paper from her box. She sat at her dressing table to write her affirmation.

Monday, 24th June 1940

My darling husband,

I must remember, before I fall to sleep, to see you and hear you and feel your arms around me. I must remember to kiss your soft, perfect lips and feel you hold me tightly to you. I must listen carefully, so I can hear you whisper softly, 'I love you, Gracie. Everything will be fine...'

Tomorrow I will wake, and the sun will have risen. Primrose will still be here, and she'll need me more than ever. I will be stronger tomorrow and stronger still the day after that... I have a strength given to me by you, and I have not forgotten it. You are not lost. You are in my heart, as I am in your pocket, always.

Forever, your own darling, Gracie x

9
Pack up your troubles

Mr Spindler had called a staff meeting to discuss Christmas. He was determined to lift the town's spirits (and his bank balance) over the festive period, so he needed his staff to be well-prepared and motivated. Although he was a Jewish man, Mr Spindler was very fond of Christmas – it was his favourite time of year: a time when, if he was lucky, the tills could ring louder than the church bells.

It was half past five, the last customers had been served and the big front doors were bolted shut. The shop floor was immaculate: Ladieswear was boasting a fine display of aprons and headscarves, and the mahogany cabinet in Menswear was perfectly organised with an array of handkerchiefs, braces and bowties. Displayed beneath polished glass, the haberdashery boasted an assortment of wools, knitting needles, patterns, buttons and coloured threads. The tills were silent, polished and emptied. The floor had been swept, and the brown wrapping paper, scissors and string had all been squared on the counters – set, ready for another day. Mr Spindler's office door was shut and locked. The large first-floor window that framed the desk in his mezzanine office (and afforded the old man his perfect view of the shop) was closed, and the curtains drawn. The shop floor was sleeping, but it was in the canteen upstairs – where the staff had gathered – that dreams were being woven and stitched together.

Gracie, Flo and Mary sat together at the meeting, grateful that Mrs Pluckrose had kindly agreed to watch the children for an hour or so. It was a gloomy, November afternoon, but the talk of festive gifts, window displays and promoting Christmas cards made everyone feel quite jolly; it gave them something to look forward to, and there had been little (if indeed anything) to look forward to for what seemed like a very long time indeed. Mary was tasked with dressing the main shop window. Her role included sourcing an appropriately angelic doll to be Jesus, and clarifying with the Reverend which animals were in the stable – following an intense debate about the donkey! Mr Spindler's plan was to invite the local schoolchildren to paint the backdrop, which was to include the animals, the star and the angel. He hoped that, by getting the local children to paint the nativity scene, he would benefit from their parents' custom when they came to view the children's masterpiece!

The nativity scene was not the only backdrop to the Christmas of 1940 in Paddock Wood. The Battle of Britain had been in full force since the July, and though the skies had calmed significantly by the October, the country was still on tenterhooks. Contrary to many people's expectations, significant bombing raids such as the Blitz in London had not only blighted big cities; much of the wider country and smaller towns had been affected too. Everyone in Paddock Wood had grown accustomed to great warplanes flying overhead to forge their way to battle. Children knew, without looking, which planes were in the sky from the specific roar of their engines. They knew when Tommy was overhead, and (more importantly) when it was Jerry. Nighttime air-raids were commonplace, and everyone was well-versed in donning their gas masks. War was very much a way of life, and life before war merely a romantic, hazy memory. In recent weeks, however, optimism had been building as it seemed that Churchill's 'Few' had shifted the odds in the Allies' favour, thanks to their bravery in the skies. There was hope that, perhaps, Christmas would afford folks in Paddock Wood time to celebrate some sort of victory: a small victory in the bigger battle of war.

As the meeting continued, Flo was charged with promoting Christmas cards. Mr Spindler was convinced that, with the right marketing, they would be more popular than ever this Christmas. The astute businessman asserted, 'Men at war need a card at Christmas to let them know we haven't forgotten them.' Flo was proud to have been given such an important role and was eager to see the cards, so she could choose the best one for her Charlie. She would need to send it with the next Red Cross parcel if it stood any chance of being received in time for Christmas.

Gracie was, as ever, in charge of balancing the books. It was a job she held dear and never took for granted. Her trusted position meant she was aware, more than the other staff, that this *had* to be a profitable Christmas if they were to secure the business' future and, in turn, their jobs. Gracie was certain that Mr Spindler's ancestors could never have seen such austere times. It was going to be a true test of the old man's character to see if he could keep his family's business afloat.

In recent times, business worries had not been the only thing keeping the old proprietor awake at night (or giving him nightmares when he eventually surrendered to sleep). Mr Spindler was gravely troubled by a much greater problem based on not-so-faraway shores: an evil machine driven by men removed from humanity – fuelled by a hatred he would never understand. He was not alone in his fitful sleep – he was spiritually bound to his fellow men, who clung tightly to their principles whilst fighting to stop the persecution of their race. He was compelled to stand his ground in the face of the terrifying machine of fascism, for the sake of his forefathers and his descendants alike. He drew strength from his faith, which drove him to protect it – and his family's future.

Mr Spindler had no control over the battle against the hideous machine of Nazism, but he did have control over his shop. He supposed that defiant, record sales, business coups and emphatic shop window displays might raise the spirits of all his allies. He struck an important blow in his unlikely corner of the battlefield by motivating his unwitting troops with his charm, wit and warmth at the meeting. He struck another by rounding off his cry to battle with mince pies and hot tea! His recruits had been called to arms successfully, and not a moment too soon, since battle was about to commence: Christmas was looming. All of Mr Spindler's staff left the shop that evening feeling buoyant. Once they had gone, the wily proprietor took a moment to look about his sleeping shop floor, breathing in the smells of polish and leather. He was assured that he had done all he could to ensure the shop's future. With a satisfied sigh, Mr Spindler climbed the stairs to his flat above the shop to the awaiting company of his widowed sister and the shop's heir: his treasured nephew, Jacob.

By nine o'clock that evening, after he had told the parable of *The Rooster Prince* to his nephew (who would soon turn eleven), Mr Spindler retired to his bed and dreamt of a merry Christmas. He dreamt of a shop filled with laughter and excited children, of ringing tills and balancing books. Almost two hours had passed when, all at once, Mr Spindler was violently shaken from his slumber. It was shortly before eleven o'clock when the nightmare unfolding – not three hundred yards away – tore the sleeping businessman from his dreams. Without warning, alarm or siren, there was an almighty explosion followed by another. The bed in which he had been sleeping was forcibly shifted across the room, and the walls surrounding him buckled. Glass was everywhere but in its frame. Terror rendered Mr Spindler immobile.

There came a call from the next room: 'Help me, Uncle! Uncle, can you hear me?'

Half-strangled with fear, Mr Spindler managed to reply, 'I'm here, my boy. I'm coming to you now. Stay still for me – quite still.'

The thought that his nephew may be hurt rallied him, and so he summoned the wherewithal to move. Dazed, he left his room and began his blackened journey to his sister's boy. His bare feet danced around shattered glass, his hands grappled with fallen furniture; Mirrors, clocks, paintings, vases, and other once-precious and reverend treasures were strewn about the place – rendered worthless obstacles to their owner's peace of mind. The glaze-less window on the landing framed a picture of horror: fire and smoke filled the street below. Mr Spindler knew the Nazis were too close now to be played with – too close to be fought off with Christmas cards and window displays. He could smell their toxic breath, and it choked him. As he walked in to see his petrified nephew, he was joined by his weeping sister. He held them both in his arms as they shook from the shock, and he thanked God they were alive and, seemingly, unhurt.

There are moments in our lives when we are presented with such unimaginable horror, such unthinkable scenes, that we strive only to survive. These moments leave us with few options, and, of course, we do not choose which of these options to take; whether we fight or flee is an impulse. Mr Spindler's impulse was to gather his vulnerable family and flee. As he was an older man, his nephew merely a young boy and his sister kind but (to his mind) fragile, his impulse was arguably rooted in some sound logic. He was scared, but he had pictured similar scenarios in his oft-sleepless nights, and, as such, he was somewhat prepared.

He ordered his nephew to dress – and to do so quickly. He told his sister to do the same, and then to pack their bags with only the bare essentials. He insisted that they were running to safety, away from the Nazis who were plainly too close now. They were on *his* street, shaking *his* home, and he was powerless to stop them. Mr Spindler quickly dressed before running to his office to empty the safe. He put the contents in an old leather holdall, then retrieved a letter from his desk drawer – a letter with details of a safe house. He took a moment to survey all he was leaving... Over ninety years in the making: his ancestry, his pride and legacy. He was leaving it all in a breath. None of it mattered now. He knew his priority, his duty, was to the young boy shaking in his mother's arms, standing at the foot of the stairs with a suitcase in his hand. They left the shop by the back door, out to the delivery yard and straight into the parked Austin. As they drove along Commercial Road, away from the train station, Mr Spindler saw in his mirror the true extent of the devastation he was leaving behind. He could not believe his eyes. He shook his head and asked himself, 'Why...? Why would they be so cruel, so evil? Why target such a place?' His sister and nephew gazed out the back window of the car and shared his disbelief.

St. Andrew's Church had been struck. The heart of Paddock Wood was seemingly obliterated – its wounds fresh, raw and bleeding fire. There was no sign of life: no sirens or alarms, no firemen or people with buckets of water to douse the flames. The erased speck of heaven had been cruelly replaced with hellish flames and devilishly precarious debris. It looked for all the world like the end had come, and for Mr Spindler and his family in Paddock Wood, it had.

As Mr Spindler turned the corner at the end of the road, Reverend Smith turned another. The sight that greeted the elderly pastor was sacrilege. The dim torch he carried provided light enough to see his beloved church had been directly struck. Destruction was evident wherever his faint beam fell, and his broken heart sank in despair.

'There's nothing to be done here, Vicar. Nothing tonight, at least.' The lone voice in the darkness came from the ARP warden, who continued in an officious manner. 'The firemen are on their way with the wagon, and I'm holding the fort 'til they get here. The Home Guard are scrambling too, but until they arrive it's all down to me.' The heat was hellish in its fury, so the shell-shocked clergyman was advised to retreat to the safety of the graveyard; he woefully resigned to do as he was told.

As the evening wore on and firemen eventually arrived, together with the Home Guard and well-meaning parishioners, Reverend Smith found himself drinking tea with his steadfast friend, Mrs Pluckrose. The two sat on a bench in the graveyard with a thick tartan blanket over their legs. They were a safe distance from the flames and firemen who were battling to control the blaze. The elderly pair sat and drank their tea from Mrs Pluckrose's flask whilst they watched the scene unfold before them. The water hoses were held by determined hands, supported in turn by robust arms and experienced shoulders. Commands were being shouted and duly followed; grit and resolve were abundant. A few feet from the firemen, at the furthest end of what was left of the church, a line of volunteers (headed up by the ARP warden and the Home Guard) were passing what little could be rescued: candlesticks, vases still holding their flowers, Bibles, tiny wooden chairs from Sunday school...remnants of their Church, of where they had been married, where they had buried loved ones and worshipped all their lives. Everyone with a part to play in the scene laid out before the Reverend Smith and Mrs Pluckrose was quite determined to save the church. Regretfully, the painfully obvious truth could only be seen from the perspective of the pair sitting on the bench. St. Andrew's was beyond rescue. It was ruined. As time raced away and the sun began to rise, tears welled in the tired old Reverend's eyes; his weak heart, soul and faith were shaken by the truth being revealed by the sun's growing light.

Mrs Pluckrose noted the dewy look in her friend's eyes and gently tried to reassure him... 'It's beautiful, really, don't you think? The promise of a new day, a fresh start... Look, He's shining His light on us all, and showing us what He's done.' The Reverend was bemused. What was his dear, old friend talking about? Perhaps she was delirious from the shock or lack of sleep. All the Reverend could see, with the aid of the sun's light, was a clearer picture of the chaos.

'You've lost me, Mrs Pluckrose. I'm afraid I don't like what I see one bit... I see no promise my dear; I see nothing these old bones can possibly cope with. Nothing at all.'

Mrs Pluckrose chuckled. 'Your old bones should be grateful! Look again... Not a single house struck, but a direct hit on the church. Imagine if that lousy bomb had struck anywhere else down the street... The fire would have swept through the terraces, and I dread to think what we'd be dealing with this morning. Come to think of it, if the bomb had hit the houses, I wouldn't be here drinking tea with you, and that's for sure!'

The Reverend placed his hand on top of Mrs Pluckrose's and gave it an appreciative squeeze. 'My dearest Mrs Pluckrose,' he smiled, 'you are a marvel and you are, of course, quite right. What a beautiful day it is and what a perfectly fine cup of tea. Cheers.'

With that, the elderly pair smiled and clinked teacups before enjoying the remainder of the sunrise together, sitting hand in hand on the bench in the graveyard – safe and warm, under their rug – watching the impromptu performance continue before them.

Gracie sat on her doorstep, halfway up Commercial Road with Primrose bundled in blankets on her knee. Mother and daughter sat quietly and watched, quite mesmerised as the flames slowly lost their strength – the rain from the persistent hoses finally claiming victory. As the smoke cleared and the exhausted firemen began to retreat, the blackened remains of the church became visible. Piles of rubble, that had hours earlier been substantial walls, were now littering the street. Remnants of stained glass hung precariously, like medieval guillotines eagerly awaiting an execution. Primrose clung tightly to her mother, and Gracie, sensing her daughter's fear, spoke softly: 'Not a soul has been hurt, Primrose. I know it looks scary, but everyone is safe. I promise Mummy's got you, sweetheart. I've got you.'

That particular weekend in Paddock Wood was like no other; the spirit of the Blitz prevailed! By lunchtime on the Saturday afternoon, an emergency disaster committee had been organised, and their first meeting took place that teatime, at the vicarage. The committee's priority was to organise Sunday's service, so as not to be beaten by the Nazi bombers. The cricket pavilion (just yards from the church) was chosen to host the service because, despite the bomb damage to the pitch, the clubhouse was intact. Committee members made it their mission to let all the parishioners know about the service by knocking on doors and spreading the word. By Sunday morning, the ardent Reverend Smith was preaching in his newly acquired, makeshift church. The number in the congregation was such that it spilled out the doors and onto the battle-scared green. A mood of defiance prevailed that morning as the congregation sang a rousing a cappella version of 'Jerusalem', and it seemed no odds were insurmountable to the bearers of the voices that rang out across the frosty green.

Bring me my bow of burning gold!
Bring me my arrows of desire!
Bring me my spear! Oh clouds, unfold!
Bring me my chariots of fire!

I will not cease from mental fight,
Nor shall my sword sleep in my hand,
Till we have built Jerusalem
In England's green and pleasant land.

It was not until the Monday that Gracie and her neighbours took any real notice of the doors that were so definitely shut at the front of Mr Spindler's shop. Perplexed staff waited outside, joined later by eager, frustrated shoppers. It was not until some two hours later that the self-declared 'person in charge' (the ARP warden) ordered the growing crowds to stand back as he performed the necessary break and enter. Upon his re-emergence to the curious, scandal-mongering crowd he declared: 'There's some nasty blast damage upstairs – glass all over the place – but there's no sign of anyone. There's empty wardrobes mind and an empty safe. The car's gone too. I reckon they've either been kidnapped or done a bunk!' Gasps rose from the crowd. 'I'll have to launch an official investigation.'

Gracie stood with Mr Spindler's books in her arms – not knowing for a moment where to turn. At last, she went the only way she could: back home to Number 77. She took a piece of precious paper from her dressing table and proceeded to tell Edward all about Mr Spindler's surprise disappearance.

Wednesday, 24th November 1940

My darling husband,

There is no way they've been kidnapped. How ridiculous! That warden thinks he's living in an Agatha Christie novel. He's done a moonlight flit. It's obvious. The first sign of trouble and he's off – and in the main, my darling, I am furious with him. It's all a bit much, don't you think? How could a grown man run away from his responsibilities? The books weren't in that

102

much of a state. It was nothing that we couldn't have overcome – not with Christmas coming and all of his rallying talk…and it's not as if the bomb landed on the shop. It only blew in a window.

Sorry, my love. I should explain… I'm rambling – well, ranting. It's Mr Spindler – he's up and gone: vanished. He's done a bunk and left us all. The selfish sod has abandoned us. Mary is suddenly without employment, as am I (obviously), but to be fair, my work has always been about the distraction as opposed to the wage packet. But for some of the others it's downright, bloody disastrous – it's their livelihoods for goodness' sake.

Who knows what will become of the store? I have no idea what to do with the books… I'll keep them safe, of course, but I wonder if perhaps they'll be needed by a solicitor – or the police even? What a t'do, my love. What a t'do…! What with the church being hit and Mr Spindler disappearing, it has been quite an unforgettable couple of days. I can't imagine life without the church and the shop…but then I suppose there are lots of things that I would never have imagined, yet here I am – living through it all.

I wish you were here by my side. Perhaps then I'd be able to say, 'Poor old Mr Spindler. He's obviously been scared off by the bomb. Pop out and find him for me. You can talk him round, and then we'll all get back to it…get back to work and carry on.' But you are not here, and I haven't the first clue where the dear old chap has run to. Who knows? Maybe he's right to have run. Maybe the Nazis are on their way… I thought we were winning, but I don't know anything anymore; nothing seems certain - nothing, that is, except for my love for you and Primrose. She misses you, my love. She's finding it harder to speak of you lately. She shrugs and nods and shakes her head when I mention you. I think she's finding it increasingly difficult to have faith that you'll be found, and I am finding it harder to reassure her that you'll return to us soon. 'When is soon, Mummy?' she used to ask, and I would say, 'I'm not sure exactly, my darling, but just as soon as he can...' She's stopped asking me now, and, in truth, I am glad that she has. It was becoming too painful to look at her sorrowful face when I offered up my inadequate nonsense. She's too smart by half to fall for my flannel.

As I write, I find myself gripped once more by the desperate longing I have to see you. I ache to hold you, my love. The pain of your absence is yet to diminish, as Mrs Pluckrose assures me it will, and I cannot begin to imagine growing accustomed to your distance from me. I yearn for your swift return and for your reassuring arms to wrap me tightly and keep me safe. I miss your arms, your hands, your eyes, your voice...

When is soon, my love? I pray it is soon enough.

Your own darling, Gracie x

10
As time goes by...

The long, dark days of winter were, at last, over, and spring was fading to make way for the long, hazy days of summer. It was a year to the day since the three men – Edward, Charlie and Thomas – had bid their farewells to the three women now sitting around the kitchen table at Number 77, Commercial Road. So much had changed...

Mary was much stronger and more outspoken than before; the fragile, porcelain doll she had once been was no more. The young, love-struck girl had grown up a great deal over the past year – she now worked as a junior nurse at Moatlands and was hopeful about training to become a midwife. Her new role at the makeshift hospital had given her the purpose and focus she had so desperately needed after Thomas' death. It turned out, her loss of employment at Mr Spindler's was, in fact, a blessing in disguise.

Flo was in employment too, working part-time as a land girl, which she enjoyed very much; she was relishing the opportunities to learn about planting and tending crops. Luckily for her, Mrs Pluckrose looked after the boys for a couple of mornings a week to help out, and both Gracie and Mary minded them as often as they could. Flo had found her vocation in life: working with food. She had also discovered the delights of taking home the fruits of her labour, without a mark being made in her ration book!

Both Flo and Mary seemed to be moving on. Mary was dealing with her grief admirably, and Flo was kept busy with her boys, work, packing Red Cross parcels and writing letters to Charlie (who, by all accounts, was doing well). Gracie, however, was still struggling. No news of Edward's whereabouts had been forthcoming, and Charlie's letters from the camp provided no clues since they were so heavily censored.

Gracie had not moved on. She still missed Edward desperately and was often consumed with thoughts of what had become of him. She wrestled with never-ending, unanswerable questions daily. The one question that haunted her most was, of course, 'Was Edward alive or dead?' Gracie's one happy distraction, and reason to wake every morning, was Primrose. She was now nearly eight years old, and her deliciously crooked, emerging front teeth were happily finding their way into the world. Her ebony hair was now much longer and thicker, and it sat perfectly in two plaits – each one proudly occupying a space on her big-girl shoulders.

As the three women waited in Gracie's kitchen for the tea to brew, they looked out through the open back door to the three children playing in the garden. The mirage that fooled the three women was one of playtime utopia: the boys were sitting down, with their backs to the women, and were very quiet. It looked for all the world as though they were watching a show being put on by Primrose and her scraggy ragdoll. Unbeknown to the mothers, however, Primrose had presented each of the boys with some tools: William with a small pail full of water, and Arthur with a trowel and bucket – and the promise of worms to be found! Primrose thought she was very clever, and so enjoyed her peaceful playtime with her scraggy ragdoll. She was oblivious to the boys who were now, happily, getting dirtier and dirtier. Three-year-old William was covering himself in a layer of mud (his war paint), and five-year-old Arthur was organising his army of worms, ready to launch a surprise attack against the aforementioned doll, his muddy brother and the unsuspecting Primrose!

'Oh, my word, would you just look at 'em – quiet as church mice,' enthused Flo.

'Ah, bless them...' sighed Gracie and Mary in unison, blissfully unaware of the messy truth.

'Edward and I often spoke about having boys.' Gracie looked at Mary. 'You know, it took me almost four years to fall for Primrose. Then, after she was born, six years of trying but never any joy.'

'She's your angel though, Gracie, my love,' reassured Flo. 'She's so good, helpful and beautiful... The good Lord blessed you with that girl, so you make the most of her. Don't waste your time on "if onlys". Having a girl is special. You can always keep a girl, even when they're grown... My boys will find themselves girls one day and they'll be off, and I'll be stuck with just my Charlie!'

Gracie smiled. 'As soon as your Charlie gets back, you'll probably fall with twin girls!'

Mary was positively giddy! 'Oh, wouldn't that be wonderful... Twin girls in beautiful bonnets with pretty little curls, sharing a Silver Cross pram.'

Flo scoffed, 'More like a cardboard box! Prams are as rare as hen's teeth, and they're only going to get rarer. I can't believe I gave my old one away! I know it was a worn-out old thing (and I said I wanted shot), but I regret it now.'

Gracie comforted Flo. 'You know you did the right thing. They needed all the prams they could get their hands on over at Moatlands. Isn't that right, Mary?' Gracie welcomed Mary's affirming nod before continuing. 'It makes my heart break to think of all those poor women bringing babies into the world over there... Tiny little babies with fathers fighting a war against Lord knows who, God knows where!'

'It's not so bad, you know, Gracie.' Mary's eyes were bright. 'All those beautiful new babies – they don't go short of love, you know.'

'Just the thought of it makes me shudder!' Flo winced as she elaborated. 'All those poor women, all in agony, screaming the place down morning, noon and night.'

Gracie shook her head as she recalled the pain of labour before stopping Flo in her tracks. 'That place needed your pram, Florence Webb. You were right to hand it in. Now, let's change the subject, shall we? All this talk of childbirth is putting me right off my tea!'

The three friends happily whiled away an hour or so. They laughed about their hardships, buoyed one another's spirits and, since there was no cake to be mustered, enjoyed sharing their slices of delicious gossip...which was particularly tasty. Flo was positively convinced that someone had bought Mr Spindler's old shop. Mary too had her suspicions, fuelled by the sighting of a well-dressed gentleman, of middling years, from behind her parlour window; he had stood opposite the store, deep in contemplation, for some twenty minutes or more.

Gracie was not convinced. 'He could have been an estate agent or from the tax office... He might have been a police officer in plain clothes. They do exist, you know.'

'Nonsense!' asserted Flo. 'Young Bill Pluckrose approached the chap, bold as brass, an' asked him what he was doing, and he said, "Looking at my new shop!".'

Mary was uncertain now. 'Bill Pluckrose? Since when did you start listening to Bill?'

This riled Flo, who continued in earnest. 'Mrs Pluckrose told me. She were queuing at the butcher's when her Bill ran off and asked the man. She were right embarrassed! Told me all about it... She spoke to this chappy herself, after she'd got her rations. Apologised to him and explained how her Bill was a bit special-like.'

Gracie winced. 'He could have been teasing poor Bill.'

Flo insisted, 'Oh no, Mrs Pluckrose said he were a right proper gent.'

As the three women debated the mysterious man further, Gracie learnt that he had a stick to accompany his significant limp. The women concluded that some terrible injury must have forced the man from active service, and that, perhaps, he was starting afresh in Paddock Wood. They wondered if he had family, if he was Jewish... They wondered what he might do with the shop, whether or not they might like to work there again... They wondered a lot. Unfortunately for the girls, their highly-consuming speculation had distracted them from the children and their exploits in the garden!

Quite suddenly, Primrose produced the shrillest scream before bursting into the kitchen. She was hotly pursued by Arthur, carrying a fistful of worms. Snapping at his heels, William followed – covered (quite literally) from head to toe in mud – roaring like a savage. The three women leapt to their feet and spontaneously joined in Primrose's screams before sweeping up the three reprobates between them. Each woman grabbed the nearest child: Mary caught Primrose and the scraggy doll; Flo caught hold of Arthur and the worms; which left Gracie with young William and the wet, cold mud. All three children were thrashing about vigorously, and the screaming and yells were escalating to fever pitch. Gracie was getting battered. Her once-prized spring frock soon resembled a well-worn dishcloth. Her prim, auburn hair was tugged at until it resembled a dishevelled bird's nest, and her pale skin was freckled with splats of mud. It was just as another sizable glob of mud landed on Gracie's eyelid that there was a loud knock at the door. As Gracie approached the door, wiping the mud from her eye (smearing it across her face), she thought to herself, 'I do hope this isn't anyone important...'

As she took hold of the doorknob, she lost her grip on the wriggling, slippery William, who ran to his mother. Gracie quickly straightened her skirt and patted her hair as she turned the lock to open the door.

'Mrs Chatley?' enquired the distinguished gentleman, with a walking stick in his hand and hat tucked neatly under his arm.

'How can I help you?' Gracie opted to act as though everything was perfectly normal. She smiled encouragingly but suspected, to her horror, that this was the man the girls had been speaking about...the walking stick being the obvious giveaway.

'I am Mr Halfpenny, the new proprietor of what was Mr Spindler's store.' To his credit, Mr Halfpenny did his utmost to reciprocate Gracie's nonchalant performance. He tried, admirably, to ignore the mud, the screams from the kitchen and the peculiar hair style that confronted him.

'Delighted to meet you, Mr Halfpenny.' Gracie extended her muddy hand, eyes fixed on Mr Halfpenny's, and maintained her perfect smile. As the gentleman reached out his hand to meet Gracie's, the screams and yells from the kitchen faded. They were replaced by stifled giggles and shushes from Flo and Mary. They watched with glee while poor Gracie tried to save face in front of her unexpected caller.

Mr Halfpenny lightly shook the muddy hand, before continuing. 'I was assured by Mr Spindler that you hold the store's accounts, and that you may very well be interested in maintaining them in the future. I'd be delighted if you would let me know your thoughts...at your leisure, of course.' Mr Halfpenny glanced down the hall, into the kitchen at the giggling, muddy melee and continued, 'I appreciate that you were not expecting me to call today.'

'Well, thank you, Mr Halfpenny. I shall call into the store tomorrow afternoon, if that is convenient? Shall we say two o'clock? I'll bring all the paperwork with me, and we can discuss matters further then.' Gracie could feel the mud drying and cracking as she increased her desperate smile...

'Perfect. Tomorrow at two, then. Good day, Mrs Chatley.' With that, Mr Halfpenny replaced his hat, inclined his head as a farewell gesture and then took his leave.

Gracie sighed, lost her fixed grin and shrank about six inches as she allowed her prim stance to collapse into itself. She happily closed the door, then leant against it before sliding down onto the floor, dissolving into fits of laughter on her journey towards the polished tiles. She was accompanied by a riotous round of applause, courtesy of Flo and Mary, and all three children joined in the fun by clapping and jumping up and down. Although the children had no idea why the grown-ups were clapping and laughing, they supposed that they were no longer in trouble – and that alone was worthy of enthusiastic celebration!

That evening, once Primrose was clean and in bed, and the kitchen had been tidied, and the worms, buckets and trowels returned to their rightful homes, Gracie dug out the books that had sat, resigned, in her mother's old dresser in the parlour. She browsed through them briefly before placing them on the kitchen table in readiness for their impending outing the following day. As she walked away from the table and out towards the stairs, she thought to herself, 'I really must make a special effort with my hair tomorrow. What must that man have thought?' It was with an amused smile of recollection, as she pictured the muddy handshake, that Gracie climbed the stairs to her bedroom.

****

Wednesday, 21st May 1941

My dearest Edward,

If only you could have seen it, my love. It really was very funny. The children were all playing in the garden when, all of a sudden, there were screams and yells and mud and worms and... Oh, poor Primrose! Well, she was beside herself. We all three

(Flo, Mary and I) grabbed a child each, when there was a knock at the door. I was in a dreadful state, all covered in mud, when I answered to – guess who? The new owner of the store: a Mr Halfpenny. What a funny thing it was. I do so wish you could have seen us – pretending that everything was fine, when, all the while, the children were screaming, and Mary and Flo were giggling like schoolgirls! I looked for all the world like I'd been dragged through the proverbial hedge backwards.

Mr Halfpenny seems to be a respectable fellow; he was terribly polite and courteous. I think you would like him very much. He's a fair bit older than us, and we assume he's been pensioned off from the army because he walks with the aid of a stick. I'll find out more tomorrow. I'm meeting with him at two o'clock to discuss the books and a possible reinstatement of my role. I shall tell him all about you. I'll introduce you in your absence.

I do so love the opportunity to talk about you... Flo and Mary avoid the subject; they are probably minding my feelings, or else they have run out of things to say. It's awkward. What is there to say that hasn't already been said? Tomorrow, though, I will have a fresh audience to impress with stories of you – of us, and of us with Primrose. I cannot wait. I will make sure that my hair is neat tomorrow, and that I am conspicuous only by my complete and utter lack of mud.

Much love to you, my darling. Check your pocket. I am there.

Your own darling, Gracie x

11
Fight for it, work for it...!

It was five minutes until two o'clock, and Gracie had butterflies dancing in her stomach. She was standing in her hall, by the front door, holding the books and looking at the second hand make its way around her watch's face. She had decided to leave the house at three minutes to two, so she would arrive exactly on time. She was worrying about which entrance to use...the main doors at the front of the store or the door at the back? Would the main door be open, she wondered? Would it be presumptuous to go around the back? A little too informal? She patted her hair, straightened her skirt, took a breath and grew an inch before making her way to the shop. It was exactly three minutes to two.

As Gracie walked, she continued to worry about which entrance to use. With her head down, looking at her polished shoes, she was deep in contemplation when she heard her name and looked up. Mr Halfpenny was standing by the front of the shop, looking as pristine as he had the previous day. His hat was, once again, in the crook of his arm and his fine walking stick was by his side. He had called, 'Mrs Chatley!' and when he was sure he had secured Gracie's attention, he continued, 'Such a beautiful morning. I thought I'd take in some of this *rural* air.'

Gracie was so relieved that the entrance dilemma had been solved that she beamed and responded with an abundance of nervously charged zeal. 'Isn't it? It's *such* wonderful weather. It puts quite a *spring* in one's step!'

'I wish I could say the same.' Mr Halfpenny gave his walking stick a gentle flick off the ground and waved it playfully before planting it back on terra firma and continuing, 'Nevertheless, it certainly lifts one's mood!

'I am *so* sorry...' Gracie was dreadfully embarrassed. Of all the things she could have said. Why, she wondered, did she have to refer to springing steps?

'Please, there is nothing to be sorry for.' Mr Halfpenny seemed reassuringly genuine in his response. Gracie smiled and shook her head simultaneously, eyes lifting to the heavens to reflect her embarrassment. She felt as though Mr Halfpenny was understanding of her frightful nerves. They shared a moment of unspoken understanding, then both smiled warmly, took a breath and happily carried on. 'I'm excited to see the books.' Mr Halfpenny raised an eyebrow towards Gracie's bundle of papers. 'Shall we go through to the office? My mother has prepared some tea.'

Mr Halfpenny led the way towards the back door, and the pair settled themselves to business. They were quite comfortable in Mr Spindler's old room. They dispensed with small talk and concentrated on facts and figures – a conversation that was most agreeable to them both. The tea went cold and the sandwiches stale, but the conversation was fresh, vibrant and flowing. Mr Halfpenny had lots of ideas and Gracie had lots of information. Between them, they breathed new life into the old, forgotten office.

As they spoke, Gracie had a few fleeting thoughts that interrupted their serious talk of business...

Fifty, perhaps fifty-two...?

His mother must be very old...mid-seventies, or even early eighties?

I wonder how long he's had that beard?

Not much grey... Perhaps forty-five then...or forty-seven...?

No wedding ring – but then Edward has no ring.

Soft, gentle hands: must have been an officer.

Flo will want to know everything!

By the end of the meeting, Gracie had agreed to resume her old duties. She also agreed to advertise the vacant posts within the store, arrange interviews and contact the local press about the store's reopening. Before leaving, she looked at the tea and sighed, 'Your poor mother. Look – I feel dreadful.' Gracie winced as she looked at the stale, cold offering.

'She'll sulk!' Mr Halfpenny looked resigned and then quickly picked up a teacup and threw back its contents.

In solidarity, Gracie shrugged and declared, 'Cheers!' before reciprocating the gesture.

'And seeing as there's a war on, I'd better make a dent in these...' Mr Halfpenny picked up two dainty sandwiches and polished them off.

Gracie took her clean, pressed, white handkerchief from her cuff, wrapped up a few of the stale delights and promptly popped them on top of her books. 'Primrose will make short work of these!'

116

'Primrose?'

'My daughter. She was in the kitchen yesterday...' Gracie stopped in her tracks, remembering the mud, screams and general chaos of the previous day.

'Ah yes! I caught a glimpse: a beautiful little girl, dark hair in plaits...high-pitched scream!'

'Yes, that's the one,'

'And the two boys, the muddy ones...are they yours too?'

'Not guilty. They're Flo's children.' Gracie elaborated, 'My friend, Florence Webb – they're her boys. Edward and I only have Primrose.'

'Lucky Edward. He has a lovely family.' Mr Halfpenny was suddenly sincere.

Gracie, delighted by his kind words smiled. 'I'll be sure to remind him of that when I next write.'

'I doubt he'll need reminding. I'm sure he thanks his lucky stars to have you every day.' Mr Halfpenny gave Gracie a knowing look, almost as though he knew Edward and the kind of fellow he must have been.

'You're right. I'm sure he does...just as we thank ours to have him.' Gracie felt as though Edward could hear her speaking, and it felt good to sing his praises; it felt good to refer to him as being alive and well. 'He's a wonderful man. I do hope you get the opportunity to meet him soon.'

'I'm sure I will...' Mr Halfpenny was aware that he had not spoken the truth. He was not *sure* at all, but it was the appropriate thing to have said.

'I'm sure you will too,' Gracie continued with the white lies. 'He'll be home before we know it, and all this war nonsense will be forgotten!'

Mr Halfpenny poured himself another cup of cold tea from the pot and declared, 'I'll drink to that – cheers!' before dutifully polishing off another cup of cold, stewed tea.

As Gracie dashed home, suddenly aware of the time and Primrose's impending return, she mused about Mr Halfpenny's story. She still knew so little about the man, yet he knew so much about her. It did not seem fair somehow, and she knew that Flo was going to be furious with her. Gracie's curiosity about her new boss served as a long overdue distraction from what had become her internal monologue of late. Her mind freed itself of morbid thoughts about Edward for a while. It filled itself, instead, with odd curiosities about her boss' age, retail experience and family life. She was busy contemplating important jobs that had to be done and deadlines that were looming. It was exciting and distracting – yes – but moreover, it gave her a special purpose. Happily, she found herself with a role to play outside of motherhood and housekeeping; she was no longer the unremarkable, nonentity she felt she had become since the shop had closed. Gracie was needed again. She mattered, and that suited her very well.

****

The run-up to the store's grand reopening invigorated the little rural town of Paddock Wood. Mrs Pluckrose was particularly excited because Gracie had put her son, Bill, forward for the job of cleaning the store's impressive, glazed façade on a weekly basis. Bill was a sizable young man – tall and wide with big hands and feet. He had a mass of black hair, rosy cheeks and tortoiseshell-rimmed glasses that were a little too small for his face. Bill was awkward and shy, a little clumsy at times, and he had never managed to read or write much at school. But he was a good boy, and Mrs Pluckrose was immensely proud of him. As well as cleaning the glass, Bill was also charged with the upkeep of the floral displays in the window boxes. He had to water the blooms and deadhead the flowers that had gone to seed. If he proved himself capable, he would also be trusted with the replanting of the boxes the following season. Mrs Pluckrose made Bill a smart, brown apron to wear whilst on duty at the store. Mr Halfpenny presented him with a bucket, chamois leather for the windows, his very own brass watering can, and gleaming, new trowel to tend the window box displays. Bill could not have been happier; he wore his uniform with pride and took the responsibilities of his long-sought-after job very seriously. On the day the store finally reopened, Bill made sure the glass was gleaming at the front of the shop. There was not a smudge to be seen, and the flowers were perfectly displayed in their boxes, heads turned in uniform towards the sun.

A photographer had been booked by Gracie, on Mr Halfpenny's instruction, to record the auspicious events of the day. The newly named *Halfpenny Stores* had sparked considerable excitement amongst shoppers. They hoped that, perhaps, the shop would be filled with goods all priced at only half a penny! Their hopes were fuelled by

Flo's naughty, playful gossip, which she shared with anyone prepared to listen: 'Yes, that's what I've heard – every single thing is going to cost a half-pen'y! It says it, plain as day, across the door. It must be true.' Flo did not stop there. She took particular pleasure in teasing the poor shop owner too, with her cheeky speculations: 'I s'pose it all balances out in't end. You overcharge on that much stuff (cottons and what-not) that the shortfall on the expensive bits is covered by that!' Richard simply lifted his eyes to the heavens, with an air of amused exasperation. *How preposterous and impossible a notion*, he thought.

The photographer positioned all the staff in front of the gleaming shop windows: Mr Halfpenny was placed in the centre of the shot, beneath the new sign that announced to the community *Halfpenny Stores*, and Gracie was positioned next to Bill, on the far left of the group. She whispered a timely reminder in Bill's ear to stay perfectly still when the photographer called for everyone to look in his direction. Meanwhile, Mrs Pluckrose stood on the opposite side of the road, with the milling crowd, and beamed with joy as the photographer recorded forever her proudest moment. The resulting photograph was published in the local newspaper, together with an optimistic report, and another copy was framed and hung in Mr Halfpenny's office. The large sepia print that hung on Mr Halfpenny's wall was glanced upon for many years to come. The new owner was immortalised, standing strong in the centre of his workforce. Bill was preserved too: standing tall at the far end of the group, wearing his pressed apron, grin fixed upon his face and his hand safely placed in Gracie's. It was the only picture of Bill as an adult, and it marked his place in history. It showed him to be a proud and capable young man – the man his mother always knew he could be if only someone would give him the chance. Mrs Pluckrose was thankful beyond measure to Gracie for being her Bill's *someone*. She prayed that, given his new and exciting prospects, Bill would at last learn to cope without her. She hoped that with the support of his new-found friends at work, and his flourishing independence, he might just manage that little bit better when she at last had to leave him to be with her beloved William.

****

Over the weeks that followed, Mr Halfpenny proved himself to be an honourable man and capable boss. He worked long hours and was often on the shop floor assisting with menial tasks. He paid wages promptly, listened to his customers and staff, and was always on top of orders and the inventory. He was never too busy, however, to sit and share some time with his beloved mother: a robust, slightly hard-of-hearing, immaculately turned-out, silver-haired, straight-talking, frail-in-body-but-not-in-spirit, perfectly delightful seventy-year-old woman. Mrs Halfpenny, known by Mrs Pluckrose as "Dottie", spent most of her days sitting in one department of the store or another, drinking tea from her fine, bone-china teacup and saucer. She enjoyed nothing more than kindling the newfound friendships she was developing with the wealth of customers pouring into the store, keen to see the changes her son was making. Mrs Halfpenny and Mrs Pluckrose (Dottie and Milly) struck up a delightful friendship over the first few weeks of the store's reopening. Both ladies were of a certain age, both had only sons, and both had husbands long since lost to the Great War. They shared their respective pride in their sons' achievements, despite their difficulties, and they happily whiled away the hours chatting and sharing their joy as they watched their boys at work. Over the weeks, Mrs

Pluckrose learnt how Mr Halfpenny had never married – there had once been a girl he had taken a shine to, but she had chosen another, so he dedicated himself to his army career and the successful pursuit of his rank of officer. When the devastating accident happened, at the beginning of the war, and Mr Halfpenny (Richard) was sent home, his mother feared he might never recover. She felt he had little, if anything, left to live for. It was Mrs Halfpenny who heard from an old friend about the store perhaps being available to purchase. It was she who pursued it, she who convinced her son that he could be the new proprietor, and, finally, she who sold the family home to finance the move and buy the preliminary stock. The little old lady who sat, unassuming, in the corner of haberdashery sipping tea, was in fact the driving force behind her son's newfound business and subsequent success. 'This little store, the town, the people – it's been my Richard's salvation. I look at him here, in his fine suit, and think how smart he looks. He reminds me of his father.'

'Well, I don't mind telling you, Dottie, that (together with Gracie) your Richard has been my Bill's saviour. He's a good boy, my Bill... I know he'll never have a head for numbers or fine words (and he'll never wear a suit to work), but he's worthy of that apron he's wearing – and it's your boy that's given him the chance to wear it. I could never thank him enough.'

'He's a cracking little worker, Milly! It's no favour – let's be clear. He deserves the job.' The ladies both sipped their tea. 'Gracie said he could do the job, and do it he can. If he was no good, he'd be gone by now.' Mrs Halfpenny delivered her words with loving sternness and finished her speech with a firm nod of her head and a brisk folding of her arms. Mrs Pluckrose was overwhelmed. She had never before heard Bill spoken about with such fervent positivity. Her chest swelled with pride and an unexpected lump rose in her throat, and tears raced to form in her eyes. To veil her brimming emotions and embarrassment, she hastily blinked away the small salty pools gathering behind her perfectly perched spectacles, and then took another sip of her tea before changing the subject.

****

As Mr Halfpenny and his mother established themselves in Paddock Wood, they soon became an intrinsic part of everyone's lives. Most residents in the town would see the new proprietors of the store at least once a week for something or other – be it a button or a thread, some candles or a handkerchief. In many cases, it was just for a chat and to pass the time. Before the new shop owners knew it, days had turned to weeks, weeks to months and, in what seemed like the blink of an eye, Mr and Mrs Halfpenny were celebrating their first anniversary as shop owners. In that time, they had become central to many people's lives, particularly Gracie's. They had become a part of her support network. In truth, they felt like a surrogate family. Gracie spent hours in the company of wily, old Mrs Halfpenny. She was a much-longed-for mother figure. They chatted about Mr Halfpenny or else about the shop and the customers or troublesome orders. They spoke about Primrose too – about how she was getting on at school and how quickly she was growing. Sometimes, although rarely, they spoke about Edward. It was an awkward subject, so Gracie did her best to avoid it whenever possible. She had always referred to Edward as simply being 'at war' when she had spoken to the Halfpennys, as opposed to being 'missing'. It had started harmlessly enough in the office when she'd had the meeting with the stale sandwiches, but now it felt too delicate a matter to resolve without hurting someone's feelings. Little did Gracie know that Mrs Halfpenny knew full well about Edward being missing. Mrs Pluckrose had seen to that, but she never mentioned it. It was not her place, and she knew Gracie would tell her in her own time if she felt the need. Mrs Halfpenny carried Gracie's secret admirably; she never mentioned it, not even to her son. She simply put it to the back of her mind.

Though the soul of discretion with the important matters in life, Mrs Halfpenny was deliciously indiscreet when it came to the trivial...particularly when the trivial involved her son! She revelled in sharing funny stories with Gracie about her son's quirks and foibles, and Gracie loved to hear them. Because of the informal manner Mrs Halfpenny adopted when talking about her son, Gracie began to look upon her boss quite differently – as though he were the big brother she had never had when growing up. He was a good big brother, not one that pulled hair or teased, but rather one who was supportive and encouraging; one who trusted his little sister with increasing responsibility as she grew and proved herself worthy. Gracie's flourishing talents paired with Mr Halfpenny's enthusiasm and dedication ensured the store became the pounding heart in the centre of Paddock Wood. Mrs Halfpenny could see it growing stronger and stronger with every passing day. She would sit quietly and smile, observing the pair at work, never saying a word but wisely watching on – teacup in one hand and fingers firmly crossed in the other.

****

Friday, 19th June 1942

My darling Edward,

Mrs Halfpenny is such a naughty woman! She is deliciously indiscreet when it comes to her poor son. She told me today how he fusses endlessly in front of the mirror with his hair in the mornings...she went on to joke about what it was he could possibly be fussing with, given the lack of material he has to work with! It is true that he has not been blessed with a crowning glory like yours, my love, but he does well enough with what he has. He is just thinning ever so slightly, that's all. I wonder if the poor man is checking and recording his hair's demise each morning? Funny really. I didn't imagine he was the kind of chap who could give two hoots about his receding hairline. What should it matter to him at his time of life?

Work is a real joy. I am being charged with ordering the stock in Womenswear as well as Homewares and Haberdashery. I am, of course, still balancing the books, which are looking surprisingly healthy given the state of the country and the war. I am happily consumed at work and time passes quickly; before I know it, it's time to go home and prepare tea for our darling girl. Primrose is happy too, more settled of late, less anxious. I suppose that may well have a lot to do with me. I am calmer than before, calmer than I was when I first received news that you were missing. I am getting used to this funny little life Primrose and I have created in your absence. We can sustain one another, my darling man, until your return. You can be proud of us, just as we are proud of you.

I imagine you, my love, not at war, not in any harm, but happily biding your time whilst we are kept apart... I picture you sometimes walking in a beautiful garden, standing tall, hands behind your back, breathing in the wonders surrounding you. I see you in my mind's eye completely at ease, resting in an old wicker chair, reading a leather-bound book, passing time until we meet again. You are safe in my heart. I am able again to smile when I think of you. I still miss you dreadfully and count the endless, unknown, perhaps never-ending days until your return, but I am no longer choked by fear when I imagine where you might be. I have put you somewhere safe, my love, and I am with you – there, in your pocket, always.

With all my love,

Your funny girl, Gracie x

12
Let us go forward together

Primrose wanted to get her mother something special for her birthday. She had no idea what to get her, nor did she have any money to go shopping with. However, what she did have was a plan. She had decided to do jobs for her mother's friends, in top secret, to earn some money. Whilst doing her jobs, she planned to ask for advice about what her mother might like for her birthday. She was incredibly excited about the whole thing, but that was before she had actually started working.

It was a blustery, wet November morning when Primrose set out to her Aunty Flo's house, just a few doors down the road from her own. Despite the grey Saturday and its best attempts to put a dampener on Primrose's spirit, she was resolutely enthusiastic. Wrapped up against the foreboding elements, with her eager fingers wriggling furiously with excitement inside her mittens, she skipped to her first job, filled with the sweet anticipation of earning a wage. Flo had decided to task Primrose with the draining task of playing with her boys for two whole hours. Primrose soon discovered it might just as well have been a lifetime... She'd hoped for cleaning or a little darning or, perhaps, polishing. What an upset! She'd been saddled with a particularly grumpy Arthur and an over-excited William. Arthur, it transpired, was grumpy because Primrose was a girl, and William was over-excited for exactly the same reason! Whilst Flo put her feet up and listened to the wireless (in a rare moment of relative peace), Primrose suffered the indignity of playing *Cowboys and Indians*. She allowed the boys to push, prod and poke her. She tolerated Arthur's taunts of *Girls are smelly*, and *You can't because you're a girl!* She showed great restraint by not lashing out at William who was, literally, hanging off her leg whilst she tried to perform Arthur's ordered 'war dance'.

When at last the two hours were over, Arthur declared, 'Good!' and stormed off in protest. William screamed, sobbed and threw himself at Primrose's feet, grabbing onto her ankles.

He was eventually prised off by his highly amused mother, who turned to Primrose and declared, 'Love a duck, Primrose. You've made an impression here, all right! Now, a promise is a promise, so here's ya thrup'nny bit.' Flo took out the jagged coin from her apron pocket and placed it into Primrose's open palm. As Primrose wrapped her tiny fingers around the coin, adorned with the Tudor rose and shield of St George, the upset of the previous two hours quickly melted away. She felt, instead, the sweet satisfaction of a job well done. She basked in the glow of pride for earning, for the first time, her very own money.

'Thank you, Aunty Flo.' Primrose was beaming from ear to ear, her crooked teeth proudly displayed.

'Mind you spend it wisely now. Perhaps get Mummy some chocolate or some nice soap. She loves sweeties too... Always has had a sweet tooth, your mam!'

With the thrup'nny bit safely stowed away in her pocket, Primrose made her way from Flo's modest terrace over to Mary's mother's house with the promise in her heart of yet more money to be made. This would be easier, she thought. How wrong she was...

Mrs Bryce was a stern, sour-faced, miserable woman. Regrettably, the war (with all its subsequent hardships) had only compounded her bitterness and tendency to administer ill-considered, short shrift to any poor soul who dared cross her path. She was crotchetier and, incredibly, more intolerable now than she had ever been. Poor, generous, gentle Mary was so ill-fated to be stuck living with such a cantankerous old bat. And to think – she was duty bound to call the old baggage 'Mother'.

'Good afternoon, Mrs Bryce,' was the greeting the merry nine-year-old offered up to the po-faced woman who stood before her.

'I see nothing good about it,' came the grim retort. Poor Primrose's heart sank as she realised it was going to be a very long afternoon. The icy wind that whipped around her pale ankles outside was easier to bear than the atmosphere inside the house. To Primrose's dismay, she discovered that Mary was not home; she was all alone with the impossible Mrs Bryce and at her mercy. 'This teapot, sugar bowl and milk jug are solid silver. It's not tat like your mother has, and the tray's silver too, so mind you be careful with it... I want it spotless. You hear me?' Mrs Bryce was standing over Primrose like an omen. 'If you make a mess, make no mistake, I shall tan your hide. If the job's not done properly, there'll be no money and no argument about it neither... If I'm not satisfied, that'll be that. So, think on!' Mrs Bryce finished barking her orders and then left the room.

Poor Primrose was left trembling with a mixture of fear and cold. Alone in the icy parlour, she was overwhelmed with fear, not daring to touch the precious silver laid out before her. As time passed and the fear grew, Primrose's eyes began to fill with tears. As the first tear fell and she lost the rhythm of her breathing, she heard a key turn in the lock of the front door. It was Mary. To Primrose's relief, Mary had returned home and rushed into the parlour to see her. 'Darling Primrose, I am so sorry. I got held up... Oh no, you're crying. Has she been terribly awful?' Mary was speaking in hushed tones so as not to alert her mother to her presence. 'I'm here now. Come on – I'll help you.'

The impossible task suddenly became a delightful, secret mission. Primrose and Mary worked as a team to polish the silver until it gleamed. Just as they were tidying away the polish at the end of a job well done, Mrs Bryce appeared at the parlour door. 'I heard you come in, Mary. I've been listening to the pair of you in here, messing about and wasting time.' Primrose thought how horrid Mrs Bryce's eyes were. As she spoke, they became thin slits, surrounded by nasty, wiry lines...

'It's all shiny though, Mrs Bryce,' announced Primrose bravely, buoyed up by Mary's presence.

Mrs Bryce, however, was not impressed... 'Clean it may be, but you only did half the work – so that's half the pay.'

The miserable Mrs Bryce only gave Primrose a farthing for all her efforts, but Mary snuck her a thrup'nny bit and some advice. 'Get Mummy something she would never get herself: a pretty scarf or some new handkerchiefs, perhaps.'

Primrose ran back home through the driving rain, safe in the knowledge that she had made over sixpence that day. As she ran home with the hard-earned fortune in her pocket, she began to anticipate seeing her beautiful mother, and she was overwhelmed with a feeling she had never felt before: appreciation. When she was greeted by her mother, she ran into her open arms and announced with a flourish, 'Thank you. Thank you for being my mummy.'

Gracie, who thought Primrose had been at a friend's playing for the afternoon, was quite taken aback. 'What's brought all this on?'

'Oh, nothing...' was Primrose's coy reply. She'd have to wait until her mother's birthday to share her stories.

Gracie smiled with intrigue, instinctively knowing something was afoot. 'Suit yourself, Fanny-Knacker-Pan. Come and have your tea.'

The following Saturday was to be Primrose's last chance to make some money and go shopping for the all-important birthday gifts. She had conspired with Mrs Pluckrose to create an alibi: she was "spending the day with her baking". It was great fun for Primrose to have the grown-ups help with the secret plan, and she was excited about taking on her last job and then spending her small fortune. Primrose's final money-making task was actually by appointment to Mrs Halfpenny. Primrose arrived at the store, with Mrs Pluckrose, at ten o'clock sharp. The playful pair went to the upstairs flat where Mrs Halfpenny was waiting. After a little chit-chat, Mrs Pluckrose left Primrose alone with her twinkly-eyed friend. Primrose was suddenly quite nervous. After all, experience had taught her that, whilst at work, she should always expect the worst.

Happily, there was no cause for upset at this place of employment. On the contrary, there was only cause for frivolity, cake and plenty of tea. Darling Mrs Halfpenny listened to Primrose's stories about her previous jobs and the money she had earned. She shook her head when she heard about the miserable Mrs Bryce and couldn't help but laugh as she listened to the tales of Flo's naughty boys! As the time flew by, the unlikely friends shared some story books, ate too much cake and drank too much tea – more tea than Primrose had ever had before. After an hour or so, Primrose asked, 'What job do I have to do today, Mrs Halfpenny?'

'Why, you've already done it! I wanted some good company, Primrose: someone to share my tea and cake with – someone to make me laugh!' Mrs Halfpenny spoke with warmth and love; she spoke as Primrose's own grandmother would have, if only she were alive. Primrose was enchanted as Mrs Halfpenny continued, 'I needed someone to keep me company whilst my little boy, Richard, is downstairs working... So you see, you've done your job already and you've done it very well!'

Primrose was astounded. 'Really? I don't have to clean anything or wash anything?'

'Most certainly not,' insisted Mrs Halfpenny. 'Now, here's another thrup'nny bit to add to the others you've got. Get Mummy something that *you* think is beautiful, Primrose. If you love it, she'll love it too.'

Shortly after Mrs Halfpenny's wise words, her son, Richard, appeared to escort Primrose around the shop floor. He was to assist her with the purchasing of her precious gift. Mr Halfpenny spoke softly to Primrose. He bent down so he could speak to her directly and not from above. He was mindful of his inexperience with children and was fearful of intimidating her. He was conscious that he might seem rather grave, given his stick, his beard, his age and his position as her mother's boss. He listened intently to Primrose's well-thought-out, well-advised ideas before offering with a gentle smile, 'We have a lovely selection of soaps, Primrose, and beautiful handkerchiefs. I have chocolates too, not many but a few, and you can just about afford them.'

Primrose looked at all the wonderful things Mr Halfpenny showed her, but they were not quite right... '*Your* mummy says I have to love whatever I get – that if I think it's beautiful, Mummy will too.' Primrose looked concerned as she spoke.

Mr Halfpenny adopted a serious tone to mirror that of his discerning customer. 'Very well – that's an important consideration. Let me think...' Mr Halfpenny paused and looked about the store. He stroked his beard as he surveyed the goods.

'It has to be so special because she's the most special mummy in the world,' insisted Primrose earnestly. It was then that Mr Halfpenny's eye was caught by some stationery, and he was struck with an idea.

'Come with me, Primrose. I think I may have just the thing.' Mr Halfpenny offered his hand to Primrose, who took it with excitement and held it tightly. He was delighted to have been so readily accepted by Primrose; he relaxed and allowed himself to get carried away with her infectious excitement. The pair hastened (as much as the limp would allow) towards a beautiful, mahogany bureau, displaying a fine selection of writing papers, envelopes, postcards and notelets.

Primrose's eyes widened, and she increased her grip before gasping, 'These are beautiful...'

Mr Halfpenny was heartened by Primrose's response. He went on to explain his thinking behind the potential gift, 'I know that your Daddy is away, Primrose, fighting the war, and I know that Mummy writes to him lots... I thought she might like to have some special paper for him. I think Daddy would love to receive it. What do you think?'

'It's perfect,' she enthused. 'It's the most perfect present in the world. Can you help me choose which bits to get? I have three thrup'nny bits and a farthing... I want to spend it all!'

Mr Halfpenny and Primrose delighted in choosing a selection of fine writing paper, delicate envelopes, postcards with illustrations of Kent, and some daintily printed, floral notelets. They agreed the notelets would be reserved for special occasions. As the happy pair made their way to the till with their bounty (still holding hands), Primrose casually announced, 'Of course, Daddy will probably never get to see any of these. I expect they'll end up on the mantelpiece with all the others, wrapped up in the ribbon. It's rotten that he's lost...missing, or whatever, you know.' Mr Halfpenny was caught off guard, for he did not know. He coughed and found his voice, 'How long has Daddy been missing for, Primrose?'

'Since almost the very beginning – ages and ages. He went away to war with Mary's Thomas (he's in heaven now) and with Aunty Flo's Charlie (he's at the camping place), but Daddy's just lost – missing, I mean. I always get that bit wrong.'

'I'm so sorry, Primrose.' Mr Halfpenny was choked by Primrose's account; he swallowed hard.

Primrose sensed his upset and felt compelled to reassure him. 'It's all right. I'm used to it. Mummy gets sad sometimes, but I don't – not anymore.' Primrose checked to be sure no one was listening before she continued. 'Can you keep a secret, Mr Halfpenny?' she asked. Mr Halfpenny nodded, and Primrose looked deep into his hazel-brown eyes to be sure she could trust him before continuing and uttering the words she had never spoken before, 'I don't think Daddy is lost. I think Jesus found him ages ago, and he's with Thomas. Don't tell Mummy though, because it would make her sad. I don't like it when Mummy is sad, Mr Halfpenny.'

Mr Richard Halfpenny had been a soldier; he had seen terrible things and was not easily moved. He had been injured in fierce battle – lost friends and comrades. He was a hero, a decorated soldier and a quietly exceptional man. He assumed he could never be shocked back on Civvy Street. Yet here he was, shocked by, and in awe of, a child who was holding him, quite literally, in her capable hands. It seemed as though Primrose was looking into his soul as he absorbed the news and began to process it.

As the shock quietly settled, he began to feel responsible for Primrose. The feeling grew at pace. In a sudden rush, he felt as though he owed it to every soldier he had ever known, to every man he had seen fall – even to Edward (a man he had never met) – to protect Primrose and keep her safe. Moreover, he realised, he owed it to Gracie. He owed it to her because she was a remarkable woman with a generous soul who had been there for him when, it transpired, he should have been there for her.

Gracie was strong, brave and resourceful – yet somehow gentle, vulnerable and wickedly witty all at the same time. She was a paradox. She had walked into his office one fateful afternoon and made him smile, although he believed he had quite forgotten how. She was the woman he admired most in the world, who happened to look impossibly pretty covered in mud. She was the woman he worked with, trusted and respected. She was, he suddenly realised, without warning, the woman he utterly and unequivocally adored.

He was in trouble – but it was delightful. It had happened implausibly quickly, but nevertheless, it was an undeniable fact. His life had changed forever: he was in love.

By acknowledging his feelings, albeit feelings he knew he could never share, he felt somehow liberated. His sudden call to duty was accompanied by an enormous rush of pride. He was no longer the unremarkable nonentity he felt he had become since losing that ill-fated battle. On the contrary, he counted. He mattered. He had responsibilities: quiet, humble, unexpected – yet dearly welcomed – responsibilities. He was alive.

****

Tuesday brought with it many happy returns, visitors, gifts, stories and laughter. Primrose delighted in giving her mother the carefully chosen, beautifully wrapped gift that she had bought with her new friend, Mr Halfpenny. The weather was dull on that Tuesday afternoon in November, but it was bright and breezy inside Number 77 Commercial Road. Flo and the boys, Mary (but not her mother!), Mrs Pluckrose, her friend Mrs Halfpenny, Reverend Smith and, of course, Richard Halfpenny had all gathered to celebrate Gracie's birthday. Primrose was beyond thrilled to have masterminded the event. The little girl revelled in telling stories about her quests to earn money and her secret shopping exploits with Mr Halfpenny. Gracie laughed and gasped. She hugged her little girl and tried to drink in every moment of the celebrations – so as always to remember the joy of the day. In particular, she wanted to remember how Primrose was so excited, how beautiful she looked, how she sounded when she laughed... As Gracie gazed upon Primrose, Richard Halfpenny found himself gazing at Gracie. He gazed at her smile. He was mesmerised by the freckles on her nose, by her eyes and her laughter. He found himself etching every part of her face into his mind's eye, so he could carry it with him always.

When at last the gathering began to disperse, it happened that Gracie, Mr Halfpenny and Primrose were left alone in the back room. Gracie told Primrose to thank Mr Halfpenny for all his help with the purchasing of the beautiful writing paper, and then sent her upstairs to get her nightie on and brush her hair. An awkwardness quickly wrapped itself around the pair left in the back room. Gracie tried to unravel it, 'The writing paper is beautiful. I expect Primrose told you all about my incessant writing to Edward...' Gracie floundered. She touched the letters on the mantelpiece. Mr Halfpenny was reassuring. 'Primrose explained everything.'

'Then I owe you an apology...' Gracie was looking down, becoming uncomfortably flushed.

'Please, absolutely not.'

'It was just easier to talk as though he were fine, but it was cowardly. I'm so sorry. I tried to tell you a few times but...'

'...Please.' Mr Halfpenny couldn't help himself. Instinctively, he took hold of Gracie's hand. Their hearts stopped, albeit for different reasons, before Richard asserted, 'There's no need for apologies or explanations.' Their eyes fixed for a brief moment before Gracie looked down again and they let go of each other's hands, returning to their proper places. The awkwardness was unbearable. 'I should be off – leave you and Primrose to your evening. I'll see myself out.' Mr Halfpenny was beside himself. He wanted to sweep away the strange atmosphere that had enveloped them, but he had no clue how it could be done.

Gracie, such was her deftness for compassion, came to his rescue. 'Not a bit of it.' She took a brave leap of faith before declaring, 'I always see my...' she hesitated, '...*friends* to the door.' Gracie had started now, so she bravely continued, 'As we are friends, I'll walk with you.' That said, she smiled and offered her arm as a witty gesture. Mr Halfpenny returned the smile, and, with a jaunty nod of his head, took hold of Gracie's arm. As they walked to the door, Mr Halfpenny was quite certain that the beating of his heart must have been deafeningly apparent.

He summoned his courage as they reached the door to say, as casually as possible, 'Then you really should call me Richard. Mr Halfpenny is so stuffy. It's fine for the shop floor, of course, but otherwise, far too stuffy!'

'Richard...' Gracie spoke his name slowly and deliberately and listened to it back. 'I think I can manage that,' she smiled. As Richard gathered his coat and his hat to place neatly in the crook of his arm, Gracie took a breath, opened the door and spoke with sincerity, 'Thank you, *Richard*, for understanding.'

Richard stepped over the threshold and then turned and stood on the pavement, looking directly at Gracie, 'Happy Birthday, Gracie.' He placed his hat on his head and reached into his top coat pocket. He produced a small, rectangular parcel and a card. 'I hope you like it. Have a lovely evening with Primrose.' Gracie took her gift. They shared a smile, and Richard turned to walk home.

Gracie ran upstairs. 'Primrose, Primrose – another present! Come and help me open it.'

The two excited, giggling girls leapt onto Gracie's bed and shook the gift. Gracie handed it to Primrose and invited her to open it. She refused and handed it back to her mother, reminding her that she was nearly ten and old enough to wait until Christmas to unwrap surprises. Gracie carefully peeled back the paper to discover a polished, wooden box. As she slowly opened it, with Primrose eagerly looking over her shoulder, she found an elegant, ornately engraved, silver pen. It was exquisite. Both girls stared in wonder and fell silent for a moment before exclaiming their combined delight. They marvelled at the pen a good while longer before Gracie became aware of the time. She hastily packed Primrose off to bed, sharing with her a quick prayer of thanks for their memorable day. When Gracie returned to her room, she sat on her bed and gazed again at the beautiful pen. She then snuggled under her covers, to escape the chilly air, and opened Richard's awaiting card.

Dear Gracie,

Happy Birthday! I hope you like the gift. It's a small token of my appreciation for all you have done to help Mother and me since we arrived in town. I saw Primrose looking at the pen in the store and thought what fun it would be to surprise you both... Use the pen to write to Edward. Primrose tells me that writing to him brings you great joy, and I want so much for you to be happy – especially today (your birthday), of course, but always. You deserve all the joy life can afford you, dearest Gracie. If it so happens that your joy sits upon the mantelpiece, tied up in a ribbon, you should write often and smile lots... Next year, I will buy you more ink.

Richard

13
Run rabbit run

For Mrs Pluckrose, the pleasure of having a strong cup of tea from her favourite china cup was unsurpassed. She loved to sit in her best chair, with her feet up on the footstool, a Garibaldi in her hand and crumbs in her lap. The decadence of the whole affair was, to her mind, unrivalled. On this particular wintry afternoon in January, the self-indulgence of the whole tea-drinking affair was especially heightened because she was having a sneaky peek at the unlikely theatre on her beloved Commercial Road. Mrs Pluckrose was incognito, thanks to the lace parlour curtains; their intricate pattern protected her furtive gaze from those who might look back from the outside world and give her away! She sat in her chair and looked on with intrigue as the stories of her neighbours – their comings and goings – unfolded before her.

Christmas had been and gone, and it had, as usual, left everyone a bit strapped for cash and rations. The community's annual festive loss, however, appeared to be the local spiv's gain because he was doing a roaring trade in the alley opposite. His trilby was perched on his head and tilted to hide his eyes. His trench coat was firmly tied shut, with the collar lifted to protect him from the wind and the gaze of any passing coppers. He leaned, audaciously, against the relative shelter of the alley's brick wall. Mrs Pluckrose watched with delight as she saw friends and neighbours braving the elements, walking suspiciously up and down the road, before ducking into the alley to get their hands on whatever contraband they could make use of. It appeared that making ends meet was forcing some of the most unlikely characters to make the perilous journey to the alley of disrepute. Mrs Pluckrose was giggling, gasping and chatting to herself as she witnessed dozens of half-frozen souls make their way up and down the icy street on their precarious bootleg missions.

Despite the bitter, northerly winds that blew outside, and the harsh, icy landscape framed by the parlour window, Mrs Pluckrose was feeling surprisingly cosy inside her little terrace. The fire was lit (just a small one), to take the edge off the chill, she had a crocheted blanket over her legs and a warm teacup in her hands. One Garibaldi remained, sitting in her saucer, and a warm contentment flowed through her veins as she reflected on the morning's completed housework. She thought about Bill at the store, working in the stock room – he had recently been promoted. As she pictured her son, she glowed with pride and became awash with a giddy, tingling sensation that flooded her from top to toe. Dear Milly Pluckrose was suddenly compelled to turn and look at the faded photograph of her beloved husband, William, on the mantelpiece. 'That's me done then, my love. Jobs all done and dusted, and Bill's sorted too, you know – he's a proper working man now. He can stand on his own two feet.' Her pride overflowed and made her feel lightheaded.

Mrs Pluckrose was taken by a deep, involuntary sigh of relief. She smiled at her darling William's picture and felt, to her surprise, a single tear of joy rolling down the paper-thin skin of her cheek. As she gently brushed the happy tear away, she was surprised to feel how chilly her skin was. She felt perfectly warm and cosy in herself, but her face was icy to the touch – bizarrely at odds with the glow she felt radiating from within. Her beautifully weathered face was like the street on the other side of the glass: uncommonly cold.

The dear old lady took a juddering inward breath and felt implausibly woozy, as if she had indulged in one too many sherries. Soft, playful pins and needles tickled her all over – working their way from her insides out. Her breathing slowed and became shallow. She was struck by a profound yet strangely comforting tiredness... The wise soul smiled and relaxed before placing her teacup safely back together with its saucer on her lap.

It took no more than a blink of the astute Mrs Pluckrose's heavy eyes for it to dawn on her that, at last, her work really was done. Not just for today – but always. It was quite unexpected, but there it was. It was time for her to rest properly now, and there was no point resisting it or fighting. There was no time to question or reflect upon it; she just accepted it for what it was and, in doing so, was gifted with a sense of pure release and joy.

In the warmth and comfort of her spic and span parlour, Mrs Pluckrose gently but purposefully placed her hands down by her sides, palms up, ready to be taken to her rest. The beautiful soul sat in her double-breasted apron, hair tied up in a scarf (with curlers adorning the front), with the finest teacup upon her lap and smiled. She closed her eyes for the last time and thanked God before she happily let Him take her hand to guide her on... It was then that she let her last breath go and heard the reassuring voice of her darling William, 'I've been waiting, my love...'

'So have I...' and with that, she was gone.

The fire continued to glow in the parlour, just as the wind continued to blow outside. The spiv continued to trade, and friends and neighbours continued to pass by the window. The indubitably glorious and unequivocally beautiful Mrs Milly Anne Pluckrose had gone, but the world she had been born into continued to spin. It was, of course, all the better because she had been a part of it.

****

It was not long after her departure that the Reverend came to call. He always popped in at the same time each week to go over the music for Sunday's service. The door was, as always, on the latch. As the Reverend entered, he called to Mrs Pluckrose (as he always did) to get the kettle on. When no reply came, he somehow knew she had gone.

As the Reverend made his way to the parlour, he braced himself. As he pushed the door open, he stood in the hall for a moment – compelled to pause. He saw William's framed photograph, turned to face his friend; he saw her eyes were closed and that she looked beautifully at peace – content with her lot.

A relief washed over the elderly pastor as he realised his dear friend had moved on peacefully, just as she deserved, and so his faith was justified and strengthened. The Reverend thanked God for His mercy as he slowly entered the room. He then drew up a chair next to his dearest friend and held her hand, gently kissing its pale, fragile skin – thankful for its remaining warmth. The Reverend then took a breath and whispered a teary, fond farewell to his best friend.

****

Last Will and Testament
Mrs Milly Anne Pluckrose

I have very little, of course. There are my clothes, I suppose, so help yourselves girls (Flo, Mary, Gracie). Feel free to cut them up and make them suit as you wish – any leftovers give to Reverend Smith to give to the needy in the parish. There's my kitchen bits and pieces which I'd like to give to Flo and my books which I should like Mary to have and enjoy. My wireless must go to Reverend Smith to make use of because his is so terribly unreliable! Gracie, you are to have my jewellery and the responsibility of passing it, in turn, to my beautiful, little Primrose. Consider it a thank you for the trench cake and flowers in the jam jar (not much gets past me girls)!

Dottie (Dorothy Halfpenny), my new-found friend – I never dreamt that at my age I might meet such a friend as you, Dottie. You have made me smile and laugh, and you have spoken so kindly of my Bill that I've been quite moved. I want you to know how much all that's meant to me. I have a small collection of glass and silver that would be nothing but a nuisance to Bill or the Reverend, so I'd like you to have it, to enjoy it, as I always did. My only hope is that you use it a little more often than I did.

I want quickly to assure Reverend Smith that the Co-Op have all the details for my funeral arrangements, and that all the necessary funds are in place. I also want to say that your friendship has been more valuable to me than all the tea in China, and (most importantly) that if you are reading this, it means I've popped my clogs before you, so I win the bet, and you owe me sixpence! Oh dear – we really didn't think that one through, did we? You'll have to put it in the offertory box for me. I don't think God's got a corner shop for me to spend it in. x

Now to Bill... My darling, darling boy...where do I begin? Just putting pen to paper breaks my heart; I can't think what to say to make this any easier for you, my love...

You are to know how proud I am of you and how proud your father would have been too, had he lived to see you grow. I promise we will both keep watch over you from up above in heaven, so mind you are good and keep working hard for Mr Halfpenny to make us proud forevermore. I want to sit with Jesus and your father and look down and say, "Look, isn't he doing well. Our boy Bill is so good and kind and hardworking. He's a credit to himself." Gracie, Flo and Mary will look out for you together with Reverend Smith and Mr and Mrs Halfpenny. You must go to them if you need help, and you must trust them as you always trusted me to know what is best for you. Be happy Bill and live your life well. It'll be just like it says in your favourite song, 'We'll Meet Again', and we'll be together, all three of us: you, me and your dad – together at last. We'll wait patiently for you, my lovely boy, but there's no rush to join us. We shall enjoy watching your adventures from afar and we'll keep you safe on your journey through life... What else can I say? I love you. Thank you for being my perfect son.

Finally, then, to Mr Halfpenny... I have left the house to Bill, but it is in trust to do with as you see fit. You are an honourable man (well raised by your mother) and a sound businessman. As such, I trust you will act only in my Bill's best interests. Please consult with Gracie in matters that may trouble you with regard to this because she knows Bill well and will guide you as I would have – I am quite certain of this. I am appointing both you and Gracie as Bill's guardians. As I write, I pray you see this as an honour and not (as my worst fears would have it) a burden. If the latter is true, I beg of you to hand your responsibility to the church under Reverend Smith's guidance. Bill is a fragile soul who, because of his special nature, demands great care. He is, however, one of

God's very own angels who will, I assure you, make all your troubles and efforts worthwhile. His smile alone was always reward enough for me. I pray you find it in your hearts to do whatever is best for my darling boy, so that I may, at last, rest in peace.

On the whole, I have led a happy life. Thank you all for keeping me company whilst I waited for my William to find me.

God bless, Milly x

14
Your country needs you

Bill was, for a time, inconsolable. The Reverend and Mrs Halfpenny seemed best suited to sit with him in the early days because they had the time and patience. The stoic pair were similar in manner to his mother, and so he responded best to their somewhat familiar ways. Over time, very gradually, Bill came to feel a little braver and a little stronger until, eventually, he was able to talk about his mother without breaking down into uncontrollable sobs.

Once the raw shock had faded and Bill could stand tall and be presentable, everyone rallied to spend time with him. They took him out for walks and invited him for supper. Mary even took him to the cinema to see his first film. The community wrapped Bill up safely under their collective wing, and the Reverend was thrilled because he knew his dear friend would be resting so very peacefully – looking down from above, with her dearest William by her side, smiling contentedly.

Mrs Halfpenny declared, on the very afternoon that Mrs Pluckrose had been found, that Bill was to move into her spare room above the store. She was insistent on the matter. Richard did not hesitate in offering his wholehearted agreement. They were both of the opinion that they had the space and, more importantly, the time to care for Bill in his great need. All this, they decided before the last will and testament had been found. When it was read, everyone was relieved that Mrs Pluckrose's wishes had, in the main, already been fulfilled.

Mrs Pluckrose was buried in the churchyard, up at the far end, near to where she had sat with the vicar on the fateful night of the bombing. The service was held in the cricket pavilion, and it was a job to fit everyone who wanted to pay their respects inside. Mrs Pluckrose had been such an integral part of the parish for so many years – she'd played at countless weddings, christenings and funerals – so unsurprisingly almost everyone from the community wanted to bid her a fond farewell. After the burial, many of the mourners went back to the vicarage for a small tea with sandwiches, sausage rolls, cake and, naturally, the obligatory sherry. It was a tight squeeze, but most of the guests were accommodated in the large dining room. The grand table had been pushed against the far wall to make room and to serve as a practical buffet area. Other guests, mainly the elderly (in need of quiet and a comfy seat), were in the informal sitting room. The ladies in charge of the food made their way from the large kitchen to the other two rooms with trays of refreshments at regular intervals to ensure everyone was well catered for. Everyone who had come to the vicarage had brought a small contribution with them, and, considering the rationing, it was a handsome spread and no one was left wanting.

Mrs Pluckrose's will had been read less than a week before the funeral, and that was when Richard and Gracie had learnt of their responsibility for Bill's guardianship. They had, however, not had the opportunity to discuss its implications as Richard had been busy working, and Gracie had been helping the vicar prepare for the gathering after the funeral. Richard's heart had been racing all day. In truth, it had been racing ever since he heard the news about the guardianship he was to share with Gracie. Its pace hastened further when he had caught sight of Gracie early that morning, walking across the frost-laced green towards the pavilion. She had been a vision – revealed by a delicate light – somehow softening the harsh edges of winter. He thought how astonishing she was: quietly giving everything and asking for nothing as she carried flowers to decorate the makeshift church in readiness for the service.

He knew he would have to talk to her about Bill – but when exactly would be appropriate? He wondered if the role would mean him spending considerably more time in her company, and, if indeed it transpired that it *did* mean just that, he wondered if his poor heart could manage it.

Richard spent a fair bit of time with Primrose after the service, whilst Gracie was busy with the food, and he was impressed by the little girl's capacity to absorb all that life threw at her... Her take on the death of Mrs Pluckrose was a practical one, peppered with fond memories and hopeful wishes for peace. 'Mrs Pluckrose was very old you see, Mr Halfpenny; she was old, tired and so very good. That's why God needed her for an angel.' There were no tears – just smiles as she continued, 'I'm sure she'll be having a lovely time in Heaven with her husband... He was lost, like my daddy. She'll find him now she's in Heaven because God will help her look.' Richard was in awe of young Primrose. Her wide, clear blue eyes melted his heart as they looked deeply and with such trust into his own. Richard's eyes reflected love and care back to Primrose, who always felt it so keenly whenever she spoke to him about *proper* things. She was safe with Mr Halfpenny; he always listened and, most importantly, Primrose didn't have to mind his feelings because he was there to mind hers. She wasn't sure how that had come to be the case, but she knew it was true. It made talking to him one of her most treasured things to do. With him, Primrose could just be herself without any worry because he was strong, honest and kind. He was like a… Well, like someone who was always there for her.

'Poor Mr Halfpenny, Primrose – you mustn't pester him so! Pop into the kitchen and get the cutlery for the table. There's a good girl for Mummy.' Primrose happily went about her grown-up task with a skip towards the kitchen.

'You know, she was being no bother. In truth, I enjoy our little chats...' Richard's heart raced. He was aware of every word he was saying, conscious of every syllable, of every move his lips made. He was trying not to look unduly flustered by Gracie, trying with all his might not to let it show how wonderful he thought she looked – how he was transfixed by her.

'You are such a dear with her...but I know how she can talk!' Gracie placed her hand on Richard's arm, just below his shoulder and continued, 'Do you think we could have a quick chat about Bill and what we should be doing with him? I spoke to Revered Smith briefly yesterday, and he suggested a few practical bits and pieces.'

As Richard nodded, finding gestures easier than speech, Flo swept into the room with another tray of sherries and a declaration that they were all to toast dear old Mrs Pluckrose. They were then to get the gramophone on and start dancing because that's what she would have wanted. There was a cheer in response and a hike in volume generally thereafter. Gracie gestured that she and Richard should leave the room, and so they made their way to the beautifully tiled, light-flooded hallway and found a quiet nook just beneath the stairs. As was usually the case, it didn't take long for Richard to be put at ease by Gracie's gentle, reassuring manner. He listened intently to what she had to say; he relaxed and found himself smiling and laughing with her. They spoke at length about Bill and agreed with one another on points they both raised. The conversation flowed, and they enthused about how they might enhance Bill's life – how they might teach him and make him feel a part of a family. They spoke of meals, days out and extra responsibilities at work to boost his confidence. They agreed to sell Mrs Pluckrose's house and then put most of the money into a trust fund. However, a small amount of the money would be used to decorate Bill's room above the shop and buy him a new wardrobe of clothes. Gracie was determined to help Bill to read a little, and Richard was going to teach him to fish, though admitted he would probably be teaching himself along the way! Without hesitation, Gracie offered the fishing tackle Edward and Primrose had so often used in the past. 'It's doing nothing but gathering dust – and don't worry, Primrose will come with you and show you everything you need to know.' The enthusiastic pair beneath the stairs wanted to enrich Bill's life – to offer the young man opportunities and challenges he had inadvertently been kept from in the past. They were speaking as parents planning for a son's future.

Flo, having helped herself to a fair few of the sherries on the tray, went by the stairs on her way back to the kitchen to replenish the stock. 'And what d'you two think you're doin', hidden away there? All secretly chitty-chatting! Come on, Mrs Chatley, there's work wants doing out here!'

Flo was clearly worse for wear, and both Gracie and Richard laughed before Gracie chastised, 'I'll come and help, alright. Give me that tray, you daft bat, before you drop it. Richard, will you get her some water please?'

As Gracie took the tray, Flo mocked, 'Ohhhh, *Richard* is it! Is *Richard* going to get me some water?'

Although both Richard and Gracie laughed at Flo's tipsy ramblings, it made them both think about how they were perhaps seen by others – drunk or otherwise. Richard resolved to be more guarded – to try harder not to let his feelings for Gracie show in any way. He would never want to jeopardise his relationship with her. He knew that, if she ever suspected he had feelings for her, he would lose her forever. Gracie was simply confused. She felt embarrassed, like a teenager, but she didn't know why. She felt guilty – like she had done something she shouldn't have, although she had done nothing at all. Was it bad form to get on so well with Richard, to enjoy his company, to enjoy talking to him? Gracie was certain that she had no 'feelings' for him. She had never even thought about him in that way until Flo had teased her. Gracie loved Richard's company, that was all. She did not love *him*. The two things were very different. There was no harm in spending time with a man she simply got on well with. And they had to spend time together because of Bill. Why had Flo been so dreadful and tainted it? She never was good on the sauce! Regardless of Flo's inebriation, Gracie resolved to be careful in the future. She did not want tongues wagging, especially not Flo's – it had a reputation for its relentless quest to find ears prepared to listen.

Gracie and Richard helped Flo home that evening. Gracie held her upright as they walked along Commercial Road (Richard's stick was not up to the challenge), and Primrose was made to hold a furious Arthur's hand to stop him from running off. This left Richard to carry William like some sort of sleepy, deflated rugby ball under one arm. Once the Webb family had been safely deposited at their threshold, Richard, Gracie and Primrose continued on their journey towards the store. Primrose thought how late it was…how very cold it was, how dark it was… But, most of all, she thought how wonderful it was. Her mother came alive when Mr Halfpenny was around – she was animated and relaxed. She laughed and smiled more – she was much less like her mother! She was more fun, that was the nub of it. Mr Halfpenny made her mother more fun to be around. The trio inadvertently walked straight past the shop and continued towards Number 77. They were so engrossed in their conversation that they quite missed Richard's 'stop'. When they arrived at Gracie's door, the two adults paused, and they both seemed to change quite suddenly. They stiffened up, became sober… Both Richard and Gracie were suddenly, horribly aware of how they might look to others, conscious of what others might think, or, worse still, what they might say. Flo's teasing words from earlier echoed in their ears. 'Gracie, I am so sorry… I've been nattering away, forgive me. It's late, of course, so I'll leave you two ladies to your evening.' Richard smiled at Primrose and patted her head.

'Thank you for walking us home and for helping with Flo. Have a good evening yourself, won't you. Take care.' As she spoke, Gracie rummaged in her pocket for the key to put in the lock. Richard smiled and walked away; he walked tall and had a smile on his face. Despite Flo's teasing, and the odd moments of awkwardness, and – of course – the fact he had been at a funeral, the day had been, on the whole, a marvellous one for him! He looked up at the heavens and very quietly thanked Mrs Pluckrose – it seemed like the right thing to do.

Little did Richard know how right he was to thank the wise, old owl who had so recently departed. Before Milly had died, she and Dottie had chatted about many things: those they loved, and their wishes and dreams for the future...not their own futures but the futures of those they would, one day, have to leave behind. Both Milly and Dottie wanted their loved ones to be happy, and they wanted them to *never* feel as they had for so many years: lonely. Milly could see all too clearly that her dear friend, Gracie, loved her missing husband, just as she loved her William. She saw in Gracie a reflection of her own self, and in the final few months before her death it began to play on her mind more and more. Milly felt as though she needed to speak to Gracie, but she could never quite find the words...

The reason for Milly's upset was the dawning realisation that to wait in hope forever, when you are so young, *is* perhaps foolish after all. Milly bravely confided in Dottie. Given her time again, if the chance presented itself whilst she was young enough to take advantage of it, and a good man came her way (a man who could care for her and keep her company as she grew old), she would take his hand and let him help her. It would not have been the betrayal to William that she had always feared, she could see that now, with the benefit of hindsight. Unfortunately, it was woefully too late for her. Mrs Pluckrose's regret played on her mind; she relived the moments on the stairs with Gracie. She heard herself speak, and she wished she could have changed her words or added to them at least – there was more she should have said, caveats that should have been added. That was where her will came into play; it had nothing to do with glass and silver or jewellery – that was simply a ruse. It was about ensuring her son, Bill, would never be lonely – that he would be cared for by two people she trusted, respected and loved. If it so happened that those two people came to see how wonderful they could be together, then there was no harm in that. Milly was happy that she was not interfering or meddling – she was convinced that she was merely assisting fate. Milly Pluckrose believed with all her heart that when she finally went to her rest, Gracie's Edward would be waiting to see her. She believed he would thank her for her efforts in ensuring Gracie's best chance of happiness. Milly knew that anyone who ever loved someone would do anything to spare them the inexplicable, aching pain of perpetual loneliness, and there was no doubt in Milly's mind that Edward loved Gracie, and so all would be well.

****

Friday, 29th January 1943

My dearest, darling man,

I needed you so desperately today, Edward, as I stood by the open grave, and they lowered our dearest Mrs Pluckrose to her rest. I needed your strong arms around me, my love...I was shaking. Why are you still not home? Why won't you return to us? Primrose and I need you. We need you to hold us tightly and tell us that everything will be fine. On days like today, it's hard to be strong. I get tired and weary and find myself wishing it all away, wishing it was all over, and that I could just join you no matter where you are...I don't care where it is...I just want to be with you.

I sometimes think that, if it weren't for Primrose, I'd run and run and run until I found you. I would never stop...I'd run until the day I died looking for you. I can't leave though, can I? I am destined to stay here, just as Mrs Pluckrose was. She was destined to stay until the day she died; eventually freed as they lowered her into the cold, hard ground – alone.

During the day, when life is busy and full, I am mostly happy. I promise I am not morose, but in the evenings (when I reflect on my life or look to my future), I can't help but feel painfully lonely. I miss you, Edward. I miss making plans with you. I miss arguing with you! What is life if it cannot be shared? A story is not a story until it is told, my love, and I have no one to listen to my story. No one wants to turn the pages of my life to find out more...

This May, it will be three years since you left us. Three years and not a word from you – not a single word. Am I destined, like Mrs Pluckrose, to be lowered into the cold, hard ground, alone, not knowing where you are? I pray to God that I am saved from such a cruel fate – that I will be released from my sentence soon. Until such time, I shall continue to live in Mrs Pluckrose's shadow; I'll do my best to live up to her example and make you proud in the process. I will make my days last for as long as possible and do all I can to wear myself out. When the evenings come, I will be so tired that I'll simply sleep – I'll have no energy left to waste on being sad or alone.

I am quite exhausted now...spent in fact. Time for bed. Time for sleep. I have yet to dream in your absence, my darling man. Dreams really have left me quite alone. I trust they will return, with you. I pray every night, that when I close my eyes to sleep, I will dream of you and the following morning you will wake me with a kiss.

Until then, my love, Gracie x

15
A nightingale sang in Berkeley Square

As Mary dashed through the deluge of rain with her sodden, bottle-green cardigan held ineffectually above her head, she lamented the absent umbrella she had left in the hall. As she ran, attempting to avoid the perilous puddles laid out before her, she was pelted mercilessly with heavy, wind-driven rain. Try as she might to sidestep the calamity of misplacing a step and ruining her precious stockings, the inevitable claimed her silk-adorned left foot just before she reached the cinema's doors. Her heart sank – just as her patent shoe had, into the grimy waters. The dire weather reflected poor Mary's mood: it was dreary and depressed, and it showed no sign of cheering up.

Every other Saturday, on her day off, Mary would catch the bus into Tunbridge Wells to see a film at the opera house. She usually breezed to the pictures with a spring in her step, full of anticipation and excitement. On this particular afternoon, however, her mood was dampened, but not only because of the weather... As the rain soaked through to her best silk slip, Mary began to wonder what romance she might have to endure on the big screen that afternoon. Who would fall in love with whom, she wondered? Which handsome hero would save the fair maiden in distress today? What fanciful nonsense, with no bearing on life in Paddock Wood (where there were no eligible men), would she have to put up with whilst she sat in the darkness, alone? Over the past few months, Mary had begun to wonder about life after Thomas – about life with another man. She had watched the romances on the big screen and been filled with hope for a romantic liaison of her own. Today, however, the rain poured down like a heavy dose of reality, and Mary concluded that such wild and passionate affairs were reserved for glamorous movie stars – not plain, drenched girls with ruined stockings in Kent.

As Mary reached the heavy doors of the opera house, she pushed with all her might to open the final barrier between her and the dry. She pushed and pushed, to no avail, and was furious that the rain had washed away every ounce of her strength. She was wholly defeated. 'Allow me,' called a voice above the noise of the rain. The arm belonging to the voice then reached over Mary's head, took hold of the brass bar running down the length of the door, and *pulled* it open. Mary, embarrassed, stumbled inside. To her utter dismay, her stumble somehow escalated into a trip. Before she knew it, she was a sodden, crumpled, mortified heap on the foyer floor. The hand, that had moments before reached above her head to open the door, was now extended in an offer to help her up from her predicament. Too embarrassed to look up and put a face to the hand, Mary accepted the outreached gesture and scurried to her feet. She then muttered a clumsy word of thanks, eyes still fixed firmly to the floor, before making a hasty retreat to the ladies to powder her flushed, rosy nose.

Whilst fixing her makeup, hair and pride in front of the mirror in the ladies, Mary contemplated leaving the picture house and returning home. By the time her appearance was remedied, however, she concluded that her hard-earned bus fare was worth more than her bruised pride, and it should not go to waste. She returned to the foyer with her head held high and joined the queue to purchase a ticket. Unbeknown to Mary, the gentleman who joined the queue behind her was the same man who had kindly opened the door to aid her escape from the rain and subsequently rescued her from the floor when she had fallen. He had waited graciously in the foyer to be sure she was unharmed when she emerged from the ladies. He gently followed her as she walked towards the queue, watching carefully to be sure she was not limping or in any obvious pain. As a consequence of his gallantry, however, the stranger found himself in the queue. Once there, he could not leave, for fear of being conspicuous and embarrassing the object of his concerns further. As they queued patiently, waiting to be served, Mary became awash with an odd feeling. She began to suspect, quite fervently, that the man in the queue behind her might well be the man who had helped her earlier. She felt her heart race a little faster and the flush return to her cheeks. She tried to turn, nonchalantly (as though trying to take in the view), so she might steal a glimpse of the fellow behind her. However, it was to no avail since the fellow behind her was determined to look at his shoes and turn away whenever her eyes drew near. At last, Mary reached the counter to be served. The lady at the counter rattled off her usual patter: 'Two tickets, madam, for the ten o'clock?'

Mary was flustered. 'Two? Oh no – just the one, thank you.' Mary felt as though her announcement was tantamount to holding a huge sign above her head that told the world she had no friends, relations or even acquaintances that could bear to accompany her to the pictures. Her cheeks felt as though they might catch fire. She quickly handed over her shilling, took her ticket and made her escape towards the darkness of the theatre.

As the titles began to roll, a lone gentleman stood by Mary's aisle seat and whispered a soft, 'Excuse me,' gesturing to the empty seat next to her. Mary was sure it was the gentleman from the queue. She smiled – caught unaware by her ease. Her embarrassment had dimmed as surely as the lights in the theatre. She stood and held the stranger's gaze for a moment longer than was necessary. As he brushed past to take his seat, he bravely whispered, 'I'm glad you're all right. It was quite a tumble...'

Mary, encouraged by the darkness, replied, 'Thank you for helping me.'

The pair sat in the auditorium for the duration of the film – staring up at the big screen but not watching a thing... By the time the film had reached its conclusion, and despite the fact they had not spoken a word, or even so much as shared a glance throughout the screening, the couple in seats ten and eleven G were no longer strangers. Mary, quite uncharacteristically, began the repartee. 'I'd like to thank you properly...' she braved, making her voice heard above the music as the credits rolled. She then offered to buy her hero a coffee, and he accepted on the proviso that she told him her name.

****

Mary's companion was courteous and charming, attentive and warm, and so she found herself smiling and sharing stories with fabulous ease. His soft, blue eyes shone out from behind his horn-rimmed spectacles, and his neat, Brylcreemed, fair hair struck Mary as being very distinguished – suave, even. She was absorbed by his every word and gesture. They laughed about their meeting, chatted about the film and others they had both seen, and soon found themselves talking about music, family, and siblings – or lack thereof... As the rain continued to fall against the window's panes and the light faded to a hazy dusk, Mary noticed the time and felt an awful jolt as she returned to a somber reality. 'The bus... I'll miss my bus, and matron will be furious with me.'

'Matron?'

It was a moment that neither Mary nor her companion would ever forget. It was the moment when they discovered what fate had in store for them both. It was the beginning of the conversation that led them to the most remarkable discovery. Mary's newfound friend was, in fact, Dr James Applebee: the new junior doctor appointed to Moatlands. He was due to start his role, alongside Mary, on Monday. Having recently completed his training in Bexley, the position at Moatlands would be his first independent posting. He had come to Tunbridge Wells for the day to discover his new local area and had stumbled upon the old opera house whilst looking for the library. He had no intention of going in, and certainly no plans to watch a film, but when he saw Mary struggling with the door, he found himself fulfilling a drastically altered afternoon's itinerary.

Dr Applebee smiled. 'Share a taxi with me. I'll get you home safely, and Matron will have no need to lose her temper.'

The doctor took Mary's hand to help her into the taxi, and he held it fast from there on in. They sat, side by side, hand in hand on the journey back to Moatlands. As they drove up the impressive drive towards the grand, old building, Mary rested her head on the doctor's shoulder and sighed, 'I can't believe we're here already. I do so wish that I didn't have to go.'

'What are your hours tomorrow?'

'I'll be finished by two.'

'Then I'll be here waiting for you. I'll take you out for a late lunch...if you'd like that?'

'I'd love it.'

The rain was still pouring, and the wind was blowing harder and faster than it had done earlier, but it was the most perfect day. As Mary ran from the taxi, leaving the doctor behind, she relished the feeling of the freezing cold rain falling on her face. As she reached the front door of Moatlands and pushed on it to open, Dr Applebee laughed. Mary stopped in her tracks, laughing out loud, and turned to share in the amusement before waving goodbye. She then *pulled* on the door and stepped inside, walking – just as they did in the movies – on air.

****

Before resting her giddy head on her pillow that night, Mary spilled her excitement onto the pages of her tatty, well-thumbed diary.

Saturday, 13th February 1943

I have just realised the date! Tomorrow is Valentine's Day, and I am going out for lunch with a handsome, charming doctor named James... Dr James Applebee. I cannot believe that any of this is happening to me. Things like this don't happen to girls like me!

I never dreamt, as the rain fell and the wind blew, and the miserable puddles ruined my stockings that I would have such an unforgettably perfect day.

I feel like fate has brought James and me to one another; that she wanted us to meet before we began to work together. Fingers, toes, arms & legs crossed that she has a good plan set out for us both. I can't help but imagine us having a future together, which I know is absurd given we've only just met, and he's a doctor and I'm just, well, me... But it was like we'd known each other forever. Oh my, the way he looked at me; the way it felt when he took my hand and didn't let go! I can't believe I rested my head on his shoulder – I was outrageous, but I don't care. I just wish so much that he'd kissed me goodbye. I think he might tomorrow. What if he's even shyer than I am? If he is shy, I'll be bold for the both of us! I don't know what's happened to me, but I am so excited and giddy. I feel as though the room is spinning. My mind is made up – tomorrow, I will kiss him. I will kiss Dr James Applebee on Valentine's Day, and it will be perfect.

Mother will be furious... How fantastic!

16
In the mood

Primrose's tenth birthday was looming, and Gracie wanted to make a real fuss of her. Her daughter was, after all, a most deserving little girl. It was hard for Gracie to believe that her only child was going to be turning ten. As a bookkeeper, she thought of the new column she would soon occupy: the *tens* column! How had this happened so quickly? Soon she would be a teenager, then a young woman, and before she knew it Primrose would be a married woman with children of her own. Gracie thought how cruel time could be. It flew by when you wanted to slow it down but dragged on when you least wanted it to. The lead up to Primrose's big day inevitably brought moments of sad and poignant reflection: she had grown up all too quickly, but Edward had been gone far too long to see her grow...

The week before the big day, Gracie asked Primrose what she would like for her birthday. 'It can be anything you like, within reason. I can't get you a bike or a dolls' house – obviously – far too expensive! I certainly can't get you a pony or a dog, or anything silly like that... Something sensible, but something you'd never usually have. Perhaps a day out somewhere, or a new dress, or maybe a party even.'

'A fishing trip! I want to go fishing with Bill and Mr Halfpenny. You've said about it lots, but we still haven't done it. The weather is fine and dry now, so that's what I want to do.'

'Fishing? You are a Contrary Mary! Most little girls would want a pretty dress.'

Gracie went about organising the trip: she dug out the old fishing tackle from the cupboard beneath the stairs, and she went through it all with Primrose to make sure they had everything they would need. She organised Primrose's clothes (including a hat and wellington boots) and arranged to go around the shop with Richard to get Bill everything he would need too. On the day before the big trip, Gracie took Primrose to Mrs Halfpenny's sitting room above the store so the pair of them could continue working on their latest, greatest jigsaw together whilst Gracie and Richard shopped with Bill.

Bill was busy organising the goods from that day's delivery in the stock room when Gracie and Richard interrupted him. 'Come on then, Bill,' rallied Richard. 'Time to get you some kit for fishing tomorrow... Do you remember? You're coming out with Primrose and me for the day.' Richard spoke deliberately but lovingly to Bill; he never patronised or belittled him, but he took great care to be steady and to the point.

Bill's response was typical – there was no eye contact, and he mumbled slightly as he spoke with his usual unease, 'Oh no, Mr Halfpenny, sir. I've got shoes to go through... Mr Young says I does them best.' Beneath Bill's ample belly and surrounding his sizable feet, shoe boxes encircled him, and yet more boxes balanced in his generous arms. It was a warm, June day and Bill, wrapped up in a woollen tank top, was hot and sweaty. His dark hair was stuck to his forehead, and his rosy cheeks were particularly flushed with responsibility.

Gracie spoke kindly, 'Then we'll leave you to it, shall we, Bill? Come back a bit later when you're finished?' Gracie knew, as did Richard, that Bill thrived on routine and order. If he felt his structure was under threat, he would get really, very upset. 'There's no rush, my love. We'll get Mr Halfpenny something to wear and then come back for you later.' Bill nodded sincerely, looking at his shoe boxes, and then happily continued stacking the shoes for his beloved Mr Young. Gracie and Richard left the stock room and immediately ducked out the back door of the store for a breath of fresh air. The stock room was stuffy, and Bill was sweaty, so the resulting aroma had been potent.

Taking a quick, refreshing breath, Gracie half-laughed as she shook her head and mused, 'Why on earth does he insist on wearing that tank top in this heat? And why doesn't he open the window in there? It's stifling!'

Richard smiled warmly, offering his hand out as he shrugged. 'The tank top is his very own, self-imposed 'stock room duties uniform', and he won't go in there without it. The window is shut because...'

The pair shared a knowing smile and nodded as they spoke in unison, '...The birds might fly in!' With her gentle laugh lingering and the warm sun playing on her back, Gracie relaxed – becoming light and free. The sun's rays calmed her, lifted her burdens and allowed her to bask in the joy of a shared moment with her friend.

Elevated and encouraged by the light dancing in the usually grey yard, Gracie found herself awash with playfulness. She smiled at Richard. 'Just because Bill has got out of his shopping trip, you, Mr Halfpenny, have not.

What are we going to get you?' She could not imagine Richard in fishing gear. He was strictly a three-piece-suit kind of a chap, and she had never seen him any other way.

'Are the silly clothes absolutely necessary? Wouldn't an old suit do? I won't wear a tie; I'll leave the jacket off and even undo the waistcoat... I could roll up my shirt sleeves too. That would surely do?' Poor Richard was desperate. He was so uncomfortable with the thought of wearing waders, a wax jacket, wellington boots and a silly hat.

'I'm not so sure you can fish properly without all the right gear. I think you need the daft green hat for camouflage!' Gracie was in her element.

'Camouflage? From fish? Utter rot!' Richard was smiling and falling deeper and deeper in love with every second.

'Let me see you then. Come on. Jacket off, waistcoat undone, tie off – the lot – then I'll decide. Come on – no shirking now. Give me your stick, and I'll help you.'

In the heat of a perfect June afternoon, hidden from view at the back of the store, Gracie helped Richard take off his jacket. She then unbuttoned his waistcoat and helped roll up his sleeves before taking off his tie. All this she had intended to do in mere jest – in the name of innocent fun. As it turned out, however, that was not how events unfolded at all...

As Gracie peeled back Richard's jacket, she was overcome with curiosity. Knowingly, she slowed her hands as they moved across her boss's broad shoulders. Though the sun shone, she felt a rush of excited shivers and caught

169

her breath in the small, unexpected thrill of it. Through the starched, white cotton of Richard's shirt she felt a robust frame; it was firm to her light, yet undeniably indulgent touch. She swallowed and tried to calm herself, but an uncontainable quiver ran through her and took over as she lingered on strong, capable shoulders. It was apparent that Richard had been keeping an illicit secret: his breadth and impressive tone had been hiding, in plain sight, beneath cunning drapery. His secrets, now exposed, proved impossible for the raptured Gracie to ignore. With no escape to be had from the heat, she was happily captured and becoming impossibly flushed. When the prim, tweed jacket fell to the floor, it was quickly forgotten, for Gracie had already turned her attention to the waistcoat...

Submitting to the stifling closeness, Gracie committed to the work of undoing each and every tiny button before her with masterful precision. She chose to let her fingers work slowly on each one, brushing against Richard's lightly concealed chest as she worked her way down towards his firm, clenched stomach. She worked silently and slowly – button by dangerous button. Once the waistcoat was undone, she edged towards the stiff shirt cuffs that she felt sure would reveal more secrets.

Richard was, by now, completely tortured by the feathered touch of Gracie, and he could not help but join his fingers with hers as she attended his shirt. The fevered pair worked together – restless fingers touching, temperatures climbing, pulses racing – all the while in absolute, petrified silence. Gracie rolled each of Richard's sleeves perfectly – slowly uncovering the strong forearms that were hidden beneath the cool, white façade.

Finally, Gracie took hold of Richard's tie – removing it with one smooth stroke before undoing the stiff, top collar button and releasing the desperate breath she had been holding. Their eyes dared not meet. They were inches apart and could feel one another's hearts pounding. They could hear the intensity of their breathing and feel the heat rising between them, but they were frozen. Neither one of them knew what to do.

'All of Mr Young's shoes are done now.' Bill had come in search of Mr Halfpenny and Gracie, ready for his shopping trip.

Gracie, with her back to Bill, put her hands on Richard's pounding chest and spoke to the floor. 'Good. Right then...' She took a deep breath to steady herself before bravely lifting her gaze to meet Richard's clear, assuring, hazel eyes. 'You'll meet us in the store in a minute or two then, will you, Mr Halfpenny?'

Richard gazed back and spoke gently, 'Absolutely. You can rely on me.' His eyes searched Gracie's as he quietly added, 'I'll be there – just as soon as you need me.'

****

The fishing trip was idyllic. Bill dozed beneath his new hat while leaning against an old tree stump. His rod was propped up by a makeshift twig and stick stand constructed by a resourceful Primrose and an encouraging Mr Halfpenny. Bill had been enthusiastic all day, despite not catching even so much as a minnow, and he had quite worn himself out. He slept soundly, and, to Primrose's great amusement, he would periodically mumble and snore with hearty contentment. As the afternoon ambled to its close, Primrose and Mr Halfpenny sat beneath the shade of an obliging apple tree and reflected on their delicious picnic, Bill's snoring, and their woefully empty buckets. The happy pair laughed and chatted together whilst savoring the last of the ginger beer, and they soaked up all the splendor the June day had left to offer them. As the sun began to ebb, Mr Halfpenny's eye was caught by a tiny, yellow flower hidden in the shade of some long grass. 'Look at that: a primrose. That's very special. It must be one of the last ones... A gift for Primrose on her tenth birthday.'

'Mum named me after the flower. She used to sit under an apple tree in her mum's garden and read stories when she was little. She said that she used to look at the primroses with her mum when they appeared under the tree every year and that they were her favourite.'

'So, she named you after them?'

'Yes.' Primrose looked wistfully out over the stream and tucked her knees up under her chin, hugging her legs tightly before continuing, 'Mum takes me to the orchard sometimes and we read there together...' Primrose was mellow and wistful as she concluded, 'It's my most favourite thing in the world to do.'

The early start, that had so obviously caught up with Bill, was now chasing Primrose; she stifled a yawn and shivered slightly, hugging her legs tighter still with her skinny, goose-pimpled arms. Mr Halfpenny picked up the folded, tartan picnic rug and wrapped it around her. He then put his arm around her and rubbed her shoulder to warm her through. Primrose smiled and snuggled in close to her companion. Resting herself into his comforting hold, she let out a soft, contented sigh as Mr Halfpenny gently kissed her forehead. Primrose was steadily edging towards sleep, and so (to help her on her way) Mr Halfpenny told her to close her eyes and make a wish...

Primrose's heavy eyes could not bring themselves to reopen once she had closed them, and so it was with her wish fresh in her mind that she joined Bill in a late-afternoon, summer snooze. She had wished that Mr Halfpenny would always be her friend. She loved how it felt when she was with him: she felt safe and looked after. It was as though he made everything brighter and more colourful – lighter and fresher than it had been before. With Mr Halfpenny, everything was simple. Primrose did not have to worry about him or take special care of his feelings like she did with her mother. If Primrose had been a little braver, she would have wished for Mr Halfpenny to be her new daddy. It had crossed her mind (it was the first thing that came into her head), but she knew it was wrong. So, she quickly revised her wish before casting it out and setting it free so as not to upset whoever it was that might catch her wish and make it come true.

Although it was not his birthday, Richard decided to make a wish too. He wished that Primrose might, one day, see him as a father figure. Perhaps the little girl he loved so dearly and held in his arms might call herself his little girl and, most importantly, be proud to do so. Although he knew it was wrong to wish for such a thing, Richard did not revoke his wish. He held it tightly and prayed that, in the fullness of time, it might come true. Glancing at Bill and smiling, he pictured family picnics, Christmas mornings, birthday teas and Sundays in church... He lightly stroked Primrose's long, dark hair as she slept soundly on his shoulder, and his aching heart longed for Gracie to be with them too – for her hand to rest on his shoulder and for her lips to kiss his cheek. He wanted her to be there with them, under the shade of the tree, to make the picture complete – to make it perfect – to make his wish come true.

'I wondered where you had all got to.' The softest, sweetest voice called out from behind the tree, and it was like music swelling in a dream. Gracie stood, subtly lit by the hazy, late-afternoon sun, and her auburn hair glistened softly in its glow. A gentle breeze carefully collected her floral shift dress and pressed it against her – hugging, as it did, her slight yet beautiful frame.

The resulting figure took Richard's breath away. Caught between his daydreams and reality, he quietly released, 'You are so beautiful.' He quickly realised his mistake. 'I'm sorry. Gracie, please, ignore me...' Poor Richard was on eggshells. He was ruined by Gracie's presence – unable to fathom what he should do or say for the best.

Richard could not help but recall Gracie's touch from the day before and remember how close they had been. Try as he might to act rationally, he was confounded. Gracie was anxious too. She had spent all day thinking about Richard. She had spent every waking hour thinking about him since their unexpected frisson at the back of the shop. They had both been so terribly polite since it had all happened – not mentioning a word, being awfully proper in one another's company. Yet they failed miserably to pretend that everything between them was as it ever was. Gracie was genuinely perplexed. Where had all these feelings come from? She had not encouraged or wanted them. They were uninvited guests – persistent and exhausting. Regardless of how hard she wished the unwelcome feelings away, they grew ever stronger and more resilient to her struggling conscience. Seeing Richard sitting underneath the apple tree, with her baby girl (so content) snuggled up beside him, helped only to confirm her greatest fear: she was falling for Richard. It was a tangled, emotional mess. She did not know if she was excited or ashamed, hopeful or fearful. She wanted to rush to him – to hold him and to be held. Yet at the same time, she wanted to run away and hide and never have to see him again. Although she had no clue how to deal with her feelings for Richard, she was certain she could not bear to see him so troubled and anxious: it upset her dreadfully. She knelt down beside him and placed her hand on his shoulder. Resting her forehead gently against his, she whispered, 'Don't apologise. Please...' With that, she closed her eyes and placed the gentlest, most heartfelt kiss on Richard's warm, softly bearded cheek. She then sat down by his side and rested her back against him before quietly confessing, 'I don't know what to do...'

'That's all right,' Richard assured her. 'Neither do I.'

****

It may not have been Richard's birthday, but he knew he had received the greatest of gifts. He felt it was a day to be remembered and recorded, so he collected his scarcely opened diary and his pen before retiring to his bed. He wrote of his dreams for a future filled with days like the one he had just enjoyed with the people he loved.

12ᵗʰ June 1943

I am daring to consider, indeed I am venturing to contemplate with considerable assurance, that my love for Gracie is not as I had once feared: destined to be unrequited forever... If I am not mistaken, and Gracie has somehow found within herself a place for my fervent affection, today is surely the greatest day of my humble and hitherto inconsequential existence.

I dared to dream today...to wish for a future with my darling Gracie – the woman I have so long admired and adored. To my surprise, to my joy and amazement, Gracie gave me reason to continue dreaming and wish harder still. I am no blinkered fool; I know the road ahead will be fraught with unknown obstacles and times of heartache, and that perhaps I am destined to be forsaken at my journey's end. However, I have to continue or else what is my life for? I believe I am here on this earth for Gracie – I am here for her, Primrose, Bill and mother, and I thank God for my chance to love them all.

17
Dig for victory

Primrose's birthday had marked the beginning of a new era for Richard, Gracie, Bill and Primrose. They spent more time together, albeit quietly, behind closed doors. Sundays were often spent reading: Gracie would share Primrose's old books with Bill, and Richard would discover new worlds with Primrose through books he bought upstairs from the shop floor. The four of them, together with Richard's mother, regularly shared meals above the shop during the week, and Mrs Halfpenny delighted in the hustle and bustle of it all. She would often offer up a wry smile towards the heavens for Mrs Pluckrose's benefit as she saw her beloved son and Gracie relax more in one another's company. As the months passed, Primrose became more confident with Richard. She would rush to him for hugs when she saw him and sit happily on his lap when she read (or when she was tired and wanted a cuddle). All the while, the turbulent undercurrent between Gracie and Richard continued to grow – relentlessly swelling and rumbling. The pair cleverly conjured the illusion of calm waters between them to fool the world and hide the turmoil beneath, but their attraction was becoming dangerously irrepressible.

By the end of the summer, and after the September harvest, Richard's thoughts turned to Gracie's impending birthday. He had long harboured an idea (planted in his mind by Primrose on the day of the fishing trip) regarding an appropriate gift for his secret love. After much deliberation with Primrose, Richard decided to make his purchase – taking Primrose with him to help choose the perfect specimen. Once the purchase was made, they were all set to surprise Gracie. On the eve of the all-important birthday, however, the carefully constructed plan was in danger of going seriously awry, so a fraught Primrose ran to the store to seek out Mr Halfpenny and share her concerns. 'Mum has the most rotten flu. I thought it was just a cold, but she's got much worse and gone off to bed.' Primrose was clearly disappointed. 'She won't be able to dig tomorrow!'

'I wasn't expecting Mummy to dig the hole, Primrose! I just thought we'd all plant the tree together.' Mr Halfpenny paused for a moment to gather his thoughts and reconstruct his plan. 'We'll plant it without her knowing – make it a surprise. Then you can get her to the window, and she can look at it from her bedroom. We'll even tie a ribbon around it.'

The following morning, Primrose gave her mother her homemade card, but she barely had the energy to open it. Primrose helped her and then proudly displayed it on the dressing table. Flo and Mary came to visit with their cards but, because of Gracie's dreadful state, the birthday greetings were left to one side. Flo took on the role of nurse – making Gracie tea, sitting with her, and cooling her burning head with soothing flannels soaked in tepid water. Whilst Flo sat with Gracie, Primrose took the opportunity to sneak away to fetch Mr Halfpenny and the all-important tree. The secretive pair tiptoed, tree and shovel in hand, through the back alley from the shop to Gracie's back gate and into the garden. Primrose had chosen the perfect spot for the tree: with plenty of space for growth, and room for a rug to be placed underneath, it was all set for years of storytelling to come. Flo became aware of a ruckus in the garden, so peeped from behind Gracie's closed curtains to discover Primrose and a rather inappropriately dressed Mr

Halfpenny trying to dig a hole for a not-insignificant apple tree.

Flo was suitably amused to see Mr Halfpenny struggle in his three-piece-suit to dig the vast hole and delighted to see Primrose so excited and expectant. Gracie slept soundly through the whole affair. As the hours passed, Flo witnessed the eventual planting of the tree and the subsequent triumphant (albeit muted) celebrations shared by Primrose and Mr Halfpenny. Given her vantage point, viewing as she was in secret from behind the glass, she saw Mr Halfpenny in a new light: through Gracie's eyes. And like Gracie, she found herself quite in awe of the man in the garden below. As Flo looked on, she decided that Mr Halfpenny was a good man...that he would be a wonderful father to Primrose. Most importantly, she concluded, he could make Gracie happy. However, as the celebrations below were drawing to a close, it dawned on Flo that the picture viewed by her, from behind the rose-tinted glass, was a work of fiction. It could never be more than a story. As long as Edward was "missing", Richard and the girls could never truly be a family or live the life Flo believed they deserved. They were destined to merely exist alongside one another. Flo was taken back to her own childhood – remembering how it felt to exist alongside her mother, watching friends and neighbours truly live, and yearning to do the same. Returning to Gracie, Flo sighed before sitting on the edge of her dearest friend's bed. She then held Gracie's hand and whispered her outrage through silent, bitter tears, 'It's not bloody fair, Gracie. Damn this soddin' war, my lovely girl. Damn it all.'

Once Mr Halfpenny was satisfied that the tree was firmly in place, he hugged Primrose and disappeared back through the gate and along the alley. He darted through the shop's back door and, after a good wash, returned to the shop floor. Primrose ran inside, took off her muddy shoes and ran on excited, quiet tiptoes to her mother's room. 'Is she awake, Aunty Flo?' she whispered.

'Sorry, my love, no. I can't let you wake her neither. She needs to rest.' Poor Primrose was desperate to show her mother the tree, but she sat patiently at the foot of her bed and waited. 'I saw what you and Mr Halfpenny were up to, my love... Y'mam'll love it, she will. She'll absolutely love it.'

Gracie slept for the best part of the day, missing lunch and dinner. Mrs Halfpenny came to call at about six o'clock with cards and neatly wrapped gifts from her, Richard and Bill. She chatted downstairs with Primrose and Flo about the tree planting; Primrose shared her concern that the day might end before her mother had a chance to see it. It was far too dark at that point to spy the tree from the bedroom window, so little Primrose's hopes of surprising her mother had been dashed. 'Even if she does wake up, and I'm guessing she *must* do soon, she won't be able to see a rotten thing out of her window... It's blacker than coal out now.' On hearing Primrose's disappointment, Mrs Halfpenny was struck by a gem of an idea: one she was quite compelled to act upon immediately. She had no time to waste, so she hurried her goodbyes before dashing back to the store without explanation, leaving Primrose and Flo quite bemused.

When Gracie eventually woke an hour or so later, she seemed a little better. Flo fetched her some tea and made sure she was comfortable before leaving her with Primrose for the evening. 'I'll leave you two now, so Primrose can tell you all about your surprise. Look after yourself.' The forlorn Primrose was certain that the tree would not be visible from the window, and so she told her mother that there had been a surprise but that it was too dark to see it now.

'Where is this surprise then, my love?' asked a curious Gracie.

Primrose mumbled with bitter disappointment, 'In the garden, but it's no good...you won't be able to see it now. We'll have to wait until tomorrow.'

'Can't you just tell me what it is then?'

'No. That wasn't the plan.'

'Well, couldn't we try to have a look? Perhaps we might be able to make something out...' Gracie could see how disheartened Primrose was.

'I suppose so, but it won't work. You won't be able to see anything, not properly...'

'Nothing ventured, nothing gained!' encouraged Gracie, with a hard-sought smile only a weary but loving mother could muster. With a faint glimmer of hope instilled, Primrose helped her mother out of bed, wrapped a shawl around her shoulders and helped her put on the slippers by the bed. Gracie ached from head to toe and felt dizzy as she stood, but she tried to appear composed for Primrose's sake. They made their way slowly over to the closed curtains, and Primrose accidentally let a small sigh of resignation escape as she began to pull back the heavy drapes. She knew that even if her mother could make out the tree, it would not be as she had imagined and dreamt it should be.

As the drapes parted, however, Primrose was stunned. Laid out before her was a magnificent scene: like a page from one of her treasured fairytales. The garden was a vision, illuminated by what seemed to Primrose like thousands of tiny lights, all twinkling in the cold night air. Bunting adorned the apple tree, and a rug was beneath it. A book was laid out ready to read together with another light flickering in a beautiful lantern. Primrose's breath was taken away. 'Wow – and I thought the tree was good!'

'It's the most beautiful thing I've ever seen,' Gracie gasped. 'Who helped you with all of this, Primrose?'

'We just planted the tree, Mr Halfpenny and me, but I didn't do any of this. I didn't know anything about this...'

Gracie stumbled – her head was spinning. She fell back towards the bed and clasped her chest. With an uneasy breathlessness, she demanded, 'Go and fetch Mr Halfpenny, Primrose. Quickly, run and fetch him, and tell him to come at once.'

Primrose was scared. She ran out of the house without her shoes or coat to protect her from the cold November air – she ran out into the darkness towards the shop and safety. At last, she banged on the front door and waited for a response. None came, and her heart was pounding. She banged louder still and called out into the darkness, 'Mr Halfpenny! It's me, Primrose. Mummy says I'm to fetch you at once.'

Mr Halfpenny quickly appeared with his walking stick in hand, turning on the store's lights and running, as best he could, towards the door. 'Whatever has happened? Is Mummy all right?'

'She told me to fetch you at once. I showed her the tree. I didn't think she'd be able to see it from the window, what with it being so dark, but it was all lit up and beautiful. Then I told her about you getting the tree, and she just sort of took a turn and told me to fetch you.' Richard quickly saw that Primrose was barefoot, so he picked her up and rested her on his good hip. He then struggled up the road as fast as his injured leg would allow, his heart thumping through his chest with every painful step. As they approached the door it opened, and a ray of light pierced the darkness. As Richard arrived with Primrose clinging to his neck, he saw Gracie standing in the hall. She had a blanket over her shoulders, Primrose's shoes in one hand and her school coat in the other.

'You'll be needing these, madam,' she smiled. 'Thank you, Richard, for coming so quickly.'

Richard was bewildered. 'I thought something terrible had happened...'

Gracie did not flinch. 'It had. It's my birthday today, and I hadn't seen you.'

Gracie led Primrose and Richard through to the kitchen where she collected the cards and presents that Mrs Halfpenny, Flo and Mary had left on the table earlier. She then led them out to the beauty of her garden. The three tightly wrapped souls, warmed by their love for one another, all sat on the rug by the newly-planted apple tree and read some of the cards by the light of the flame that danced in the lantern. Richard then read the first chapter of *The Magic Faraway Tree*, the book he had placed by the lantern, with Primrose on one side of him and Gracie on the other. All the while the happy trio sat beneath the tree,

Mrs Halfpenny was looking on from her window above the store, just about able to make out the shadow of her son and her dearest girls under the tree. They were all illuminated by the wealth of candles she'd had the good sense to provide Richard with, not even so much as an hour earlier. Once the chapter of the book was completed, Gracie ushered Primrose off to bed, and she obliged without complaint (such was her tiredness from all the digging). Before she left, however, Primrose kissed her mother, gave her a small hug and told her that she loved her. She then turned to Mr Halfpenny and did the same... Richard managed to find his voice somewhere in the swell of his emotions. 'I love you too, my darling girl.' As he spoke, Gracie placed her hand in his and held it tightly. Gracie and Richard watched Primrose disappear into the house and then sat quietly for a moment before Richard ventured. 'You must be frozen.'

Gracie whispered in reply, 'Quite the opposite...' before making her way to her feet and helping Richard to do the same. As she passed him his walking stick, she continued, 'We should blow out the candles, in case we get into trouble with the warden.'

'Most of them have burned themselves out. Couldn't we leave the rest to do the same?'

Gracie had spotted the figure of Mrs Halfpenny sometime earlier, gingerly peering down from her window above the store, so she was eager to extinguish all the flames that illuminated Richard and herself. She whispered to Richard as she subtly gestured towards the first-floor window of the store, 'It's not just the warden I'm worried about!' Richard was amused by his mother and impressed by Gracie's sterling observation. The couple parted so they could quickly extinguish the potentially incriminating flames before meeting again under the cover of darkness, by the apple tree. As Gracie returned, Richard was holding a gift, outstretched, ready for her to open. 'But you've already given me a gift! The tree is so beautiful.'

'I made you a promise last year – do you remember...?'

'You promised to buy me more ink.'

Richard hesitated. 'It's up to you what you do with it. It must be your decision.' Richard was standing before Gracie with the neatly wrapped gift in his hand.

Gracie took the pretty parcel and looked at it with painful confusion before putting it in her pocket and exclaiming with hushed desperation, 'But I don't know what to do. It's impossible. It's just impossible.'

Richard was at his wits end. The months and months of harbouring his love, then the madness at the back of the store in June, the fishing trip, the months that had followed...living for every second he might share with Gracie. The sheer agony of it all was simply too much to bear. Without thinking, he took a breath and spilled out, 'I am so hopelessly in love with you, Gracie.' As the words fell from Richard's mouth, he felt a rush of release. 'I spend every moment of every day thinking about you, and at night I can't sleep because I can't hold you. And God knows I understand it's impossible for you, Gracie, I swear I understand – but please, you must realise that it's impossible for me too.' Richard shook his head in despair. 'I have no say in all of this. I'm powerless. I can't tell you what to do... I can't even touch you.' He reached out a trembling hand towards Gracie's delicate face but dare not lay a finger on her beautiful, lightly freckled cheek. He paused and frowned, then he slowly withdrew his hand... He took a moment to catch his breath and then continued, with a look of desperate longing, 'I can't kiss you. I can't hold you in my arms or...' Gracie placed her finger on Richard's exasperated lips, and he fell silent. With Gracie's touch, the turbulent undercurrent that had raged between them for so long suddenly quelled and was replaced by a force drawing them together until, at last, there was nothing between them at all. Slowly, taking hold of Richard's face, Gracie looked deep into his hazel eyes, assuring him of her complete surrender. They both held fast, gazing into one another's eyes, before Gracie raised herself up on to her tiptoes and trusted her lips to Richard. In the midst of the lingering kiss that followed, they were safe. They were home.

When at last the couple parted, Richard uttered in disbelief, 'What a way to catch the flu!'

****

17th November 1943

Richard,

For years I have written to Edward, and for years the letters I have so carefully penned have collected on the mantelpiece. Not one line has ever been heard. Not one sentiment has ever been appreciated; not even so much as a single word has ever been read or pondered upon... No comfort has been given to another living soul by my writing: no reassurance received, or anguish quelled, and yet I have continued to write. On reflection, I believe I have done so simply to hear myself think.

Tonight is different. I am writing because I want so very much to be heard, at last, by someone other than myself: to be heard by you. So much of me wishes that you were here by my side, Richard – that we could be together tonight and hold one another until morning. If you were here, I could tell you how I love your smile and how your touch leaves me breathless; I would kiss you, if you were here – that is what I would do.

But you are not here, my darling. You cannot be here, not tonight, not tomorrow night or perhaps ever...Understand that despite your feelings for me, regardless of our foolishness, our holding of hands and stealing of kisses in the dark, that I am not a free woman. I am married to Edward, albeit perhaps to the memory of him, but I am married nonetheless – until I know for certain otherwise. I have long since suspected that Edward is a terribly long, long way away from home – far removed from our world and waiting for my prayers to soothe him in the next. The truth is, however, I do not know. Our affair has no future, Richard. All the while Edward is missing, all the while this terrible war rages on, we cannot be together because tomorrow Edward might just return. If that were to happen, I would somehow have to learn to be his wife again and, in doing so, I would have to learn to forget my feelings for you... Everything is so hopelessly impossible.

Help me, Richard. I beg of you please to help me. Help me to find out what has become of Edward, to find some peace at last, even if it means you running the risk of finding him. Say you will do it for Primrose and for me. We have no future, my darling man, until we can resolve my past. No matter how much I may want to give my heart to you, it is not yet mine to give away – it is still my husband's. You must also understand, no matter how much Primrose loves you (and I do not deny that she does) she loved her father more. I am so sorry if that is difficult for you to hear, but it is true. Primrose may not remember the relationship she shared with her father, but I do, and I owe it to her to be certain he is gone forever before I allow her to move on. I owe myself much the same certainty for much the same reason.

Edward was serving with The Queen Victoria's Rifles, and he left home on the 21st May 1940. I enclose all the information I have received from the records office, which is precious little I am afraid. I trust you implicitly, Richard, and so I place our fate firmly and safely in your strong and capable hands.

Thank you for loving me and for loving Bill and Primrose as though they were your own. Thank you for the apple tree and for all the time you must have spent planting it. Thank you for all the candles and ribbons and bunting... I will never forget this evening. You made such an effort to make my birthday a memorable one; believe me when I say, I will never forget a moment...

I trust you will understand that we should not be alone in one another's company until all the matters that concern us are resolved. I know that I cannot trust myself in your presence, such is my unquestionable desire for every glorious part of you. Be patient with me, my love. Have faith and wait for me, and I promise to be worth every moment of the waiting.

Thank you for the ink. I hope you believe I have used it wisely...
Gracie x

18
Roll out the barrel

The shop was uncommonly busy: it was the week before Christmas and the eve of the parish council's annual party. Consequently, the haberdashery was a blur of women with threads, elastic, buttons, needles, pins and zips. The hustle and bustle of it all was wonderful, and Gracie was glad to have been enlisted to help with the unexpected clamour for glamour. The chatter about ingenious fixes to old frocks and adornments to new ones (that were affordable if a little plain) seemed infectious. Ideas were flying around like snowflakes whipped up in a storm, and Gracie was in her element. There was nothing more satisfying than seeing the shop alive with customers. She revelled in its success, knowing that it was thriving – despite the war – in part because of her efforts. The shop was at the heart of the community, Gracie was at the heart of the shop, and that was a source of great pride.

'Gracie! Gracie...' A timid voice somehow cut through the chaos, and Gracie turned to see Mary. Her tiny frame was supported by teetering tiptoes as she waved some lemon ribbon above her head.

Gracie excused herself, wove through the bustling throng, and made her way over to her dear friend. 'It's so lovely to see you.'

The friends briefly and lightly embraced before Mary hurriedly explained, 'I've only got fifteen minutes left of lunch, and then I have to be back, or Sister will have my guts for garters.' Mary was obviously in a hurry, but, moreover, she was excited about something, and Gracie wanted to know what. 'Can you pretty please put this ribbon by for me? I'll give you the money tonight. I could pop into yours after tea and give it to you then, if that's all right?'

Keen to know the full story, Gracie wasted no time in extending her hospitality. 'Why not come to ours for your tea? Primrose would love to see you. It's only brisket and mash but you're welcome.'

'A night away from mother! You're on. See you at five thirty-ish then?'

'Perfect.'

With that, Gracie took the ribbon and rolled it around her hand as Mary hastened, as fast as the melee would allow, towards the shop's grand front doors. As Mary reached the door, Bill took pride in opening it for her and wishing her a good day before closing it again and gently rubbing the brass handle with his soft polishing cloth. Richard happened by and smiled at Bill. 'Good job, Bill. The storefront looks perfect. The decorations are just right and you, young man, look very smart indeed. You make your Aunty Gracie and I extremely proud.'

'Thank you, Uncle Richard.' As Bill spoke, he addressed the ground, but he smiled and went a little red, so Richard knew he was happy.

'Keep up the good work! I'm off to help Aunty Gracie...she looks a little snowed under.' Richard gently and calmly placed his hand on Bill's shoulder and gave it a congratulatory squeeze before heading off towards the storm that was haberdashery. 'Need a hand?'

'What do you think?' The following few hours flew by in a whirl. Gracie and Richard knew their parts well: they danced around customers, sidestepped one another gracefully and completed sale after sale.

With every brush past one another, however, the tension grew. With every glance, the need to be together intensified. They were consumed with illicit thoughts. An energy was building between them: their hearts were pounding, and their skin was hot and flushed. At last, the final customers were served and, together with the rest of the staff on the shop floor, Gracie and Richard went about the business of tidying their stations. Gracie did her jobs as slowly as she could, trying to look busy whilst doing nothing in particular. Eventually, all the staff bid their goodnights and peeled away home leaving her alone with Richard. As Richard rolled down the large blinds of the shop's impressive façade and finally shut out the world, Gracie moved to the Christmas tree at the far end of the store. She waited with her heart racing. Christmas music played softly in the background as Richard turned and walked back up the store towards the freshly cut, elegantly dressed tree – and Gracie. Because most of the store's lights had been switched off by diligent employees, a soft hue fell on the store which caught the Christmas decorations and ornaments beautifully. They, in turn, caught Gracie's skin, lighting her eyes and her smile – creating a vision for Richard to drink in as he slowly drew nearer. Gracie and Richard had yearned for hours to be together, to hold one another, to spend a moment without the world looking on and casting judgement on their unlikely affair. Now, thanks to a mixture of Christmas shopping fever and gently coaxed fate, they had their chance...

Richard tentatively approached Gracie. 'May I have this dance?' he ventured with a smile. Gracie's heart calmed, and she felt herself falling further for the handsome, gentle and quietly remarkable man before her.

'I thought you'd never ask.'

Gracie returned Richard's smile, and then took his stick and leant it against the haberdashery counter. She then slowly gathered herself and stood before him. Taking Gracie into his arms, Richard felt strong. As Gracie rested one hand lightly on his shoulder, and the other into his waiting palm, he knew without reserve she was lost to him. Together, they slowly began to waltz. It was not as Gracie had imagined dancing with Richard might be – it was quite the contrary. He danced with more ease than he walked. The rhythm of the music carried him away, and with Gracie in his arms he moved confidently around the unlikely dance floor; he pulled Gracie a little closer to him, and she, in turn, rested her head on his chest, closing her eyes. She allowed herself to be lost in the arms of the man she felt safe with – the man she was, undoubtedly, falling in love with. As the song ended, a moment of stillness settled between them. Neither could bear to let go; neither wanted it to end. Richard, however, remembering Gracie's words in the letter she had penned on the evening of her birthday, eventually did the proper thing and eased away from his hold, gently kissing Gracie's hand, leaving her aching for more. Gracie could not bear the pain. Her heart was crushed. Richard looked lovingly into her longing eyes and shared his thoughts.

'I don't imagine we'll be dancing together at the Christmas party, so I'll remember this dance when I see you across the room tomorrow, and it will make me smile.' Richard then broke away and collected his stick before continuing, gently reassuring Gracie: 'I've been digging, asking questions, calling in a few favours from chaps I used to know... I haven't come up with anything concrete yet, but not a day goes by, Gracie...'

'...I know. I trust you. I know you're doing your best.' Gracie's heart was growing heavier. She could not bear the reality a moment longer. She just wanted Richard to hold her.

'Lots of this stuff is secret, you see – there's red tape, Whitehall and the bog-standard official statements to negotiate. Then there's the fact that I'm not a relation – that throws up problems too.'

'If you need me to do anything...' Gracie just wanted to kiss Richard. It was all she could think about.

'No, not at all. I've stumbled over that hurdle now. A good friend of mine is seeing what he can uncover for me. He's a decent chap, and I trust him.'

Gracie could stand it no more. She went to Richard and held his hand, then leaned in and kissed his cheek. 'Thank you. You know, you mean the world to me.'

'Do I?' Richard looked for reassurance, and Gracie gave it to him by kissing his unprepared lips.

'The world...' To be sure Richard was in no doubt, Gracie kissed him again. It was a kiss that should have led to much more – a kiss that would have moved them to the bedroom, if only they had one. Reluctantly, they eventually broke away from one another, yearning all the while to be closer still. Their parting was done in silence. They were both breathless, both speechless…and even if they could have spoken, they would never have found the words to say.

****

'Mum, you're late! Was the store really, really busy? Did you end up on the shop floor again? Was it fun?' Primrose was excited. It had been her last day at school before the Christmas holidays (reason enough to be joyful), and she loved the idea of her mum working on the shop floor; it was so glamorous. It made her all fidgety.

'You'll get a stitch or hiccups or both if you keep all on like that. Take a breath, child, and stand still. You look like you've got ants in your pants! Now listen to your mother for a minute…' Gracie purposely paused to make sure she had Primrose's full attention, and for dramatic effect, as she knew Primrose was going to be thrilled by her announcement. 'I need your help because your Aunty Mary is coming over for her tea.'

'Aaahhhh… This is the best day ever.' Primrose was struck all at once by a mixture of growing excitement, pride and urgency. 'Of all the days that you're late home! I'll get the best linen for the table and the best crockery, and I'll quickly lay it before I get changed. Can I wear my Sunday best, please, Mum, can I, can I?' Primrose's enthusiasm was infectious.

'Why not! And I'll get out the best glasses. Let's have some fun.'

It was peculiar, but in those few moments, from when Gracie had come home to when they both set about their jobs, Primrose grew up a little. They both felt it — it was oddly tangible. Happily, however, for both parties, the little step towards adulthood was devoid of any pangs of regret or longing for days gone by. It was a glimpse into the future, and it was fun! By the time Mary arrived, the table was perfectly set. The brisket was prepared, and both Primrose and Gracie looked beautiful, if a little flushed from their hurried efforts.

'This looks wonderful, Primrose, and so do you. You're growing up on me! I won't have it. You must stop at once,' Mary joked, but Primrose thought it was fabulous to be seen as a young lady. The evening sailed by and the three 'ladies' enjoyed their meal and the sweets that Mary provided (unearthed from her cardigan pockets) before Primrose was demoted to her original rank of little girl and packed off to bed. Primrose was trusted, however, to clean her own hands, face and teeth — so she consoled herself that perhaps, all was not lost.

Conversation soon turned to the upcoming Christmas party, and Gracie questioned Mary about the yard and a half of two-and-a-quarter-inch lemon ribbon she had been so eager to secure earlier that day. Mary was coy at first, but, after a glass and a half of sherry, she soon loosened up. She began to confide in Gracie about her suspicions that her beau might be thinking about popping a certain question! Gracie was spellbound; she was transported back to the days before the war when the girls would get together and listen to Mary swoon about her dear Thomas. Perhaps it was the sherry, perhaps it was time or even the blasted war itself, but Gracie did not flinch once at the idea of Mary moving on with her life. She knew, more than most, that love was love and ought to be grabbed. She wasn't counting the months or years since

Thomas had died, nor the time since the good doctor appeared, to try and work out if this was an "appropriate" love affair. Who could waste time on that sort of nonsense these days? Gracie mustered all her strength to stop herself from telling Mary about Richard. So much of her wanted to share the excitement with her friend, but she knew she must not. Mary's affair was legitimate; hers was not, and she had to remember that. Not that it was an affair. Not a *proper* one... Not yet, at least.

The two women did not avoid speaking Thomas' name; he was as much a part of the conversation as anyone. They reflected happily, imagining how thrilled he would be that his girl had done so well. 'I'll always be Thomas' girl, you know that, Gracie – but it's time for me to move on. It's time for me to grow up... I'm ready to be someone else's *woman* now.' There was a gleam in Mary's eye.

'Mary! You haven't...have you?' Gracie was beaming from ear to ear.

Mary's defence came incredulously and with a tongue planted well and truly in her cheek, 'Oh, that you could suggest such a thing, Gracie Chatley!' Gracie probed no more but suspected plenty!

****

The party was such a to-do... Punch flowed, the Reverend was escorted back to the vicarage at a little after nine (very much the worse for wear), and all the ladies looked spectacular. The evening surpassed everyone's expectations, and Mary, with her handsome Doctor Applebee by her side, was the toast of the night. Mary was a picture: her dress was black with yellow piping, and the

196

ribbon she had bought cinched her tiny waist to highlight her elegant frame. Doctor Applebee was a tall, fresh-faced, handsome, young man with fair hair and, thanks to nerves, two left feet. He wore a black dinner jacket, a broad smile and his pride at having Mary on his arm like a badge of honour. Together, Mary and James shone through the night and lit up everyone's hearts with joy.

A handful of local servicemen were on leave for Christmas, and they danced with their girls in the hope that morning would never come. The war had not ruined everything: it had not ruined Christmas, and it had not ruined love. In the middle of the festivities, Richard, who was serving behind the makeshift bar, caught Gracie's eye across the room. They fixed their gaze on one another before they smiled and danced. They may not have moved from where they stood, but they danced together, nevertheless. In their imagination, they kissed under the mistletoe and held hands until dawn. *'One day'*, thought Richard on his walk home in solitude, *'One day, we will all meet at that place again... I will dance with Gracie, and everyone will look and smile and be happy for us – just as they were happy for Mary.'*

****

8th December 1943

My darling James,

I cannot sleep. I may never be able to sleep again...

I am dizzy with a heady mix of excitement and nerves. The thought of you arriving tomorrow to formally ask my mother for my hand in marriage makes me shake from

197

head to toe. I cannot believe any of this is true. To think that I once lay in this very bed and cried myself to sleep night after heart-breaking night...when now, here I am unable to sleep for happiness.

I will make you such a fine wife. I will keep a beautiful home, and I'll cook you the finest meals rations will allow. I'll launder your clothes, darn your socks and listen to your troubles. I'll love you too, whenever you need me; I'll be yours for the taking. I'll love you forever and make you the proudest man. We'll have children, as many as you wish... I have always imagined five or six, but if you imagine more, then I'm sure I will manage with you by my side. I picture boys that are handsome and strong because they take after you, and girls who are gentle and mild, who sit on your knee and listen to your stories before bed.

It will be my life's work to make you happy, just as you have made me the happiest woman alive tonight.

I love you, Doctor James Applebee,

Until tomorrow,

Your very own, Mary x

19
Careless talk costs lives

May's blossom was raining down on the Green by the cricket pavilion, and a mix of white and pink petals showered Primrose as she played in the warmth of the afternoon sun. Together with the delicately entwined flowers in her hair, the falling blossom adorned the ten-year-old's long, ebony locks until it inevitably became the unspoken envy of her friends. May Day was an excuse for Primrose to practise cartwheels instead of times tables, and, although she may not have known it, she was having the time of her life.

The children were waiting to perform their maypole dance, the highlight of the afternoon's festivities, for which they had been practising in earnest for weeks. All the children had a position, a ribbon and very real fear of going wrong to contend with. Unsurprisingly then, as the performance neared, the butterflies in Primrose's tummy began a dance all of their own. At long last, and mid-cartwheel, the call to begin the annual dance ritual rang out from the megaphone in Mrs Bremner's hand. 'Would the children kindly take their places around the maypole now, please. If the Morris Dancers would also gather on the bandstand with their instruments to accompany the children...' There was a sudden rush of activity as everyone jostled for position: children to their ribbons; Morris men (dressed in white with handkerchiefs waving in the breeze) to their bells, sticks and accordions; parents to their vantage points and teachers to their posts. 'Ladies and gentlemen,' came the voice over the megaphone. There was a pause and then an irritated repeat, 'Ladies and gentlemen!' A hush began to fall. 'Daisy Patterson, you are in the wrong place, child. How many times? Swap with Arthur, quickly, quickly...' Poor Daisy, flummoxed and embarrassed, tripped over her own feet as she made her way to a confused Arthur. He reluctantly gave up his position but, alas, not his ribbon. 'Arthur!' bleated the voice through the amplifier. 'Arthur, give Daisy your ribbon!' Arthur promptly did as he was told, released his ribbon and took Daisy's in return. Finally, the children were in the correct places and ready to begin. Mrs Bremner gave the nod to the musicians, who dutifully set to work, and so the nervous dancers began.

'Trust my Arthur to be in the wrong bloomin' place! Would you look at the state of him too...grass stains everywhere. Your Primrose looks a picture, my love.' Flo was cringing with embarrassment and peeking out from behind Gracie's shoulder to watch proceedings.

'He looks a bit muddled, Flo. Bless his heart. He's concentrating so hard on the skipping that he can't remember where he's meant to be going...!' Gracie was biting her cheeks so as not to laugh, as were the rest of the audience.

'Oh, Gracie, this is awful. He's useless! Just like his father – two left feet!' Flo shook her head, covered her smiling mouth and raised her eyebrows as the music reached its crescendo and all the ribbons were beginning to weave, except Arthur's.

'I thought your Charlie was a good dancer,' recalled Gracie as Arthur bumped into an unsuspecting (and soon to be furious) Audrey Middleton.

'He was fair enough, I s'pose, after years of me getting squashed toes, like that poor lass Arthur's just ploughed into! Nowhere near as good as your Edward, mind.'

As the dance ended and the applause swelled, the children peeled away from the brightly adorned maypole and back to their parents, to be welcomed with open arms and warm smiles. Arthur, conversely, was greeted with a stern glower and a clip around the ear. Gracie went through the motions of congratulating Primrose, but all the while she was consumed with thoughts of dancing with Edward. She was trying to remember how it felt...how it felt to be held by her husband. However, all she could feel was Richard. No matter how hard she tried, she could only feel Richard's hand in hers. An unexpected, vile anger began to rise up from within her. Gracie was furious. She wanted to remember dancing with her husband. How could Richard have taken that away from her? Gracie's heart raced, and she began to panic. She suddenly turned cold and clammy; she felt sick with guilt and shaken by rage. Richard had somehow played with her mind; he had wooed her, kissed her and danced with her when he had no right. Had he turned her against her husband without her realising what he was doing? Had she fallen under some sort of illicit spell? Did Richard really love her, or was he playing with her – only interested in one thing? In the months that had passed, he had offered no news on Edward's disappearance. He had kept her waiting. Had he withheld information, or, worse still, was he using his friends and his influence to fabricate lies or hide the truth?

'Did you like it, Mummy? Did you see my toes? I was really pointing them for you.' Primrose was out of breath and gazing at her mother expectantly.

201

Gracie was shaken from her racing thoughts and asserted, 'You dance beautifully, just like your father – just like him.' Primrose was taken aback; her mother had not uttered her father's name in months. She was unsettled and did not know how to respond.

Luckily for Primrose, but unfortunately for him, an unsuspecting Richard came over to congratulate the radiant dancer. 'The most beautiful dancer by far.' Richard beamed and presented Primrose with a small posy of spring blooms that he had cheekily pinched from the shop's display. 'You were as pretty as a picture, just like your mother.' Richard was uncommonly relaxed and comfortable. It was unusual for him to feel so liberated in Gracie's company, but the sun was shining, the mood was bright, and love was in the air; the resulting, potent combination lulled Richard into a dangerously false sense of security.

Gracie was cutting. She tested Richard to his limits. 'She danced like her father. She's the spitting image of him. She's kind, thoughtful and generous like him. She's patient like him – and loving too. You couldn't begin to understand how alike they are. They're like two peas in a pod.' Gracie was engulfed with guilt, regret and angst. She was frantically trying to recall every quality her husband possessed in a bid to ease her guilt at forgetting his touch. She hastily continued, clinging to Primrose like a shield for protection. 'She's irreplaceable...'

Richard was stricken – crushed by Gracie's torrent of ill-thought ramblings. '...Just like her father?' Richard granted himself the dignity of striking his own final blow before throwing in the towel and bravely smiling at Primrose. 'I'd better get back to work before I get into trouble with Mrs Halfpenny. Be sure to pop those flowers in some water when you get home.' He turned, lowered his head and made his way silently through the bustling crowd. He was hurt deeply, perhaps irrevocably. He had no clue why Gracie had been so vile towards him, but he supposed the cause did not matter. The effect was clear enough.

Gracie resisted every fibre in her being not to run after Richard and beg for his forgiveness. She stood, instead, and watched him walk away, conceding that it was no less than she deserved. She was an unfaithful wife, a tempestuous excuse of a mistress and a selfish fool. She was not worthy of Richard's forgiveness or of Edward's memory. Perhaps, then, she had better concentrate on being a fit mother – that was the least she should do. She took a breath, defied her welling tears and hugged her daughter before taking her to the refreshment tent for some bitter-sweet lemonade.

As Gracie stepped inside the airless canvas, she was greeted by Mary and her wide-eyed fiancé, and by Flo and the boys. Mary casually enquired as she looked beyond the tent's drawn back opening, 'Where's your Mr Halfpenny off to so early?'

Gracie bit back. 'He's not *my* Mr Halfpenny.'

Flo backed Mary... 'He looks out for you and your Primrose, and Mary meant no 'arm did she! So step down off that horse of yours.' Gracie felt herself blush and her heart race. 'Boys, you play nicely with Primrose now. I'm taking your Aunty Gracie for a cup of tea.' With that, Flo pointed and stared at Arthur before clipping him around the ear for good measure. She then took Gracie's arm and led her off towards the steaming urns and giant teapots. As the unwitting Arthur rubbed his stinging ear, Dr Applebee tapped William on the shoulder and declared – *It* – before running out of the tent, hotly pursued by Mary, William, Arthur and Primrose.

The bunting in the stifling tent was motionless; the air was heavy with the scent of cakes, jams and wilting grass; the clatter of teacups and spoons provided accompaniment to the various conversations being held about the place, and smiling people bustled around cotton and lace-draped tables to enjoy one another's company. Gracie sat alone on a small table waiting for Flo who had joined the busy queue for tea. As she waited, she found herself overawed by everyone's happiness. She could sense the joy all around her, but it was no use – she could secure none for her own keeping. Eventually, Flo returned. 'Chaos! Marjorie from the W.I. was just saying they never expected so many people to turn up. They've got poor Doris out the back with a bucket, washing up cups ten t'dozen! I said I'd give 'em a 'and in a bit. Not til I've had my say here, mind. So, drink up, shut up and listen up.' Gracie did as she was told. She had learnt over the years that it was the best way with Flo. The boys were not the only ones to be a little bit scared of her. 'What on earth is going on with you and Mr Halfpenny?' Gracie sat dumbfounded. 'Well? Come on, it's a simple enough question.'

'Nothing...' Gracie chanced.

'Nothing my eye! In my experience, a woman only gets that flustered and that inexplicably angry with a fella when she hates him or...' Flo raised both eyebrows, lowered her chin and tilted her head towards Gracie by way of intimation.

'What do you mean, flustered and rude?' Gracie opted for attack as her defence. 'Were you listening in on a private conversation?'

Flo continued in a hushed voice, '*This* is a private conversation. You were practically shouting at the poor chap in the middle of the green. I'm surprised you didn't ask to use Mrs Bremner's megaphone to finish the poor bloke off!'

Gracie covered her mouth with her hand and winced at her inappropriate outburst before rallying and accusing Flo. 'It's because of what *you* said about Edward's dancing... I couldn't remember how it felt to dance with Edward.' She took a chance and decided to confide in Flo. 'I tried to remember Edward holding me and dancing with me, but I couldn't.' She took a breath and looked down. 'But I *could* remember dancing with... Richard.'

'Marjorie and the cups can bloody well wait!'

Gracie went on to explain – in hushed, furtive tones – what had happened behind the store the previous June: the fishing trip; the meals they had shared, almost like a family, with Bill and Mrs Halfpenny; even her birthday and the dance in the store the week before Christmas. Flo was aghast. 'Almost a year this has been going on. Almost a year, and this is the first I hear of it?'

'I haven't known what to do. Besides, nothing's really been *going on*... I know I shouldn't have, but I swear it's only been the odd kiss, nothing more. I would never...not all the while Edward is...' Gracie stopped.

205

'Edward is *what*, Gracie?' Flo continued in earnest, spurred on by her memory of Richard digging in the garden in preparation for the apple tree. 'In your heart, what do you believe, after all this time? Be honest with me.'

Gracie stared at her teaspoon as she nervously stirred. She then looked Flo in the eye and rounded on her. 'What do *you* think? *You* be honest with me...' Flo was surprised to find herself on the defensive again. Should she say what she thought Gracie wanted to hear? Did she even know what that was? Should she avoid answering and turn the question back on Gracie, or should she be a friend and tell the truth, regardless of the fall out that might follow?

Given their delicately public position, Flo opted for what she hoped was the appropriate course of action. 'It's not for *me* to say what *I* think. It's what *you believe*, in your heart, Gracie. That's what counts.'

Gracie was at her wits' end. 'And what if I have no idea what to think or believe anymore?'

Flo continued to pursue Gracie. She was not going to let it go. She knew her friend needed to face herself even if she was scared half to death of what she might find. 'Do you still love Edward?'

Gracie's eyes welled. She was petrified of hearing her own voice's response. 'I, I think so...' Gracie was trembling. The thought of what question might follow suddenly struck her, and she turned white with fear. She was right to be concerned; Flo was relentless.

'And Richard?' Flo moved a little closer, subtly looking about her as she did, before continuing in a slow whisper, partly covering her lips with her hand to ensure they could not be read. 'Do you *love* Richard?'

Gracie took a breath and held it tight. She stared into her teacup before confessing in a terrified whisper, 'I think so...'

Flo sighed and thought for a moment before asserting, 'Then you have some serious thinking to do – and you owe that poor man an apology!'

****

On the whole, Gracie was relieved to have confided in Flo. She felt as though their chat over the china teacups had forced her to the crossroads she had been avoiding for far too long. As Flo made her way to help the ladies of the W.I., Gracie made her way home, safe in the knowledge that Primrose was going to spend the night with her Aunty Flo, so she was free to do her 'serious thinking'. As Gracie approached the store on her walk home, she hesitated and thought about seeking out Richard to ask for his forgiveness. After a moment's pause, however, she elected to continue on the path towards home, to her sanctuary, to think alone. Seeing Richard, she decided, would skew her thoughts and confuse the issue; she could not see Edward, after all, so it would be unfair to give Richard any advantage – given the gravity of the situation. As Gracie approached her door, she was resolute. *Her* future was in *her* hands. It was not in Richard's because he had obviously failed in his attempt to find any news of Edward. It was not in Edward's either because he was clearly not coming home to her rescue – all hope there was long gone. Only *she* could sort out this mess. What was she going to do? Was she contemplating an affair? Could it even be called that? What would it be? Who would know? What about Primrose? What about God?

Gracie went straight to the mantelpiece and took the letters she had written to Edward and quickly untied the ribbon that bound them together. She then sat in Edward's chair and held the letters close to her chest before tearing open the first one and reading it aloud to herself. She read it over and over again until she knew it off by heart. She then set it aside and opened the next. All night long, she read the letters... She read them until her eyes stung, until she blinked so slowly that her eyes did not open again, and she unwittingly fell asleep.

Edward's chair was Gracie's bed until the milkman's footsteps awoke her from her dreamless slumber. With the clink of the glass bottles on the doorstep, she rose from the chair and ran upstairs to the papers in her bedroom and feverishly began to write, even though she was hardly awake.

2ⁿᵈ May 1944

Dearest Edward,

It has been quite some time since I wrote to you last. Forgive me...

Primrose danced around the maypole yesterday, and she looked beautiful. Flo said how she danced like you. It was a harmless thing to have said, but it upset me so very much. I was heartbroken because I could not remember how it felt to dance with you; how it felt to hold your hand; to touch your face or to have your arm around me. I felt suddenly as though I had lost your memory as well as everything else, and I was angry. I spent

208

all night reading the letters I have written to you in a vain attempt to find you somewhere within me - to recapture how it felt when you first went away, when I could still feel your touch even though you were no longer here to hold me. I read until my eyes could see no more, and I fell into my dreamless sleep. I tried so hard, but it was no use. Edward, my love, your touch has left me. I fear I may never get it back.

My heart is broken. It is torn in two, and the pain is simply unimaginable. Has the memory of your touch left me because it's time for me to let you go? Or is it because I have drifted so far away that I can no longer reach you? Either way, I am lost, without a hand to guide me and, as ever, I am all alone. I need time — time to heal my broken heart, to make it whole and worthy again. Please, forgive me.

Until I am found,

Your own darling, Gracie x

With that, Gracie folded the page before her and placed it in the awaiting envelope. As the seal was set, she looked out on the beautiful May day that was gently unfolding before her and resolved to give herself until September to be found.

20
You always hurt the one you love

The relationship between Gracie and Richard rapidly dissolved into one of boss and employee. Neither one of them was able to mend the rift that had been so hastily torn between them on May Day. Cosy teas were a thing of the past, and Gracie worked as few hours as were practicable to get her jobs in the store completed. Primrose, Mrs Halfpenny and even Bill felt the tension between them, but they were too young, too wise and too uncertain respectively to say a word to either one of the stubborn pair about it. Business matters between Gracie and Richard were dealt with professionally and swiftly, and, as time went on, Gracie felt certain that Richard had lost all feelings for her; Richard, in turn, was convinced of Gracie's indifference towards him.

By the time June came, and the enormity of the D-day landings was beginning to unravel in the press, Gracie felt desperately isolated. As stories of triumph and sad losses played out on the wireless, and newspapers featured little else but news from Normandy, the war felt closer to home. Friends and neighbours inevitably received news of loved ones. In all too many cases, the news was of tragic losses. With each revelation, Gracie felt herself falling a little deeper into despair...their news somehow exacerbating her own painful state of limbo. She yearned to talk to someone – to be freed from her solitary confinement, to be heard by someone who knew her heart and understood. Flo was of no use; she just got cross with her for not clearing the air with Richard. She did not understand that Gracie didn't want to give him false hope.

In July, Richard received a dossier in the post containing all the information on Edward that had been found. It was a sizable document, bound with string, with a brief covering letter. Richard, though tempted, did not so much as glance at the first page. Instead, he gathered up the bundle and took it straight to Gracie's house. Primrose answered the door. She was delighted to see Richard, as was Richard to see her, but neither one quite knew how to greet the other. There was an awkward exchange... 'These are for Mummy,' Richard began.

'The apple tree has tiny apples on it...' Primrose wanted to take Richard's hand and lead him through the kitchen into the back garden but knew she mustn't.

Richard wanted to scoop Primrose up and hold her tightly. He wanted to tell her how much he had missed her. 'They're very important, Primrose, so make sure you give them to Mummy straight away.'

'She's just in the kitchen; I can get her for...'

'...Can't stop, I'm afraid. Must dash.' Richard nodded his regretful goodbye and headed back up the road towards the store, his heart becoming heavier and more sorrowful with every step.

Primrose watched him walking away until her mother called, 'Who was that?'

'Mr Halfpenny. He said to give you these.'

The papers were a heavy read. Night after night, Gracie battled through the documents. She checked in her dictionary for unfamiliar words and re-read countless paragraphs in a bid to make sense of the military phrases, expressions and baffling acronyms. Eventually, after weeks of reading and note-taking, she reflected on her findings:

None of Edward's battalion had returned home.

The majority were dead and identified as such.

Nearly all the remainder were prisoners of war.

The few men that were unaccounted for were classed as 'missing' and would be classified 'presumed dead' seven years from when they originally disappeared.

Gracie felt as though she had been on a long, heartbreaking journey to nowhere. She was left feeling bitterly disappointed. Edward was not certainly dead; she could not mourn. She could not move on, and so, she was still in limbo. In being disappointed, she realised (to her utter shame) that she must have, subconsciously at least, wished her husband dead.

The guilt hit hard.

Gracie disappeared into herself, leaving poor Primrose floundering in her attempts to be self-sufficient, just as she had been when her father had first disappeared... However, Primrose was older now – she was wiser too. Although she had no Mrs Pluckrose to turn to, she still had the Reverend, and he – in turn – had his angels.

It was after Sunday school (on a particularly scorching day at the end of July) that the tatty-haired, hot, flustered and flush-cheeked Primrose gathered the courage to approach the Reverend. 'Mummy's gone funny again, like before. It was a letter that did it – a letter Mr Halfpenny gave her. She's not eating, not doing anything...'

'What did the letter look like, Primrose? Was it a telegram?'

'No, it was huge! More like a book someone forgot to stick together. There were pages and pages and Mummy must have read it a hundred times over.'

The Reverend took a moment to think of who he could turn to. Who could be his angel today? 'Let's get you over to Mrs Halfpenny's for some lunch, shall we? Would you like that, Primrose?'

'I would but... I don't know if I'm allowed. I'm properly hungry though.'

'You're allowed, Primrose. I'll sort it all out. You mustn't worry – you're a good girl, and you were *right* to have told me about Mummy.'

The Reverend shepherded Primrose towards the church door and then accompanied her on the walk to the safety of the flat above the store. Mr Halfpenny was out, but both Bill and Mrs Halfpenny were home and delighted to see Primrose in their doorway. The Reverend explained their unannounced visit, 'It seems that Primrose's mummy is a little under-the-weather, and I wondered if she might join you for lunch today?'

'We'd be delighted to have her, and you too, Reverend, if you haven't a prior engagement?'

'Only with my armchair and the papers, and both can wait.'

Primrose and Bill busied themselves with a jigsaw, playing alongside one another – although not necessarily together. The pair were perfectly absorbed and happy in their chosen tasks: Primrose completing a spray of flowers whilst Bill completed the straight edges. Meanwhile, Mrs Halfpenny and Reverend Smith shared a cup of tea. 'She was brave to have told me. I've told her I'll sort it out, but I haven't the faintest clue what I'm going to do as yet. She said her mother went 'funny' when Mr Halfpenny gave her a letter. Do you know anything about it?' The Reverend was pinning his hopes on old-Mrs Halfpenny.

'Gracie and my Richard have both been acting very strangely of late. We've all been dancing on eggshells around the pair of them. They've had some sort of falling out, that's for certain.' The Reverend was encouraged that he was making way, so he prompted Mrs Halfpenny to continue and she obliged. 'Richard did have a dossier of papers the other day – military looking. They arrived, and he disappeared with them straight away. Then he came back, just as quickly, without them.'

'Will Richard be gone for long, do you think?'

Mrs Halfpenny was uncertain. 'There's no knowing how long he'll be. He's taken to disappearing for hours at a time... He's miserable. I don't know what to do with him.'

The penny dropped. 'Two lovely, young people, both miserable, both suffering...'

Mrs Halfpenny encouraged his line of thinking, '...and each one needing the other to heal their broken hearts...'

The Reverend suddenly saw everything very clearly indeed. 'This is a cruel war, Mrs Halfpenny, and not just for the boys on the front line.' Mrs Halfpenny agreed, and the tea continued to flow until the Reverend became aware of the unmistakable sound of Mr Halfpenny's heavy footsteps, punctuated by his walking stick, raising from within the stairwell. 'It sounds as though the man I need to talk to is on his way...'

As Richard walked in, he spoke before even raising his head to see who was in the room. 'Good God! It's damned stifling out there. I couldn't take another soddin' step...' Richard looked up and saw the Reverend. 'Oh goodness me, Reverend Smith! Sorry about that. I had no idea...'

The Reverend gently chuckled to himself. 'I'll assume you were just having a chat with the man upstairs as opposed to taking any names in vain... I shouldn't worry too much. I've done much worse, trust me!' Primrose jumped up and rushed over to Richard and hugged him. She felt safe because her mother was not there to scold her, and so she happily held on tightly. Richard hugged her back, feeling safe for much the same reason. The Reverend took his opportunity. 'Goodness me, Primrose, it looks as though you've been waiting to share that hug for a while. Has it been bubbling up inside of you there?'

Primrose answered freely, 'Forever and ever.'

Mr Halfpenny kissed Primrose's forehead. 'Too long. I'm so sorry, Primrose. It's complicated. Your mother and I... well, like I say, it's complicated.'

215

Mrs Halfpenny stepped in and took Primrose's hand. 'You can't just stand around here all day, Primrose, my love. We've a lunch needs preparing and these old hands of mine could do with some help, so come on.' Mrs Halfpenny called over to Bill, 'You too Billy-Boy! Up you get, and give me a hand in the kitchen, a minute.' Bill dutifully did as he was told, and, as Mrs Halfpenny disappeared with Bill and Primrose, she cautioned to the men, 'I won't be able to keep them out of your hair for long, so don't beat about the bush either of you.'

Richard invited the Reverend to join him in the seating area of the flat. The Reverend sat in the impressive wing-backed armchair whist Richard lent against the large window frame opposite. 'How can I help you, Reverend?'

The Reverend answered in muted tones so as not to be overheard by those just the other side of the wall. 'Like your mother said, there's no time to beat about the bush. I'm too old and too tired for "softly, softly", I'm afraid. So, here's how I see it...you tell me if I'm wrong or if I'm interfering or if you'd rather sort it out for yourself. I won't be offended. I'll just eat my lunch and get Primrose out of your way.' Richard was nervous but invited the Reverend to continue. 'It's easily done, you see. I've seen it time and time again, and Mrs Pluckrose (God rest her soul) warned me about all this. She told me to keep an eye out, but I'm getting on and I forget things...'

Richard was confused. 'I'm sorry, Reverend, but you've quite lost me, I'm afraid. What's "easily done"? She warned you about all of what?'

The Reverend gathered himself. 'Rambling again, aren't I? Agnes said I always rambled... Right, well, in a nutshell then…' The old man packed up his inhibitions and placed them neatly to one side. He then drew a not insubstantial breath before taking the plunge with no regard for style, only substance. 'You have fallen in love with Gracie, and I assume Gracie has fallen in love with you (which seems perfectly reasonable), but the pair of you have had some sort of fall out (that must be where the letter fits into all this), and so, all-in-all, you both feel pretty hopeless because of course it's ridiculously complicated, what with Edward still being missing.' The Reverend gasped for breath then sighed with relief before concluding, 'I think that's pretty much it, in a nutshell, as they say.'

Richard was stunned. He had no idea that a man of the cloth could be so candid and non-judgmental, and so his reply was marred by his disbelief. He stuttered dreadfully and drew breaths ever more rapidly as the heat rose from under his collar. 'To an extent, I suppose… I certainly feel very strongly toward Gracie. That is to say, I do indeed have, well, yes, as you say, umm, absolutely…but I, I fear Gracie feels somewhat indifferently towards me. As for the letter, I, I have no idea.' Richard looked out of the window and caught sight of Gracie's apple tree in her back garden, and his heart sank.

'You must know something of what the letter contained. Your mother said it looked military, and Primrose told me that after her mother had read it (countless times by all accounts), she went into herself and is now refusing to "come back".'

Richard sighed, and then woefully shared his story. 'Gracie asked me to find out about Edward: to do some digging, pull in some favours, that sort of thing, to see if we could establish the facts surrounding his disappearance. Gracie and I were quite close at that point, intimate even.' Richard suddenly remembered who he was talking to. 'Although nothing inappropriate happened between us, you understand...but I was hopeful, then. I was hopeful that Gracie was considering moving on, that perhaps the two of us, Bill and Primrose might be a real family. *If,* that was, I could establish once and for all that there was no hope of Edward's return. It turns out, however, I was a hopeless fool. It was May Day, you see, long before the paperwork turned up that Gracie made her feelings clear. She told me how irreplaceable Edward was, and, well, I've just had to accept it. Things have been frosty between us ever since, but when the papers turned up (the ones my friend had managed to gather), I took them straight to her because I owed her that. As for what was in them, I have no idea...'

The Reverend was pensive. 'Well, whatever it was, it's sent her into herself, and Primrose is suffering the consequences. I'll have to go and talk to Gracie to get to the bottom of this. Can I leave Primrose with you?' Richard did not hesitate in confirming that Primrose was always welcome. Reverend Smith continued, happy to be making progress, 'I think it's best that I get over to Gracie now, strike whilst the iron's hot and all that. Your mother's doing me some lunch, so I'll be back as soon as possible. You'll say my excuses for me, won't you?'

'Of course, and if there's anything I can do?' Richard looked forlorn.

'You could send her your love. I could tell Gracie that you send your love. I think that would help.'

Richard looked out of the window towards the apple tree as he replied, his mind replaying the evening he had shared with Gracie in the garden on her birthday, 'Send her *all* my love, would you? Wish her well for me.'

Reverend Smith agreed to Richard's request and then made his way to Gracie's. On the short walk, in the blistering heat, the Reverend had a quick chat with Mrs Pluckrose. 'And what on earth am I going to say when I get there? There's going to be tears. I know there'll be tears, and I've no clean hanky on me! The things I do for you, you old know-it-all with your angel wings...all comfy on some cloud, looking down and laughing at me, no doubt. Right, well, here we are. I'm not going in there alone, you're coming too. You can tell me what to say.' Reverend Smith knocked on the door, and, as he suspected, there was no reply. He pushed, therefore, on the latched door and gently edged in. 'Gracie, Gracie, it's me. It's Reverend Smith. Shall I get the kettle on, love?' Thank goodness, he thought. Mrs Pluckrose had got him off to a good start.

As the Reverend ventured through the house, towards the back room, Gracie stood from Edward's armchair. She was still in her nightgown, hair unkempt, face pale and thin, frame weak and crumpled. On seeing the Reverend, Gracie smiled and gently laughed before speaking with bittersweet recollection, 'Here we are again.' Gracie shrugged and offered herself up... 'Only this time we've no Mrs Pluckrose on hand to speak words of wisdom, and I'm all out of milk.'

The Reverend sighed. 'Then it's a good job I've got my flask to hand. A drop of whisky is just what I need!' The Reverend took his trusty flask from his inside jacket pocket and gave it a little shake to ensure it held the required goods. 'I'm sure that even Mrs Pluckrose, God rest her soul, would approve... So, come on, you, and indulge an old man. Join me at the kitchen table and grab a couple of glasses.'

Once oiled by his whisky, the old Reverend Smith threw caution to the wind and spoke from his heart. He told Gracie how Mrs Pluckrose had predicted that Richard would fall in love with her and how painful a dilemma it would prove to be all round... He also reassured her that Mrs Pluckrose was confident, as was he, that in the fullness of time all would be resolved; life would carry on again quite happily. The Reverend then asserted, 'It's how you deal with the here and now though, Gracie, that's what concerns me. Poor Richard is broken-hearted, Primrose is at a loss, and as for what our poor Billy must be going through... Well, that's anyone's guess.' Gracie lowered her head, suddenly aware of her self-indulgence. 'You need to talk to Richard, not necessarily today or tomorrow but soon, my love. You need to build a bridge and ask for his forgiveness because (as far as I can see) he's done no wrong. But you've seen fit to punish him...and for what?' The Reverend made sure he'd collected Gracie's gaze, and he held it tightly before venturing, 'Loving you?' A pause followed to allow Gracie the time to digest the truth. 'As far as I can see, Richard's been the perfect gentleman in all of this. The poor man didn't plan on falling in love with you, Gracie, and I'd wager that you've been no angel in all this...' The Reverend smiled as Gracie blushed.

'You're right. I know you're right, but I need to get my head straight before I talk to Richard or else, I'll blurt out some nonsense, and I'll make such a fool of myself.'

The Reverend did not hesitate. 'You've made Richard feel a fool for long enough. Why not join him and be fools together?'

'The fact of the matter, Reverend, is that Richard has had enough of me. I've driven the poor man to despair. I accept that I owe him an apology, of course I do. There's no guarantee that he'll accept it, obviously, and even if he does, things between us could never be how they used to be...'

Reverend Smith smiled knowingly. 'That reminds me, honestly I'd forget my head if it wasn't screwed on! Richard sends you his love. No, let me get this right, he sends you *all* his love and wishes you well.'

The Reverend raised an eyebrow towards Gracie, who stifled a smile before taking a hearty breath...but as the breath was let go, she was compelled to offer up her obvious dilemma... 'And Edward? What about Edward in all this, have you forgotten about him?'

The Reverend did not falter. 'It seems to me that perhaps *you* might have, Gracie, but, no, I have not...' The Reverend decided to speak from his heart the words he believed Mrs Pluckrose had wanted to say before she had passed away. 'My darling girl, you of all people know Edward. You must know that if he were alive, he'd have got word to you; if he were a prisoner you'd have been told; if he were lost, he'd have been found by now; there is no logical explanation for such a long disappearance, except for one...' The Reverend took hold of Gracie's hands, as he began to spell out the truth as he and Mrs Pluckrose saw it. 'You don't need a piece of paper from a man in an office, a man who knows less about your husband than you, to tell you that Edward has gone, Gracie... The formality of time passing by to make a death official is nothing but manmade, bureaucratic nonsense. It's a hollow, preposterous gesture dreamt up by men in suits to fulfil their own ridiculous notions of correctness.' The Reverend, caught quite unaware by his own outburst and believing it to have been gifted to him by Mrs Pluckrose, took a short breath before continuing in his own humble words, 'Listen to your heart, child, not to a stranger sitting poised at a desk with a rubber stamp waiting for the years to pass. What could he possibly know that you don't already know in your heart?' The Reverend squeezed Gracie's hand to reiterate his final point. 'God decides when a man leaves this earth, Gracie…no one else.' He offered his arms out to Gracie, and she fell happily into their safety. 'If Richard wants to love you and you love Richard, look after one another and wait patiently until the silly man in the office stamps his wretched piece of paper.' With her beloved, steadfast Reverend Smith's arms around her, Gracie felt as though she were a child, wrapped in her father's arms. Everything was magically better and nothing more needed to be said.

The Reverend promised to return Primrose to Gracie after Sunday lunch, and he suggested that she clean herself and the house up before he returned. Gracie agreed, and, as soon as the Reverend left, she set to work. She started her chores in the kitchen and soon realised the Reverend had forgotten his ornate, silver whisky caddy. She picked up the half-empty canister and, as she took a cheeky nip, she pondered what Mrs Pluckrose must have seen in Richard and her that she had not.

Once the house was clean and tidy, and Gracie herself was feeling more ordered (and certainly looking more respectable), she ambled out into the garden and settled down by her beloved apple tree. To her amazement and with thanks to the fair weather, she spied a ripe Early Worcester ready for the taking. It felt as though it was a gift from her mother. With hope in her heart that she was being looked after by both her mother and the apparently prophetic Mrs Pluckrose, Gracie plucked the fruit from the tree and took a moment's pause. As the fruit filled her hand, she became aware of a song. It was coming from a neighbour's wireless, carried through the air with ease thanks to the terraces' open doors and windows. The song filled her heart just as surely as the apple filled her palm. Without a second thought, she hastened to action, polishing the apple on her sleeve as she ran indoors, up to her bedroom. She sat at her dressing table and placed the apple by her tarnished mirror. She took out one of the notelets, bought by Primrose for special occasions, and then her beautiful pen. With the song still filling the air, and the whisky warming her heart, she quickly wrote down the words that had moved her so.

Richard,

> *'You always hurt the one you love,*
> *The one you shouldn't hurt at all.*
> *You always take the sweetest rose,*
> *And crush it till the petals fall.*
> *You always break the kindest heart,*
> *With a hasty word you can't recall.*
> *So, if I broke your heart last night,*
> *It's because I love you most of all.'*

I'm so sorry to have hurt you. Please find it in your heart to forgive my selfishness and trust, if you can, that as friends we will survive this dreadful war. We'll be all the stronger for it too when at last we emerge, together, on the other side. Thanks to the Reverend, I now understand that, in the fullness of time (if we are patient and look after one another), we will one day be content and where we are supposed to be.

Enjoy the apple, the first of many for years to come, I hope!

Your dearest, Gracie x

As Gracie lowered her pen, the door was lightly rapped. She hastily folded the page, and collected her apple, all set to give both to the Reverend. She hoped he would pass them to Richard, by way of a peace offering. Gracie positively skipped down the stairs, such was her anticipation at seeing Primrose and the Reverend, and so when she threw open the door, the resulting shock knocked her sideways...

21
We'll meet again...

'Hello, Gracie, my love. Long time no see.'

Gracie stood aghast. Before her (although almost unrecognizable: a whisper of his former self) was Charlie Webb. He was desperately, no, *painfully* thin – distorted and somehow twisted. 'Are you gonna invite me in, girl, or just stand there?'

'But I've run out of milk! Will whisky do?'

Charlie had escaped. It was all quite unbelievable... Gracie had read similar stories in the papers (stories she had deliberately kept from Flo and her over-active imagination), but there was no denying it – this was not her imagination – this was Charlie. It transpired that he had successfully escaped the horrors of the camp. He'd negotiated (with a few friends) huge, unfathomable swathes of Europe, before miraculously making it home, safely to Britain. Gracie listened earnestly as Charlie recalled the escape and the planning that had been involved. He explained the frightening near misses where recapture had only just been averted. Gracie thought it would make for a smashing film at the pictures. She would go and watch it with the girls. She was put in mind of Flo and suddenly blurted, 'Good Lord! Does Flo know you're back?'

Charlie laughed. 'Of course she does, you dozy mare... She'd have had me guts for garters if I'd come here before seeing her and the boys! I got home late last night. I think she's still in shock 'cos she's hardly said a word, and there's been no sign of me double egg, gammon and chips!' Gracie laughed, amused at the idea of Flo being speechless. 'I didn't want no fuss though, Gracie. Seriously, it's not as though I'm a returning hero from battle or anything. I'm more of a lucky stow-away, really...' Gracie felt the mood change. Charlie became tense and awkward. It was clear he was building up to something. 'It was Flo said I should call round. She'd have come too if it weren't for the boys. Arthur's got a fever see, and William's off colour too now, or else...'

Gracie was impatient. 'Why did Flo say you should call? It's to do with Edward, isn't it? Tell me, Charlie. Dear God, if you know something...' Gracie suddenly felt lightheaded. It was the shock, she supposed – combined with the whisky.

Charlie drew her a chair and helped her to sit at the table before getting her a glass of water. He continued slowly and deliberately, 'Flo told me you'd been sent a telegram, about the same time as she got hers, telling you that Edward was missing?' Charlie wanted to make sure he'd got everything right, that Flo had not been muddled or confused about events...

'That's right. We all found out on the same day. You and Edward were missing, and poor, young Thomas was dead. Then a few weeks later, we got news that you were a prisoner of war. We haven't heard any more about Edward. Nothing – not a word since that first day.'

Charlie had known all along that this day would come, that one day (if he survived the war) he would have to face Gracie and Mary and explain what had happened. Charlie had rehearsed the encounters many times over, but, despite his hours of practise, he was still horribly under-prepared. 'We'd been dug in for days. We had no food left and water was like liquid gold. We were under-resourced, overwhelmed, and we all knew it was hopeless... We must have been outnumbered ten to one – at least that's how it felt. They had tanks and heavy shells; we had pistols and not enough ammunition.' Gracie hung on Charlie's every word as he described how they'd come under attack and how young Thomas, half out of his mind with hunger, suddenly, without warning, ran out into the battle ground without any cover, his gun blazing up towards the sky... 'It was suicide, Gracie. Edward was screaming out after Thomas, but it was no use. The poor lad had lost his mind...' Charlie reflected before continuing, '...or else, he was the only one left with a mind of his own, and he was going to end it all on his terms and no one else's. I guess we'll never know, but either way it was bad, Gracie. Edward and I both saw it, and it was really bad...' There was a chilling silence.

Eventually, Gracie dared to ask, '...and Edward? What happened to him?' Gracie's hands were clasped and resting on the kitchen table.

Charlie slowly sat down on the chair opposite Gracie and purposefully placed his hands over hers. He started out as he had always practiced, 'Edward was a hero...'

Charlie went on to explain how Edward blamed himself for Thomas' death. Apparently, Edward had felt guilty and had replayed the events all night long, wishing he'd done something differently – wishing he'd grabbed Thomas and pulled him down. 'I told him, there was nothing he could have done. If he'd run out after him, he'd have been a goner too, but he was having none of it. When he eventually fell asleep, I'll be honest with ya, Gracie, I was glad of the peace.' Charlie continued with his tale, describing how (when Edward drifted off to sleep) he lit up a crafty fag to calm his nerves, when all of a sudden, all hell had let loose. Charlie explained that heavy shells had started raining down just across from where he and Edward had bedded down. One of the shells struck a small barn opposite, where some of the others in the battalion had taken refuge for the night. 'I put my head down, Gracie, and prayed those shells would leave me alone, but Edward (suddenly very soddin' awake) grabbed me and told me to run. So, I got up and started to run, just like my Flo had said, "in the opposite direction", away from the shellin'. Your Edward, though…he ran straight towards the barn, to help the other men. I threw myself down behind a pile of old rubble and screamed at him. It was no use.' Charlie's eyes took on a distant look as he slowly relived the moment. 'Edward was there, right in front of me, and I looked at him – looked him straight in the eye. He looked back, just for a second, as if to say, "I'm not gonna sit and watch another of my boys go down without a fight" and then…' Charlie paused and returned his eyes to Gracie, fixing his gaze on hers in an act of duty as he recalled the final, exact detail. 'Then there was this blast. One God almighty blast, and that was it. He was gone. In the blink of an eye, Gracie, it was over. It was as quick as that.' Gracie stared at Charlie. She was not upset or angry or sad; she was numb with disbelief that, after all the years of waiting, she was hearing at last what had become of her husband. Charlie continued with his story, 'The next thing I knew, there was Nazis everywhere, and our blokes were emerging left, right and centre with their hands up. They weren't being shot at, so I joined 'em, and that was the end of that. I weren't a soldier no more. I was just a good-for-nothin' – a coward.' Gracie sat staring blankly through

228

Charlie, and he felt he had to keep talking, to avoid the silence or prevent any tears that may soon follow. 'I'm so sorry, Gracie. Sorry that I'm here and your Edward isn't. He was a man of honour – a hero. Gracie, I'm so sorry.' Gracie heard nothing. She had heard nothing after, '*He was gone.*'

Charlie made his awkward goodbyes as Gracie sat staring blankly. He then made his way to the front door where, upon opening it, he was greeted by a man with a hat in the crook of his arm and a cane in his hand. The two men looked quizzically at one another before Charlie announced, 'The lady of the house is indisposed.'

Richard assured the stranger: 'That is why I'm here.' With that, the men crossed on the threshold, and Richard made his way to find Gracie at the kitchen table, with three glasses of whisky and a glass of water in front of her. 'There was a man on his way out – he let me in,' Richard began with a puzzled expression.

Gracie stood in a wave of emotion and cut Richard off with a torrent of rambling words, 'I have been so foolish. I've known for so long that he wasn't coming home, but I wouldn't admit it to myself... I don't know if it was fear or guilt, shame or dread or what it was. Was I scared of what others might think, of how Primrose might react? Perhaps I was scared of what it might mean for us, if people were to judge us... I was scared that people would think badly, can you understand that? I was too concerned about doing the right thing, you see, about being proper. I was worrying about all the wrong things and all the wrong people...' Gracie suddenly slowed and cupped Richard's perplexed face in her hands. 'In the middle of it all was us, and I lost sight of that. I am so desperately sorry.' Gracie slowly took Richard's cane and placed it on the table before holding him as if to dance. 'You know, you are a wonderful dancer...' She mocked her own misgivings. 'You are kind, handsome, strong and gorgeous and above all, despite all I have put you through...you're here.'

Richard smiled. 'Gracie, are you drunk?'

'I'm not drunk, Richard. I'm free... Free to dance with whomever I choose.'

The music from the neighbour's wireless was still floating through the house, and so Gracie and Richard danced. They danced before they kissed and then they danced some more, but in the end (as the music began to fade) the kissing, the soft, lingering, long-hungered for kisses happily continued.

****

Lost in one another's embrace, Gracie and Richard were quite unaware of Primrose's return to the house or of the Reverend and Mrs Halfpenny who had accompanied her. The mischievous three had snuck in, quite unnoticed, and tiptoed upstairs in a bid to get Primrose into bed without interrupting whatever it was they *hoped* was going on in the kitchen. Once Primrose was settled, the playful Reverend and his accomplice, Mrs Halfpenny, made mock, heavy footsteps towards the kitchen door. They then coughed loudly before knocking, with humorous rhythm, the wooden panel before them. Gracie laughed and composed herself before quickly sitting at the table, and Richard took up his cane and tried to pose nonchalantly against the kitchen wall.

'Gracie, it's me. It's Reverend Smith, dear,' the old man cautioned from behind the door.

'Reverend, how lovely. Do come in. I have your flask.' Gracie was flushed and failing to sound composed. The Reverend slowly entered with Mrs Halfpenny.

Richard was taken aback. 'Mother, you're here too. What a lovely surprise!'

Mrs Halfpenny smiled and gave her son a knowing look... 'Well, I spoke to the Reverend here, and we decided that (seeing as you'd been gone for so long) we'd better bring little Primrose back and get her ready for bed.'

Embarrassed, Richard turned to Gracie to explain. 'I was supposed to be checking that you were alright before I went back home to collect Primrose for you.'

Gracie spoke apologetically to Mrs Halfpenny, 'Thank you for bringing her back for me. I'm sorry but we got...' Gracie searched for an appropriate word, but the best she could come up with was, 'waylaid?'.

Mrs Halfpenny smiled. 'I'm jolly pleased to hear it!'

The Reverend and Mrs Halfpenny offered their goodbyes. Gracie assured the Reverend that she would catch up with him the next day, feeling that she owed him an explanation. Richard had a similar, brief conversation with his mother, but he was a little more vague – not yet knowing what his explanation was going to be. Gracie had spoken very little that evening (apart from her initial outburst), and so Richard was still rather at a loss as to what had happened to turn his life so drastically upside down. As Gracie and Richard stood by the door of Number 77

231

and waved goodbye to the Reverend and Mrs Halfpenny, Richard spotted the apple and the notelet on the small windowsill in Gracie's hall. 'What's this?'

As the couple sat wrapped in one another's arms in the back room, Gracie took delight in explaining to Richard that she had spotted the apple and penned the words in the notelet *before* she had been paid a visit by her neighbour. 'The Reverend made me think, made me realise, how selfish I had been. Then, when I saw the apple, and heard the music, I didn't need to think anymore – I just knew.'

Richard was intrigued... 'What? What did you know?'

Gracie spoke in a whisper of sincerity, 'I knew that I loved you.' She kissed Richard's soft, perfect lips. 'I knew that Edward was my past and that you were my future. No matter how long I was made to wait, I would do so with you by my side, as my friend, until you could be more.'

Richard was confused. 'But friends don't do this...' He kissed Gracie's lips, once, twice, three times. He kissed her cheek, then her neck, easing down the shoulder of her dress to press his lips against the warm, soft, tempting skin beneath...

Gracie was breathless. 'If you do that, I'll never be able to tell you...'

Richard, amused by Gracie's predicament, continued in earnest. Gracie protested with a breath-filled plea, 'Oh my God, Richard, please!' He was unrelenting... Gracie knew she had to explain what had happened earlier that day before she could let herself go, and so she tore herself away and set herself squarely, facing Richard. 'The man you passed in the hall was Charlie Webb.' Richard looked blankly, so Gracie prompted, 'Flo's husband...' Richard was, understandably, shocked. Gracie quickly continued so as not to get too bogged down in the details. 'It's a fairly long story, but the upshot of it all is that Edward isn't coming home. He's been at *rest* for a *very long time*. Just as I'd secretly prayed. He hasn't been lost or afraid for years, trapped or tortured. He's been at *peace*. Charlie saw it all. He was with Edward, and it was all over, just as I suspected, a very long time ago.'

Richard was stunned. 'I thought you'd just decided to move on – that life was too short. I had no idea...' Richard didn't know what he was supposed to say, how to feel or what to do. He suddenly felt himself shift to the defensive. 'So, what's this? Is this shock or grief or madness? I don't understand, Gracie. What's going on?'

Gracie was calm and clear. She gave Richard the note to read... Once he had finished, she continued. 'See? I let myself love you *before* Charlie came to call, and that's the proof.' Gracie pointed to the letter. 'I let Edward go before I was told he was gone. The only sadness in my heart, before Charlie called, was that I didn't know how or when Edward had died. I *knew* in my heart he was gone, though. I wasn't going to wait for a man in an office to 'confirm' it. Reverend Smith made me see that was ridiculous. And I was frustrated, if I'm honest, that I couldn't be with you *properly* until the authorities had reached the same conclusion as me. I was livid about it if I'm completely truthful. Mary is getting on with her life, and I suppose I was jealous. I wanted to get on with mine. I was cross that I had to waste more time, but I was prepared to, for you...for us. I was prepared to do anything for us to be together. I know you'll think badly of me, that I must be some kind of monster to find out my husband is dead and then seconds later throw myself at you, but it's not like that. It's messy, I know, but I'm trying to explain, to be honest with you.' Richard looked into Gracie's green eyes as her brow furrowed, and he listened intently as she continued. 'When Charlie told me that Edward really had gone forever, I was numb, of course I was. Then, the second I saw you, I felt as though everything made sense. We've waited long enough. Edward has been gone long enough. I've mourned since the day I got that bloody telegram. I knew he was gone there and then, I think... I've grieved my husband. My mourning is done. I want to start living. Can you understand? Do you think I'm awful? I'm just trying to explain...'

Richard held Gracie's tiny waist. 'I've never thought you were awful, and you are certainly no monster! I know, more than anyone, how much you've struggled in your grief. So, if there really are no catches, and I *really* don't have to worry about you? You're not on the brink of madness or despair, and you're not drunk, and I wouldn't be taking advantage? Might I trouble you for another kiss?'

Gracie rested her tiny wrists on Richard's shoulders and let her hands fall before seductively biting her lip and whispering, 'I wish you would take advantage, Mr Halfpenny.'

Richard quickly pulled Gracie into him and kissed her passionately as her hands ran across the back of his shoulders. They did not speak, but it was clear that both Richard and Gracie agreed that life was too short to wait for officials in offices to declare what was right or wrong.

They knew that this was their chance, regardless of licenses and certificates, and so they took it and ran.

****

In the hazy light of the following morning, Richard woke and gazed at Gracie in disbelief. She was curled up on the couch, nestled in his arms, with a hand-crocheted blanket covering her delicate frame. Although they had not quite consummated their relationship, Richard was in no doubt that Gracie was his and he was hers. He discovered a lot about himself that night, things he'd never even dreamed, but he discovered even more about Gracie. What a woman she was; what an astonishingly glorious, outrageous, accomplished woman she was. As he gazed at her, he hoped he would never recover from the shock of the night they had shared.

Despite knowing their love must remain a secret for the time being, he was carefree. He knew that, one day soon, he would be able to shout from the rooftops that he loved Gracie, and it would not matter who heard him. For now, however, he was wise enough to know he had to get home... He carefully peeled away from his love, gently resting her head on a cushion, before creeping quietly upstairs in search of the box of writing papers and the pen he had given her when he fell in love with her, all those years ago.

My own darling, Gracie,

The sun is in danger of giving us away, and so I must make my way home with regretful haste. I have dreamt of being with you for so long, but I never dared to imagine it would be so perfect. I feel every inch a new man this morning, my love. It's with thanks to you and your surprising nature that I do!

Come to Mother and me, with Primrose, for your supper this evening. Bill will be thrilled to see you, even though we both know he will not show it. Mother (I am sure) will greet you with open arms. We can relax in her company – I am quite certain of that. She will not judge or condemn us. She will only coo and be overjoyed that we are, at last, together.

I love you. A million times, I love you – and a million times more besides. I am a young man today thanks to you; I am no longer an old soldier with a cane. I am a young man who happens to carry a stick, so he can conduct the orchestra playing in his heart. Today, I will conduct every happy tune ever composed by a man in love, and what a concert it shall be...

Until this evening, my love,

Your very own Mr Halfpenny

22
Goodnight sweetheart

Gracie woke when she heard the door close, and she allowed herself a moment... She had not dreamt, which she thought was a shame. She wondered if, perhaps, being happy would take a little practice, and once she was accomplished, dreams might return to her. She dressed before making a pot of tea. She then prepared a tray to take up to Primrose, wanting to spoil her and to explain everything that had unfolded over the past few weeks. Most of all, of course, she needed to tell her about her father... Primrose was sound asleep after her eventful Sunday evening, and, when Gracie woke her, she was slow to open her eyes and see the tray.

'Is that tea, Mummy? Can I have some? In bed?!' Gracie laughed at her daughter's disbelief. She then sat on the edge of her bed and rested the tray between the pair of them. Primrose sat up and huddled under her blankets whilst her mother poured the hot brew. As Primrose blew gently on her precious cup of tea, she listened intently as her mother explained that Charlie was home, and he had brought sad news: Daddy would not be coming home. He was gone. Forever...

It was a curious moment for Primrose. She was sad that her father was gone, but she felt an undeniable sense of ease wash over her. She was aware of a lightness replacing a heaviness she had, until that moment, been unaware of. Primrose thought that perhaps she should cry, for her mother's sake. Alas, there were no tears to be found. She was unsure of what to do or say for the best. 'Are you all right, Mummy? Would you like a cuddle?'

Gracie was confounded. 'It's Mummy that should be asking you that...'

Primrose felt the need to confess. 'But I knew Daddy wasn't coming home a long time ago. I just sort of knew, so I'm, well, used to it, I suppose...' Primrose was worried about how her mother might react to her shocking confession.

Gracie smiled. 'I sort of knew too... I'm sorry, sweetheart, for not talking to you about it before, for sort of ignoring it all for so long.'

Primrose smiled before comforting her fragile mother with words beyond her years. 'That's ok, Mummy. There was nothing to be said.' Primrose had a warming thought. 'At least now we can both say goodbye to Daddy, properly.' Gracie took Primrose's lead and declared (to Primrose's delight) that she would not be going to school that day. Instead, the two girls were to get ready for something altogether more important: saying goodbye to Edward, to Daddy – at last.

Once dressed in their finest, Gracie and Primrose headed towards the cricket pavilion (come make-shift church) where, thanks to an earlier phone call, the Reverend Smith was waiting. On arrival, Gracie explained Charlie's surprise visit and the news he had brought. Gracie then asked if Primrose and she could quietly say their goodbyes to Edward in church; they wanted the Reverend's help to do it properly, to be able to mourn one last time before, at last, moving on. The Reverend was kind, gentle and informal. He offered up prayers of thanks bor the long-awaited conclusion to Edward's disappearance, and he gave thanks too, that

Edward had left this world swiftly and without suffering. Primrose then lit a candle with the Reverend's help, before being escorted by the old man into the small rose garden behind the pavilion. She was to choose a spot to plant a rose in her father's memory. Primrose felt relieved; she was free to talk openly about her father and anticipate a future without him returning, and she could do so without judgement.

Gracie sat alone on a salvaged pew. She had lit her candle and placed it next to Primrose's. She sat quietly, in the middle of the ramshackle church, alone with her thoughts. As Gracie sat perfectly still, her head filled with pictures of her wedding day. To her utter joy and surprise, she saw Edward's face as he turned to see her beneath her veil. His clear blue eyes were mesmerizing, and his smile melted her heart... She felt Edward's hand – the softness of his fingers wrapping around hers as they walked, hand in hand, husband and wife, along the aisle of the church towards the doors. As she stepped over the threshold of the church with Edward by her side, her heart skipped, and it sailed happily forward in time to when Primrose had been born. She saw Edward holding Primrose in his arms – a father at last. She saw the tears of joy in his eyes, and Gracie knew she was safe. She'd be wrapped forever in Edward's unconditional love. Finally, she heard Edward say, '*I love you, Gracie. Everything will be fine.*'

Gracie thanked her husband for loving her. She thanked him for Primrose and for making her the woman she was. She thanked him for making her strong enough to carry on through the war without him – for making her strong enough to love again, without fear or regret but with hope and faith. Finally, Gracie gave thanks for her memories. She vowed never to forget how much she loved the man she had married...the man with the clear blue eyes who, as she now quite vividly recalled, danced very well indeed.

Before Gracie left the church, she took a note from her pocket and placed it next to her candle.

My dear, departed Edward,

What a journey we have had. What an adventure we have shared. What a life we have created in our darling Primrose... Thank you, my love.

Rest well now, in peace and glory. Until we meet again...

Your funny girl, Gracie x

23
V for victory

Mary's wedding had been meticulously planned down to the very last snowdrop. It was to be on the first Saturday of January 1945, and no one but Charlie Webb was considered good enough to give Mary away. The only bridesmaid was to be Primrose and, naturally, Arthur and William were named as pageboys. Mary's dress had been slaved over for nights on end by Flo, Gracie, Mary and Mrs Halfpenny. Even Mary's mother had contributed – donating some lace she had kept by in case it came in handy...which it did, for Mary's short but perfectly styled veil.

Dr Applebee had grown more and more nervous as the big day grew nearer. By the time the stag night came around, his nerves were completely wrecked. Charlie was therefore in his element... 'You shouldn't be nervous, James, me old china. You're a doctor, for goodness' sake! You're a doctor that deals with women on a daily basis, which means that even though (as I suspect) you haven't any *practical* experience for ya wedding night, you are at least a master of the theory!' Dr Applebee downed his half-a-bitter in one, desperate gulp and then landed his empty glass back on the richly stained bar of the Kent Arms.

Filled to the brim with Dutch courage, the doctor exclaimed, 'But I *am* nervous! That "experience", or rather lack of it, has got me worried sick... What if it goes wrong? What if I'm so nervous that I can't, you know...'

Charlie laughed and slapped poor James on the back with considerable force. 'Well, James, my man, if you have any problems "rising" to the occasion, you know what you'll have to do – call the doctor!' Charlie laughed at his own joke, but poor James turned green.

Richard, who was propping up the bar on the other side of James, stepped in with some encouraging words. 'Ignore Mister Webb, James, my friend. I think it's admirable that you've *waited* for young Mary like you have. You'll see, when it comes to it, you won't even have to think about it. You'll be fine, and everything will "work" perfectly. You mark my words.'

Charlie was not done... 'What would you know, Richy-boy? You're a single man – you shouldn't know nothing about any of this sort of stuff!'

Richard, who'd had very little to drink, was not going to be drawn. 'I know enough, Charlie. Let's leave it at that, shall we?'

Charlie rallied. 'The sly old dog's got a gleam in his eye! Good on ya, Richy-boy! I didn't think you had it in ya.'

By now, James was very drunk, feeling extremely sick and very confused. 'I don't see how any of this helps me...'

Richard laughed, 'The only help you need is help getting home and into bed. Charlie – give a sly old dog with a stick a hand, would you?' Charlie downed his pint before taking hold of the very unstable doctor, together with Richard.

As the three men snuck James out of the bar, leaving the other young doctors to their fill of beer, Charlie reminisced. 'They don't make 'em like they used to, Richard; the old doc used to drink me under the table.'

Richard and Charlie helped the intoxicated doctor back home, to his quarters at Moatlands, being as quiet as they could so as not to disturb the newborn residents and their mothers. A stern-faced matron met them at the door and took hold of the doctor before directing his two inebriated accomplices off the premises. It was a freezing night; the frost had set hard, so Charlie and Richard walked as briskly as they could to reach home. As they walked, Richard mustered his mettle and asked Charlie, 'What was he like? I'm guessing he must have been quite something...'

'What, Ed?' Richard nodded. 'He was a good bloke. A really good bloke. He loved Gracie with all his heart, and Primrose was the apple of his eye.' Charlie nodded back towards Moatlands. 'He'd have loved more little 'uns, but it wasn't to be, you know how it is sometimes.' Richard listened intently as Charlie spoke about his friend, 'Ed was honest and reliable... He was me best mate.'

Richard lamented... '*Irreplaceable*, I once heard someone say.'

Charlie stopped in his tracks and faced Richard, his breath white with the cold. 'This is none of my business, I know that, but my Flo says you're a good bloke; says you've looked after Gracie these past few years...' Richard wondered where the conversation was leading and felt a familiar knot in his stomach. 'Gracie means a lot to me, so does Primrose.' Charlie put his hand squarely on Richard's shoulder. 'You've fought hard for your country, for freedom, for a life and a future for the likes of our Gracie.' Charlie squeezed Richard's shoulder. 'You may not have known Gracie when you took that bullet, but, as far as I'm concerned, you took it for her.' He glanced at Richard's leg before reassuring him. 'To my mind, the day you signed up to fight was the day you became worthy of Gracie and our Primrose.'

Richard was taken aback, and he questioned, 'With your blessing?'

Charlie smiled. 'With my blessing, with Flo's and Mary's and everyone else who's been struggling through this bloody war. Life's too short, mate. You of all people should know that.'

****

The wedding day was absolutely picture-perfect. There was a light flurry of snow to dust the pavilion and the green, and the congregation were warmed by the glow created by Mary and James as they made their vows. Mary was particularly heartened to see her friend Dorothy Brunt and her little sister, Isobel, in the congregation. Their brother, "Young John", (as everyone called him) had been killed in action, in Italy just before Christmas. Mary knew how awful things had been for them at home, so her wedding day was made all the more special because they were there, smiling and in their finery. They had promised Mary they would not miss her wedding for the world, and they were true to their word. Dorothy was a dear friend of Mary's from school, and the day wouldn't have been the same without her. Young John had been friends with Thomas; Mary believed they would be together, watching the ceremony from heaven and enjoying the view.

Gracie stood by Richard's side throughout the ceremony. As they sang *All Things Bright and Beautiful*, Gracie smiled at the surprisingly warm tone of Richard's voice. 'I never knew you could sing,' Gracie whispered as they sat down.

'I'm full of surprises!'

By the end of the service, Gracie and Richard were holding hands. It was the first time they had shown their affection for one another in public, and they had butterflies in their stomachs as testament. Their public display of affection had not been prearranged or discussed in any way – it just happened spontaneously. It felt right. It felt like it was time. Once the photographs had been taken and everyone had made their way over to the Vicarage for the reception, the snow was falling heavily. Primrose, William and Arthur were aching to play in the snow, but they were forbidden until the formality of the toasts and the cutting of the cake had been completed. When Mary at last gave the all-clear, the children ran out into the snow followed by the vast majority of the adults...even the Reverend joined them and could not resist throwing a snowball or two. It was not long, however, before he felt the pinch of the cold and so returned to the warmth of the fire and Mrs Halfpenny's knowing look of, '*I told you so!*'

The Reverend's garden was, in many ways, better kept and more impressive than his house. It had a generous pond, immaculate lawns and a stunning array of old trees (including an impressive willow that wept close to the water's edge). In the summer, borders overflowed with colour, butterflies, sweet scents and honeybees. The garden was the secret, sinful envy of many a parishioner. Gracie and Richard stood huddled together beneath the old willow tree, close to the ice-patched pond, and watched from a safe distance as the frivolity unfurled. The old tree was collecting snow on its long, delicate branches, becoming more beautiful with every minute that passed. Richard knew, as he stood beneath the tree's icy majesty, that Gracie and he had at last arrived... Friends and neighbours, covered in snow and smiles, shouted towards Gracie and Richard, encouraging them to join in the games. They simply smiled back and held one another tighter still, both quite overwhelmed by the love and acceptance that was so generously being granted. The snow continued to fall, taking the temperature with it, but they stood fast beneath the relative shelter of the tree, watching the fun and games. The tingling of their fingers and toes and the numbness of their wind-chilled faces did not bother them in the least. Richard was standing behind Gracie, his strong arms wrapped around her, and despite the cold she felt herself melting; closing her eyes, she softened further into Richard's arms as he quietly began to sing one of her favourite songs, '*I've Got My Love to Keep Me Warm*'. With that, she melted a little more...

After twenty minutes or so, once everyone had become cold and wet and the children had begun to whine, Mary and James returned to the warmth of the Vicarage, dutifully followed by their guests. The wedding party was greeted with hot tea, towels and a roaring fire thanks to the efficiency of Mrs Halfpenny (and the compliance of Reverend Smith). Once everyone was well warmed and dry, Mary and James decided to take their leave, back to Moatlands and their new, married quarters. They were to spend their first night as husband and wife in their new home before setting off the following day to the Belvidere Bed and Breakfast in Broadstairs for their eagerly anticipated Honeymoon. Charlie had managed to borrow a car, from one of his friends at the brewery, to escort the newlyweds up to Moatlands as a bit of a surprise wedding gift. He was tickled pink at the prospect of seeing Mary's face when she saw the gleaming white Austin FL1 parked and ready to take her away. Charlie, together with young William and Arthur, had dressed the car's bonnet with a yard or so of white ribbon, and then littered the bumper with old cans and shoes, tied on with string. As Mary and James were led by the excited guests out onto the Vicarage driveway, their surprise and thanks were evident and plentiful. They kissed and hugged their friends goodbye, and then made their way to the car before Mary suddenly exclaimed, 'My bouquet! Girls, quickly...' All the ladies and young girls, including Gracie (who was dragged by an eager Primrose), gathered and jostled for position in front of the vicarage door. Mary turned her back on the keen, excited gathering and prepared to throw her bouquet. However, she paused and, instead, turned back to face the expectant throng. 'It's no good, girls,' she determined. 'I can't risk it!' With that, she ran to Gracie and gave her the bouquet together with a kiss on the cheek before whispering, 'We all want you to be happy, Gracie. Richard makes you happy, so why not?' Everyone spontaneously cheered and clapped, and Gracie blushed. Richard looked on in wonder.

****

It was gone midnight by the time Gracie got around to putting the flowers into a vase. She sat at the kitchen table and gazed at the winter blooms of gorse, hellebores and witch hazel with bright, hopeful eyes. Perhaps, she thought, once the war was over, her time might come. Gracie continued, as though in a trance, to gaze at the flowers and wonder about her future when her thoughts were suddenly interrupted by a faint, single wrap of the letterbox and the sound of a letter falling to the mat. Gracie raced to see what it could possibly be at such an hour and saw, to her delight, the familiar sight of Richard's handwriting. She opened the door in a heartbeat and startled Richard, who had begun his journey back towards the shop. As Richard turned back in shock, he whispered, 'I just jumped out of my skin!'

Gracie laughed quietly and beckoned Richard to hurry inside. 'Shhh. You'll wake the neighbours and get me into trouble. Quick.'

The moment Richard made it over the threshold and Gracie shut the door they took hold of one another and kissed passionately. There were no pleasantries or gentle romantic courtesies, only feverish advances. Gracie knew in an instant that she was not going to let Richard go home that evening, and as Richard realised how hungry Gracie was to be with him, the kissing grew all the more urgent. Kiss by kiss, touch by touch, button by button, Gracie and Richard both found what they were searching for. They teased one another until they longed to move upstairs to Gracie's bedroom. Richard took hold of Gracie's hand and kissed it before whispering to her, his nose rubbing her soft, downy ear, 'Have you made any plans for this evening?'

Gracie tilted her head to feel Richard's lips on the pulse of her neck. 'No…no plans.'

Richard smiled and fell in behind Gracie, wrapping his arms about her waist and kissing her lightly freckled neck before chancing… 'Well, seeing as it's so late, I thought that perhaps we might tiptoe, oh so very quietly, up to your room and snuggle down for the night. What do you think?'

'But I'm not tired.'

'Who said anything about sleeping?' Gracie led Richard quickly and quietly up the stairs, her fingers entwined in his. However, before they reached halfway, Richard paused and felt himself hold Gracie back, fighting his urge to be with her. 'Are you sure, Gracie? I mean, really sure about all this?'

Gracie, suddenly very sober, thought of Primrose sleeping in her room and of the nights she had climbed the stairs with Edward...but it made her angry. She did not want to be sober. She wanted to be giddy and irresponsible. She wanted Richard and was suddenly determined. Turning on the stair to face the man holding her back, she looked deep into his eyes, resting her hands on his barely covered chest, before asserting in a whisper, 'I'm going to take you upstairs, Richard.' Gracie smiled a mischievous smile. 'I'm going to take you to bed.' She paused to kiss Richard's soft, bearded lips by way of affirmation. 'I'm not some fragile doll, too precious to be touched.' To prove her point, Gracie dared to undo another button before encouraging Richard's hand to the bare skin beneath her loosened blouse. 'We have unfinished business to attend to, Mr Halfpenny.' Gracie half-laughed as she continued, 'I pride myself on completing all tasks to the very best of my ability.' Richard could not believe what Gracie was saying. She kissed him again, caressing the back of his neck, pulling him closer to her. She spoke again, her lips still touching Richard's, 'Now, do as you're told, and come to bed.' Richard was overcome. He softly bit Gracie's bottom lip, and she lost her breath in the thrill; she had never felt anything like it before.

Happily, Richard forgot what it was to be a gentleman for the rest of the night. By morning – much to his surprise, and Gracie's delight – he was no longer in a position to consider himself her boss. Oh, how the tables had turned...

****

Gracie was shocked by how she had behaved. She had never known such lust was possible. As she rested, she could not help but think of Edward. He had never really spoken in the bedroom or dared to play like Richard. Edward had been a careful, gentle lover. Gracie suspected that his mind had often enjoyed thoughts he never shared with her. Regardless, he had *never* made her feel or behave as Richard just had. Richard was older, more experienced, perhaps? Whatever it was, she loved every dangerous, thrilling, unpredictable moment, and she wanted more... Perhaps it wasn't just Richard that was different. Perhaps she had changed too.

The war had changed everyone. The rigours and demands that had befallen Gracie over the past few years meant she was no longer simply the passive, meek wife she once was. She was a woman of substance now, with demands and expectations of her own. She was a woman prepared to push every boundary she encountered, if she so desired. Gracie wanted to take all she could from every moment, to dare and risk and try everything because she would never again count on there being a tomorrow. But she was no less loving or giving – if anything, she was more so now. As for Richard, he had been freed by the war because it had introduced him to Gracie. He had learnt to take without apology and give for giving's sake. He had found trust with the only woman who had ever really known him, and he had never felt more alive. The war had shown him how cruel life could be, but Gracie had shown him how beautiful it was. He supposed that, perhaps, you could not have one without the other. Life was a balance, and Gracie had helped him, at last, to find his...

****

'Richard is here early this morning, Mummy. He must have been very hungry and dashed here first thing for breakfast.'

Richard was fetching the letter he had posted the night before, but he heard Primrose's observation. So, as he walked into the kitchen, he declared, 'I was up with the lark, Primrose, and you're right, I'm starving!' Gracie poured her tea and then began to read her letter...

My own, darling Gracie,

To see you surrounded by your friends with Mary's bouquet deliberately placed in your perfect, delicate hands was blissful. To hear the outpourings of joy and acceptance, to see Primrose's excited face and then your cheeks so flushed with adorable coyness...it was all more than I could comprehend. It was more joyful a day than I could have ever dreamed.

Imagine my joy when later, as you were busy with your friends, chatting with Flo and sorting out the children, the Reverend sought me out to, "have a word". I suspect he had been prompted by my mother! He was keen to explain that I need not wait much longer to ask you the one question I am not yet at liberty to ask... The Reverend went on to explain that in his experience, a simple statement to the relevant authorities from a witness (in our case, Charlie) would be all that was needed to set the wheels in motion, to at last furnish you with the necessary paperwork, securing your status as a single woman. A woman free to answer any questions put to her.

To leave you tonight was sheer agony, my love; to set you and my darling Primrose to your door and then return home to my lonely bed was unbearable. I cannot sleep...it is impossible without you. To have enjoyed such a day, to have been a couple as we were, to have been accepted with such generosity, only to have it all end so abruptly...I am devastated. If you feel as I do, my love, I will move heaven and earth to ensure we do not suffer such indignities as we did this evening for very much longer.

I cannot bear the wrench of leaving you at the threshold, Gracie, not when I want so desperately to carry you over it...

One word from you, my love, and I will begin to move heaven and earth.

Forever yours, R x

Gracie looked up from her letter and looked at Richard who was busy buttering Primrose's toast. 'Are you still here?' Gracie smiled and put her hand on Richard's thigh. 'Shouldn't you be round at Charlie's, moving heaven and earth?' Richard, quick as a flash, kissed Gracie's cheek and began to move.

Primrose was confused. 'Why is Uncle Charlie trying to move heaven and earth, Mummy? He'll never manage that, even if he gets help.'

'You never know, my love. You never know what's possible until you try.'

24
There'll always be an England

The Reverend was either mistaken, optimistic or just plain barmy when he assured Richard that the process of securing the paperwork he needed was a simple formality – one that would take "no time at all". Months of procedures, form-filling, phone calls and chasing documents was hardly the quick, simple process Richard had been hoping for, but Gracie constantly encouraged and supported him. She reminded Richard that it would be foolhardy to imagine moving both heaven and earth would be an easy task. She revelled in reminding him that his struggles through tangled, red tape would eventually lead to her – in soft satin and white lace.

As winter gave way to spring, Gracie was still (to all intents and *legal* purposes) a married woman. In her heart, however, she was a blossoming, single flower, enjoying the growing heat of her springtime courtship. The horrors of the war were melting away under the promise of the warm spring sun. The country's mood was lifting. There was a heady hope for peace thanks to the confirmation of Hitler's death in the papers at the beginning of May.

Unbeknown to Gracie, and on the self-same day as Hitler's death was reported, Richard at last received the paperwork he had been waiting for. Unsure of what to do next, of how best to tell Gracie the news, Richard went to Charlie and Flo for advice. 'What do you think, Flo? Should I tell her they've arrived? Should I give her the certificate?'

Flo was in no doubt. 'Of course not! She don't need to see some morbid bit of paper tellin' her what she already knows, man... She needs you to surprise her, to sweep her off her feet, to get her a ring and get down on one knee!'

Charlie was curious. 'Can you get down on one knee with that leg of yours, Richy-boy?'

'Not without help!'

Charlie laughed. 'Blimey, mate – this is gonna need some careful plannin'.' He turned to Flo. 'Come on, girl – get that paper and pencil a yours out – we've got ourselves a proposal to organise.'

With Flo's guidance and vow of secrecy, Richard set about planning his proposal. The first job, to Flo's mind, was securing the perfect ring. Richard had a suggestion that Flo agreed with... His grandmother's ring, a small cluster of diamonds on a thin band of gold, would be perfect. It was decided that on Saturday the 12th of May (exactly one month before Primrose's twelfth birthday), Charlie and Flo would take Primrose out for the day, on the ruse that they would be away for her *actual* big day, and Charlie did not want to miss making a fuss of his little princess. Gracie, unfortunately, would not be able to join them because she would not fit in the car Charlie was going to borrow. Flo was overcome with excitement. She was over the moon with her contribution to the mischievous plans, remembering Primrose's birthday as she had. With fingers crossed for dry weather, Richard was going to prepare a picnic, a *champagne* picnic, and take Gracie to the orchard... He was going to read to her, most likely a sonnet, since he knew Gracie loved to be read to. If he was already sitting (and the tree was there to lean on), he should just about manage to get on one knee, produce the ring and pop the question. Flo was beside herself. 'You must learn that sonnet thingy off by heart. 'ave the book with yer (that'll look good), but don't look at the words. Look into her eyes.'

Charlie teased. 'You're a daft old bat! You don't half make me laugh... What do you know about flammin' sonnets?'

'I know they're romantic, you old sod, which is more than can be said for you!' Flo clipped Charlie's ear.

Charlie shrugged at Richard and playfully tried to defend himself. 'I proposed with a cream stout, a bag a chips and the promise of a good time if she said yes! I don't know what she's moaning about.' Charlie kissed Flo's cheek and tapped her ample bottom.

Richard shook his head and smiled. 'There's not much written on that bit of paper of yours, Flo... Why don't I jot down the words of that sonnet, and you can read them through later and tell me what you think.' Flo passed Richard the blank paper and pencil, then looked on in disbelief as he proceeded to write the words of Shakespeare on the scrap of paper.

When Richard finished, Flo was stunned. 'How the heck did you ever learn all that?'

'Gracie, of course. She was the one that read it to me in the first place.'

'Blimey! That's amazin' is that. 'ere, think on, Charlie. I reckon you've got some wooin' to catch up on!'

Everything was set. Flo had arranged to have Primrose the following Saturday, and Richard had organised the champagne and ordered the food. The ring had been polished and the sonnet practiced.

What is it they say about the best-laid plans...?

It was the 8th of May when the announcement was made, and the whole street had tuned their wirelesses in to hear it. Rumours were rife, but no one dared believe it was true until they heard it for themselves. Silence fell as Churchill spoke,

"Hostilities will end officially at one minute after midnight tonight (Tuesday, May 8), but in the interests of saving lives the "Cease fire" began yesterday to be sounded all along the front, and our dear Channel Islands are also to be freed to-day. The Germans are still in places resisting the Russian troops, but should they continue to do so after midnight they will, of course, deprive themselves of the protection of the laws of war, and will be attacked from all quarters by the Allied troops. It is not surprising that on such long fronts and in the existing disorder of the enemy the orders of the German High Command should not in every case be obeyed immediately. This does not, in our opinion, with the best military advice at our disposal, constitute any reason for withholding from the nation the facts communicated to us by General Eisenhower of the unconditional surrender already signed at Rheims,

nor should it prevent us from celebrating to-day and tomorrow (Wednesday) as Victory in Europe days...

We may allow ourselves a brief period of rejoicing; but let us not forget for a moment the toil and efforts that lie ahead. Japan, with all her treachery and greed, remains unsubdued. The injury she has inflicted on Great Britain, the United States, and other countries, and her detestable cruelties, call for justice and retribution. We must now devote all our strength and resources to the completion of our task, both at home and abroad. Advance, Britannia! Long live the cause of freedom! God save the King!"

Gracie and Primrose were above the store, standing with Richard, Mrs Halfpenny and Bill when the announcement was made. Once it was complete, the outpouring from them all, even Bill, was without parallel. With Churchill's words still ringing in their ears, Richard led his family out to the street and the crowds that had already gathered there. They ran to their neighbours and friends and shared in their delight. As Richard surveyed the scene, he saw tears of joy and faces lost in shock and disbelief. He saw impromptu dancing and heard spontaneous singing, but he saw tired faces too – brows heavy with sadness, framing haunted eyes. Richard could hardly breathe, such was the force of the collective, emotional release. He saw the faces of the men he had lost, he felt the bullet hit his leg, he felt the cold mud all about him and the rain stinging his face.

'It's over!' Gracie took a hold of Richard in an enthusiastic wave of joy and, in so doing, brought him home safely to her. Richard was surrounded by everyone he loved: his Mother and Primrose were there, standing either side of Bill; Mary and James were wrapped in one another's arms; Reverend Smith was by Gracie's side; Flo was there too, with Charlie; William was on his father's shoulders and Arthur was pulling at his mother's pinny. Most importantly, Gracie was in his arms.

Without a thought, Richard turned to her and loudly released, 'Marry me! Marry me tomorrow and make me the happiest man alive.'

'But – what about heaven and earth? They still need to be moved!'

Gracie's heart was racing, and Richard smiled as he felt in his jacket pocket for the ring he'd been keeping close to his heart... 'Heaven and earth have been moved.'

Flo was fit to burst with excitement and could not help but interrupt in an urgent whisper, 'Don't forget ya poem...' She looked at Richard and encouraged him to begin, but he returned her look with one of blankness because the words he knew so well (and had rehearsed countless times) had completely escaped him.

Charlie, to everyone's astonishment, (and his own slight embarrassment) prompted his friend in his moment of need. 'Let me not to the marriage of true minds admit impediments...

Flo stared at Charlie in disbelief. Meanwhile, thanks to his prompt, Richard continued the sonnet whilst holding Gracie's hands in his... 'Love is not love which alters when it alteration finds, or bends with the remover to remove: O no! It is an ever-fixed mark that looks on tempests and is never shaken.' By now, a hush had fallen over the street and a throng of revellers were suddenly silent witnesses. 'It is the star to every wandering bark, whose worth's unknown, although his height be taken. Love's not time's fool, though rosy lips and cheeks within his bending sickle's compass come: Love alters not with his brief hours and weeks, but bears it out even to the edge of doom.' Flo took a hanky from her pocket and dried her eyes. Charlie sniffed and used his sleeve. 'If this be error and upon me proved, I never writ, nor no man ever loved.' Silence hung in the air as Richard passed Flo his cane, and Charlie helped him to his knee. 'I love you, Gracie. I have always loved you.' Richard presented the old, but cherished, ring to Gracie. 'Marry me tomorrow at the pavilion, and then let's all gather here in the street afterwards and celebrate for all we are worth.' Not a soul, not even the children, dared to breathe.

All eyes fell on Gracie... She smiled, but her eyes filled with tears. She was quite overcome as she gazed into Richard's longing hazel eyes. She drew a breath and stared hard to prevent a tear from falling before whispering, 'Yes. Yes please!' The throng cheered and clapped as Gracie accepted the ring. She then suddenly turned to Reverend Smith and spoke, cutting through the celebrations, 'If that's alright with you?' The impromptu congregation all turned to look at the Reverend with expectant faces. 'If it's allowed, I mean... What about the banns being read and all the formalities?'

'On this occasion, Gracie, my love, I think we can put the cart before the horse (if you know what I mean)!' Richard made his way to his feet, with Gracie's help, and then shook the Reverend's hand with grateful thanks. 'We can play around with the paperwork and legal nonsense later. I'll marry you tomorrow, Gracie love, and God will be glad. That's all you need worry about.'

****

The remainder of the day was frantic. With the help of Reverend Smith, Charlie, James, Bill and his mother, Richard set to work organising a wedding *and* VE Day street-party. They had less than twenty-four hours to conjure a miracle. Reverend Smith instructed them all to pray! Gracie, meanwhile, met with Flo and Mary to alter Mary's wedding dress with lightning efficiency. It was a big day for Primrose too because her mother allowed her to make the tea, all by herself, for the first time. 'Needs must, Primrose, my love. Just be careful not to scald yourself. I haven't the time to deal with that today!'

****

It was midday on the 9th of May when Gracie, at last, walked into the pavilion, proudly led by Bill, to become Mrs Halfpenny. She was a vision for Richard to behold: a dream in ivory silk. Her soft, sweet skin was concealed, but her figure was clear and beautifully suggested for Richard to adore. Standing at the far end of the makeshift aisle, her face was a hazy, distant promise – just as her love had once been. Though lace veiled her dewy, green eyes and soft, balm-kissed lips, her beauty could not be hidden; it shone for all to see. With every step she took, the distant promise of love and marriage came closer to deliverance. This was it – the final steps. After everything they had been through, after all this time, at last, it was here. When Gracie finally stood before Richard, he slowly lifted her veil – the final obstacle between them. Their dreams of being together were coming true, and neither of them could quite believe it was happening.

There were no bridesmaids. Primrose was sitting happily with Mrs Halfpenny, holding her hand, and there were no page boys or maids of honour. Nothing distracted from the pure and simple beauty of Gracie arriving to become Richard's wife. The service was simple and short. Charlie read the sonnet Richard had voiced in the street the previous day (to Flo's utter delight), and there was only one hymn, at Primrose's request, *Jesus Christ the Apple Tree*. Thankfully, no one seemed to know of any lawful impediment as to why the wedding should not proceed (though everyone suspected there were probably plenty), and so, before the clock struck half-past twelve, Gracie and Richard were kissing as husband and wife.

The street party was an unparalleled success. The sun shone, food was plentiful and music played. As the VE Day (come-wedding) celebrations continued into the early hours and the street revelled in its post-war delirium, Gracie and Richard quietly snuck away. At Number 77 Commercial Road, Gracie and Richard were enjoying a party of their very own!

Despite the sanctity of marriage, Gracie and Richard's wedding night was just as thrilling and exciting as the nights they had secretly shared before, and both were relieved to find it so. They fell asleep with blankets in disarray, pillows on the floor, wedding cards strewn about the place and Richard's suit crumpled into a hurried heap in the corner. Gracie's dress, however, was hung neatly, thanks to Richard's patient hands. It was perfectly placed on a fine, silk-covered hanger to be preserved for whomever might need it next!

To the happy couple,

God's blessings to you both! This is the happiest day - the most joyous day of all...

May the love shown to you today be with you always. May it carry you through your lives together as husband and wife. Peace, faith, hope and love be with you both...

Reverend Smith x

p.s. If you happen to bump into the Bishop, no need to mention any of this at all...!

25
Coughs and sneezes spread diseases

The following morning saw the whole of Paddock Wood wake with a hangover of some sort or another... The street was littered with broken bunting and paper plates, and trestle tables had spilt over onto their sides. It was a little after eight when Gracie woke Richard's thumping head with a kiss. He groaned, 'I think I need an aspirin, Mrs Halfpenny.' Gracie laughed and fetched the much-needed glass of water, laced with the necessary cure. By nine o'clock, thanks to Gracie's enthusiasm, she had rallied Richard and Primrose to the shop floor, ready to start their new lives together. Gracie felt as though it were New Year's Day.

She was standing on the brink of her new life. Her hair was dressed. She was wearing her favourite frock.

Gracie was ready to face whatever came her way, and Primrose was holding her hand...eager to jump with her mother into an exciting, new world full of adventures. As Gracie and Richard were discussing plans for the shop, and Primrose was trying her best to interrupt and persuade the newlyweds to expand the toy department, a train drew in at the station.

A man, with expectant eyes and flowers in his grasp, began walking the streets he had left five years previously. He pictured his wife: dressed to the nines, hair neat and prim, his daughter by her side. As the man walked, he wondered how his child might have grown. She was six when he had left, nearly seven, but now she would be almost twelve. As the man felt in his pocket for a length of ribbon and a tattered note, he was struck by a thought. He wanted to buy a gift for his daughter – a toy perhaps or maybe a new teddy.

'We should have more children's things: more toys and teddies!' insisted Primrose.

Richard laughed. 'Aren't you getting a bit old for teddies?'

Gracie held Richard's hand and assured him. 'You are *never* too old for teddies, sweetheart.' As Gracie and Richard stood in the centre of the shop, their backs turned on the glass façade, Primrose plucked a teddy from the small display of toys and made her way to the front window, imagining it full of toys at Christmas.

The man in the street passed the tumbled trestle tables and lamented the party he must have missed. He trod on the strewn bunting – walking over the patriotic shades of red, white and blue that had fallen prey to the night's eager breeze. He decided to call into the shop on his way to the house – he would buy his daughter a teddy and tie the ribbon she had once given him around its neck. '*You are never too old for teddies*', he thought. The man arrived at the shop's impressive door and noted that the sign above it had changed. He supposed that, in all probability, many things would have changed since he had left.

Primrose was sitting in the window of the store, holding the teddy in her arms. She was imagining being surrounded by many more... With a start, she was shaken from her childish daydreams and suddenly aware of a man hesitating at the door. She was transfixed – impossibly drawn to his eyes. She saw him look at her mother. She saw him stare at

Richard as he kissed her mother's cheek and pulled her close with the hand he held around her waist.

The stranger took a step back, as though he had been pushed, then his eyes turned quickly to meet Primrose's. The child sitting in the window of the shop, clutched her teddy, frozen in time. The strangers looked at one another, defencelessly. Neither one could comprehend what their eyes were showing them. A stab of pain rose up inside them both, and their chests caved. They were helpless – incapable of drawing breath. Their perfectly matched eyes filled rapidly with tears, and, as they blinked, their tears began to fall.

In the end, the man summoned more strength than he had ever needed before, and more courage than he had thought possible, to turn away. He lowered his head. The soldier was silent and resigned to his duty. He was not needed there. The teddy had already been bought, so he made his way back to the train station. His steps were heavier than they had ever been, and tears rolled down his face. The cold reality of the streets bore no comfort for the man stepping on the ruined red, white and blue of yesterday, and, despite the warmth of the shop (no matter how tightly Primrose held her teddy), there was an unmistakable chill from which she could not escape.

****

That night, as Primrose climbed into her bed, her mother comforted her. 'You don't seem at all well, my love.' Gracie felt Primrose's forehead. 'I think you're coming down with a little fever.' Primrose could not speak. 'A good night's sleep will do you the world of good. You'll see, things will be better in the morning.' Gracie gave

Primrose her teddy and spoke assuringly, 'Give him a good cuddle, and he'll make you feel all better.' With that, Gracie took herself off to bed.

Primrose was in a deep state of shock. The result was a complete shutdown. She had shut down just as surely as her mother had done, all those years ago, when her father had gone missing – for the first time.

The ticking of the clock from the landing was growing louder and ever more urgent, and Primrose's heart raced to overtake it. She lay quite still, her teddy nuzzled into her neck. Thoughts of girls in faraway lands, ribbons and heroes played on her mind as she grappled with the crushing weight in her chest. She was, once again, six years old...

As the clock continued to tick, and the seconds turned to minutes, the pain in Primrose's chest worsened. Her fragile frame struggled to cope. She was drowning in painful, vivid memories of her father – her beautiful, perfect, brave, strong, *irreplaceable* father. The pain in her chest slowly grew and raised up, gripping her little throat in its clutches. She struggled for air. She tried to draw deeper and deeper breaths, as though she were trying to rescue herself, as she had once before: sitting at the kitchen table, on her father's lap. Her mind raced. *'It was him. Wasn't it? Surely, it must have been... But, then again, how could it have been? Oh...but it was. It was Daddy, but he turned away and left.'* She sobbed muffled tears into her pillow until she fell into a fitful, troubled sleep.

Gracie snuggled up in bed with Richard. He had already sought refuge from his long, hungover day. She laughed.

'You look how I feel! Budge over and make some room for a small one.'

Gracie slept soundly and deeply in the comfort of Richard's arms, and, for the first time since Edward had left, she fell into her dreams... She dreamt vividly of *Edward*. She dreamt as though he had never left, and they were living their lives as though the war had never started. They had more children in her dream: two little boys, handsome and clever like their father. Edward was charming and funny. He danced with Gracie around the kitchen table and kissed her neck when the children weren't looking. He called her his 'funny girl'. Gracie made them tea and then sat with Edward in the back room, keeping him company whilst he read his paper. He occasionally shared the odd line or two with her, interrupting her sewing and making her lose her thread...

When morning came and Richard awoke, he gazed on Gracie and smiled. She was still fast asleep, still dreaming. He slowly lent into her and softly woke her with a tender kiss. Gracie continued to dream, and she kissed Edward back. She kissed him again and again until she eventually opened her eyes. The moment she opened her dream-filled eyes and found her new husband instead of the one from her dream, she unravelled in shock.

'Gracie, whatever is the matter? What's wrong?' Richard was terribly worried. He thought Gracie must have somehow hurt herself or suddenly fallen ill. 'Gracie, talk to me. Does something hurt? Gracie, my love, you're scaring me now. Whatever has happened to you? Why are you crying?'

Gracie gasped. 'It was a dream.'

'Oh, my darling, whatever was it about?'

'It was just a silly dream...' Gracie fell into her loving husband's arms and let go of all her long-held defences. The dream had felt so real, and the shock of waking was too much for her to bear. She allowed her tears to fall. It had been five long years since she had cried. Now she had started, however, it seemed impossible to stop. Thank goodness Richard was there for her. How lucky she was to have him by her side. Imagine, she thought, where she'd be without him?

****

10th May 1945

My lost love,

If I am to live, Gracie, I must believe that you never saw a word I ever wrote. I must trust that you believed I was gone and that my letters to you sat in some God-forsaken place, leaving you lost and mourning.

I wrote to you often, my love, and trusted those about me to deliver my words to you – all on the understanding that it would be impossible to ever receive word back (such were the dangers all about us). How cruelly it appears we have been deceived. How our lives together have been played with, my darling girl. How sorry I am that all at once our life together is over – lost forever to some cruel twist of fate.

To see you as I did, in another man's arms, was the saddest of affairs. I felt such unfathomable pain. I was filled with anger but silenced by grief... I felt the rip in my heart as you were torn from me; I mourned your loss, Gracie, as truly as a widower at the mouth of a grave. As I write to you now, nothing has changed. I am still wrecked by your loss.

To walk away from you, to leave you to your happiness, was all I could think to do given what I saw. I knew, in that instant (as I stood by the shop's door), how you had suffered over the years. I felt your pain, Gracie. I saw your journey in my mind's eye: I saw you fight back tears, I heard your angry questioning, and I saw your heart torn between my memory and the man who held you in his arms...

I love you, my darling, and that is why I left you to your peace. I imagine you have suffered enough in my name, and I am damned if I should cause you another moment's heartache. I will not be that man, Gracie. I am better than that.

Primrose will recover from her sighting of the stranger in the doorway – I'll fade away. Perhaps I'll become a curious feeling that puzzles her but makes her smile. Perhaps I'll transform into a comforting whisper she sometimes hears on the wind. Maybe I'll fade like a watercolour left in the rain: once perfect but, in time, nothing more than a softened wash of familiar hues... Whatever I become, I trust she is safe and happy without me.

She looked well. No, she looked perfect. She was clearly at home there with you both. You must have worked hard to ensure that. He must love her very much. I have to believe you wouldn't have chosen him if he didn't love Primrose with all his heart – as I do. As I always will.

I trust Primrose to you Gracie, and I trust the man you chose to hold you in his arms because I trust your judgement. I trust you as surely as I did when I walked out to war all those years ago. The pain is no less unbearable today than it was then. My only consolation is that the war is over, and I played my part. so Primrose can grow up in a world at peace, safe in your care.

I will write to you often, Gracie, and the letters I write will collect on my mantelpiece. Not one will ever be sent. Your eyes will never see a word, but I will write just the same and tie my letters with Primrose's ribbon. I'll keep the letters safe, and on days when the pain of your loss is too hard to bear, I will take them down to read and pray they bring me comfort. I will share the rest of my life with you, Gracie. You will always be my wife.

I will pray for you every night, my darling, and, before I go to my sleep, I will hold you in my arms and I will kiss your soft, perfect lips. I will whisper softly to you, 'I love you, Gracie. Everything will be fine.'

God bless, my funny girl,

Edward x

A Love Letter to Paddock Wood

My little hometown of Paddock Wood is very dear to my heart, but I admit it is an unlikely setting for a grand romance novel. There are no breath-taking landmarks or awe-inspiring vistas…it is far from extraordinary. In fact, it is arguably the epitome of a mundane, rural town.

I came to live in Paddock Wood in 2004, after leaving the Medway Towns, to set up my family home. It was a world away from where I had been. I moved to a little farmer's cottage on a rural track that looked out over fields… Horses lent over my garden fence, and I had an apple tree in my garden. I genuinely couldn't believe my luck.

In the holidays and on weekends, I would take my girls to Barsleys, the department store in the centre of our new, rural town. The store had wooden drawers for tills, and staff added up our purchases using pencil and paper – steadfastly resisting the march of time. The store was a little refuge for my girls and me, and we usually found ourselves there when we fancied a treat. The café was our favourite spot. Whilst nursing a pot of tea, we loved looking at the old sepia photographs proudly displayed on the walls there. On one visit – whilst reading a local history leaflet – we discovered that during the Second World War, the manager (Mr Barsley) mustered clean socks and hot teas to pass through train windows (at Paddock Wood Station) to troops evacuated from Dunkirk. That story never left me – I thought he must have been such a gent.

When we moved to Paddock Wood, I worked as a primary school teacher, and I enjoyed researching for school projects and plays. As part of one such project, I found myself looking into my local area's role in the war. I uncovered fascinating details about our town's involvement: I learned about John Brunt VC, a fearless young war hero, and General Sir Frederick 'Freddy' Morgan, the brilliant mind behind the D-Day landings. I discovered that Moatlands had been a home for mothers and babies, and that the Hop Farm had, for a time, sheltered the Queen Victoria's Rifles. I had more material than I could ever fit into a school play, but these stories stayed with me.

Time rolled by in Paddock Wood, and characters for a story began to develop. They were mainly echoes of my great-grandparents and grandparents. Their wartime experiences and gutsy resolve were woven into my DNA through the stories they shared. My nans always seemed quite jolly when they reflected on the war – a contradiction that puzzled me as a child. As an adult, I realised there must have been a certain thrill in the peril they faced. A few salacious stories were kept from me for years – secrets and scandals unfit for a child's ears. When the revelations came, I was shocked, but not as shocked as Grandad must have been when my uncle was born in 1946!

As the pieces of *A Very British Affair* started to reveal themselves, I kept coming back to the Queen Victoria's Rifles. I couldn't stop thinking about how impossible it must have been for them and those they left behind... Their collective plight compelled me to put pen to paper.

A Place Worth Remembering

If you ever find yourself in Paddock Wood, I invite you to step into the history that inspired this novel. Pop into Barsleys for a cream tea and some socks! You'll see how it influenced the store in my story. Visit the war memorial near the station, where you can pay your respects to those who served. Cross the road, and you'll find The John Brunt VC – formerly The Kent Arms – renamed in 1947 to honour our local hero. While you're there, stop by the Red Cross charity shop, then take a short walk to the churchyard nearby. You will notice that the church itself is missing – but, of course, we know why that is the case.

Paddock Wood may look like any other rural town – and in many ways, it is. But during the Second World War, like so many villages, towns, and cities across Britain, it played its part. The people who lived here rose to extraordinary challenges, and their stories deserve to be remembered.

Though this novel is fiction, it is inspired by real events. I hope it encourages you to delve into your own local history. You may be astonished by the stories of heroism, resilience and sacrifice that unfold on your very own doorstep.

Printed in Dunstable, United Kingdom